BREAKING

Maggie Makepeace was born in Buckinghamshire and went to school in Devon. She has BSc in Zoology from Newcastle University and an MSc in Ecology from Aberdeen. She has worked as a TV presenter, for the Scottish Wildlife Trust and in the Wales office of the RSPB. She is married and lives in Somerset. The author of several scientific publications, *Breaking the Chain* is her first novel.

BREAKING
THE CHAIN

Maggie Makepeace

ARROW

First published by Arrow in 1995

Copyright © Maggie Makepeace 1994

Maggie Makepeace has asserted her right under the
Copyright, Designs and Patents Act, 1988, to be identified as
the author of this work

First published in the United Kingdom in 1994 by

Century, 20 Vauxhall Bridge Road, London SW1V 2SA

Random House Australia (Pty) Limited
20 Alfred Street, Milsons Point, Sydney
New South Wales 2061, Australia

Random House New Zealand Limitd
18 Poland Road, Glenfield
Auckland 10, New Zealand

Random House South Africa (Pty) Limited
PO Box 337, Bergvlei, South Africa

Random House UK Limited Reg. No. 954009

A CIP catalogue record for this book
is available from the British Library

Papers used by Random House UK Limited are natural,
recyclable products made from wood grown in sustainable
forests. The manufacturing processes conform to the
environmental regulations of the country of origin.

ISBN 0 09 943141 6

Printed and bound in Great Britain by
Cox & Wyman Ltd, Reading Berkshire

For Tim, with love

Chapter One

When summoned urgently at seven o'clock in the morning to the bedside of a dying friend, Peter Moon, QC paused only long enough to cook and eat a large unfilleted kipper, before rushing to the well-known London hospital. He was too late. Nancy Sedgemoor was already dead.

'She passed away five minutes ago,' the nurse said, 'and you were her only visitor. Wasn't that a shame?'

'Oh.' He found that his predominant emotion was one of relief. Poor Nancy; but it was probably all for the best.

'Would you like to see her?'

'What? Oh no . . . no, thank you.' It would be too gruesome, and it wouldn't help her now. He should have gone to see her before. He had always meant to. It must be all of ten – no, more like twenty years . . . He sighed and ran a hand through his thick white hair.

'I'm very sorry,' the nurse said. 'Is there anything . . . ?' Peter looked at her properly for the first time. She had dark eyes and smooth fudge-coloured skin, and she had pursed her full lips together in a sympathetic line as though she felt for him. 'How about sitting down a minute,' she suggested, 'to get over the shock?'

'No, thank you very much. You're most kind.' He smiled appreciatively at her. In his youth, he might have paid her a compliment; chanced his arm? Well, perhaps not, under the circumstances. But it was very pleasant to be sympathized with. He turned to go.

'Don't forget your stick!' She pointed to where he had parked it, propped against a trolley.

'Indeed no. Goodbye.' He picked it up and shook it at her in mock salute. Then he walked back along the hollow cream-painted corridors, using it for support, and moving, it seemed to him, even more slowly than usual. He appeared to the casual observer to be weighed down with grief, but in fact it was just

1

a twinge of arthritis. His spirits were already resuming their normal buoyancy. No serious suggestion of guilt presented itself to him. He was not a man who entertained self-indulgent emotions. He slipped his right hand inside the jacket of his elegant pin-striped suit and held out an antique watch on a gold chain. He could just read it without his glasses. Good, he thought to himself, plenty of time to get to Chambers for my meeting. It will undoubtedly take all morning; what a good thing I had the foresight to make myself a decent breakfast.

That evening, alone as often in his flat in the Temple, Peter Moon lay back comfortably in his best armchair with a glass of whisky in one hand, his stockinged feet up on the coffee table, and the news on Channel 4. Only then did it occur to him that he ought to let his wife know about Nancy. He supposed he'd better phone her. He put the whisky down, stretched out a hand for the remote control and zapped the television off with a flourish. The telephone was also within reach. He was halfway through dialling the number of their house in Somerset, when he remembered that he hadn't done any of the things on the list that Hope had given to him the weekend before, and it was now already Wednesday. He put the receiver down and took another mouthful of whisky. He didn't feel like being nagged.

He glanced round the large sitting room, taking in his familiar surroundings in a complacent glance. He had always liked the long shape of it, with the bulge at the far end, the balding Persian carpet, the dark wallpaper which showed off his treasured oil paintings, the shelves full of rare books, and the expensive heavy furniture. The green velvet curtains hung in heavy folds beside the tall mullioned windows with their view out over the immaculate Temple gardens below, to the Embankment and the River Thames beyond. Now the summer evening sun slanted in sideways through them and glinted on the silver frames of photographs grouped together on top of Hope's harpsichord. They were mostly of the weddings of his sons, and other family occasions, with the odd picture of himself in a group of similar old men at some function or another. He saw that one of them seemed to have got knocked over, perhaps when the daily woman did the dusting. He hauled himself awkwardly out of his chair and went to stand it up again. It was the one of his eldest son, Duncan, wearing, for the first and only time in his life, a dark suit and with his plump, smiling, thirty-ish bride on his arm.

His eldest son and probably the last of the bunch to get married; strange that, Peter thought idly. Nice that they lived so close to the house in the country. Duncan always had, of course, but he hadn't been much help to his mother. Peter still rather hoped that Duncan's wife might become the daughter that Hope had always wanted. At first he had had the notion that Hope would take to her instantly, in spite of the fact that she was no great beauty. She was sensible enough and she had shown every sign that she would sort poor old Duncan out. But somehow it hadn't happened like that. The two women had lived barely a mile apart for the last four years, and yet scarcely saw each other. It was a great pity. It might have distracted Hope, and indirectly taken the heat off him. An on-the-spot daughter-in-law had the potential to be so useful . . . Of course! Inspired idea; he'd try to encourage a greater intimacy between them himself. And for a start he would telephone her – whatsername? – and get her to pass on to Hope the message about Nancy.

Phoebe Moon picked up the telephone and the patrician, rather fruity voice of her father-in-law said, 'Ah, now to whom am I speaking?'

He always said that. The first time he had rung her up, in the early months of her marriage, Phoebe had been nonplussed. If you phoned somebody, you were surely speaking to *them*, weren't you? She could remember the conversation of that day almost verbatim. It still rankled.

'To whom am I speaking?' the voice had said.

'Who d'you want?' she had asked cautiously.

'Why, my daughter-in-law, Duncan's wife.'

'Oh Peter! I'm sorry, I'm not used to your voice yet. This is me, Phoebe.'

'Of course it is. Phoebe . . .!' He sounded as though he were trying it out for the first time. We've been married for three

3

whole months and he's forgotten my bloody name, Phoebe thought, hurt.

'*Bright Phoebus in his strength*,' Peter went on. 'Where does that quotation come from, do you know?'

'No. I don't think . . .'

'*The Winter's Tale*,' he said triumphantly.

'Oh.' Phoebe felt put down and thought crossly, So why ask me if you already know?

'I'm surprised you don't know that; intelligent girl like you,' he said. 'Phoebus is, of course, Apollo the Sun God, is he not? So what does that make you, a sun goddess? The sun wife of the son of Moon.' He chuckled at his own joke.

'Actually,' Phoebe said, having looked it up in a book of names when she was ten, and knowing she was on firm ground, 'it means bright and shining and it also means the moon, not the sun.' She had felt like adding, So there!

'How very apt,' her father-in-law said jovially. 'I can see we shall have to call you Mrs Moon Moon.'

Perhaps it was his way of giving her an affectionate fatherly nickname, Phoebe wondered. Somehow at the time, it hadn't felt very paternal or even very friendly. It still didn't. But in those days she was newly married and generous of spirit; prepared to give him the benefit of the doubt. She had thought, He's not being unkind on purpose. I expect I'll soon get used to his funny ways. And so she had laughed politely.

Now she recognized his voice at once. It always irritated her that none of the family ever bothered to identify themselves on the telephone. She wondered if they did it on purpose, to give themselves an advantage over the person they were calling.

So she said, 'Hello, Peter. You know fine who you're speaking to. How are you?'

'I'm well, thank you.'

'Were you wanting to talk to Duncan?' she asked. 'Only I'm afraid he's out every day until dark in this good weather, cutting people's lawns. I —'

'No,' Peter interrupted. 'It was you I wanted. I wonder if you could do a small favour for me?'

When Phoebe had first met Duncan's parents, on a wet day in April, she had initially been surprised and then not a little overawed. They were not a Mum and Dad, they were a Father and Mother. They were not demonstrative and they did not invite confidences. They made Phoebe feel decidedly uneasy. They challenged her only-child's preconceptions about life in large families. People, especially women, who had lots of children were warm and welcoming, calm and sociable, weren't they? After all, even in those days, back in the forties, you surely didn't *have* to have children if you didn't want them, did you . . .? So a woman who had had four and then adopted another, must be really maternal; a comfortable sort of person who would listen to you? Phoebe quite realized that you didn't have to be fat to be comfortable, but nevertheless she was shocked at how thin Hope was, and how drawn she looked.

'W-Well, she is n-nearly 70 and she's suffered from depression for m-m-most of that time,' Duncan explained. 'It runs in the f-family.'

'But you don't get it, do you?'

'N-Now and then.'

'Oh you'll be all right when you've got me looking after you,' Phoebe said lovingly. 'Anyone would get depressed, living alone like you've done for so long. It'll be totally different when we're married, you'll see.' She didn't say then that she expected Duncan in his turn to look after her. That went without saying. He had already proved that he could, when he had rescued her from that dog, on the day they met. To Phoebe, being looked after was what marriage was all about, and large families were things one rested in the bosom of. She had been looking forward to that bit, never having had one. She was sure she'd get the hang of this one in time. She was, after all, not an innocent young bride, and she was entirely confident of her capacity to guide Duncan gently into the rôle of loving husband. She was sure they would both quickly adjust to living together and, from then on, would support and encourage each other whenever necessary. Instead of 'I', they would become 'we'.

Poor Duncan had had a bad time, living rough in his overgrown stone cottage for years and years with no proper income, and working irregularly as a jobbing gardener for anyone who would employ him. It had occurred to Phoebe to wonder why his mother hadn't occasionally driven over from the big house at the other end of the village, bringing with her a Hoover and some Flash. But when she met Hope it was obvious why not. Hope didn't do housework. Hope apparently didn't cook either. Perhaps, Phoebe wondered, she didn't because she couldn't? Phoebe herself had long ago learnt to say 'I don't play tennis' rather than 'I can't play tennis'. It made you sound more in charge of things.

When she was about 7, her great-aunt had told her that if you learnt to play mixed doubles well, you would meet a nice young man. Phoebe, then more interested in climbing trees than in boys, vowed never to learn and was completely successful at school in failing to achieve any degree of competence in the sport. She never met many nice young men either, but got involved at 20 with a married teacher in his forties and stayed trapped in the affair, veering wildly between optimistic joy and black despair for the next ten years. Then in July 1986, she met Duncan Moon.

Their wedding took place eleven months later in a rather decrepit register office in the small town in Northumberland where Phoebe and her divorced mother both (separately) lived. They were due to go in at eleven o'clock but were held up for half an hour by the wedding before theirs, which was running late. Running was hardly the word; none of the participants looked able to do anything quite so active. The bride was heavily pregnant and dressed entirely in orange. She was attended by two small children — her own? — some dozy youths and four old women who swayed alarmingly and looked as though they had already been to a reception. Her groom eventually appeared looking sheepish, and they all trooped off to the room next door.

Phoebe, who had worried for weeks as to whether her family and the Moons would get on together, looked anxiously across the waiting room over the heads of friends and relations, to where Hope and Peter were sitting with Duncan. Hope's thin mouth looked particularly unamused. Peter was writing something on the back of an envelope with a fountain pen. Phoebe hoped he hadn't left it until now to compose his speech. He had accepted the job with alacrity, on learning that Duncan's future father-in-law would not be present. Duncan looked up and smiled at her. Phoebe blew him a kiss.

'Is the famous one coming?' Wynne, her mother, whispered beside her. 'The actor, what's his name again?'

'Roderick. The family call him Rick. No, I don't think so. He's filming abroad somewhere. Conrad and his wife said they would be at the reception. Herry won't come though, Duncan says. It's a pity. You know, I still haven't met any of his brothers.'

'Who did you say last?'

'Hereward, the third son.'

'Snooty sort of names if you ask me,' her mother said, pulling a face.

'How can you say that? You called me Phoebe!'

'That's different. Your name's been in our family for generations; my mother, her grandmother . . . way back. It's traditional.'

Phoebe smiled at her affectionately. 'Have you talked much to Hope?' she asked.

'Long enough. We met in the entrance hall. She said, "We're very pleased about this marriage," in a toffee-nosed sort of voice, which made me feel I ought to curtsey or something, and that was about it. She's not the sort of woman you could confide in about your varicose veins, is she?'

'*Please*, Mum, for my sake. It's only for a few hours. Couldn't you just pretend to like her?'

'Don't worry, my pet. I won't let you down. But who'd a thought your man would have her ladyship for a mother! He's all right though, is Duncan's dad; lovely manners. I should think he likes his own way, mind, and I'll bet any money he can't change a plug. I can't bear a man who's no good with his hands!'

'Duncan's very practical.'

'I know, bless him. He's a dear. The only thing I can't understand is how a man like him can have got to 45 and never been married. He's not one of *those*, I hope?'

'*Mum!* Of course he's not.'

At that moment a man of about forty sauntered in. He was wearing khaki shorts, a pink flowery shirt and flip-flops on his feet. All his exposed skin was darkly tanned and his hair and beard had been sun-bleached almost to white. He had three gold earrings in one ear and he carried in one hand, and upside-down, a bunch of roses in a paper funnel. Peter raised a hand in greeting and the man went over and sat beside them, holding the flowers between his knees.

'Who's *that*?' asked Phoebe's mother, forgetting to whisper.

'I don't know . . . Oh yes I do. I think it must be Brendan, Peter's son; Duncan's half-brother. He delivers yachts and things all over the world. Duncan said he might be in Newcastle about now. Doesn't he look brown?'

'Brown be blowed! You'd think he'd put on proper clothes for an occasion like this, wouldn't you? Who's his mother then?' But before Phoebe could reply, the Registrar appeared at the door and invited them all in to the wedding room.

As soon as they had been through the simple formalities in front of the Registrar, and she was officially Mrs Moon, Phoebe stopped worrying and gave herself up to the blissful realization that she was finally irrevocably a *wife*. She looked at Duncan with love as he gave her the customary kiss. He was so tall and handsome, and he looked so good in that lovely suit. Phoebe was, for the first time, completely and utterly content.

They drove to a nearby hotel for the reception. Peter consulted his envelope and made a witty speech which made even Hope laugh. Then Duncan did his. He stammered badly, and forgot to thank Phoebe's mother for all she'd done. Everyone was rather relieved when he stopped early on and shrugged his shoulders shyly, spreading his large hands in a gesture of defeat. Public speaking was so tough for someone like him, Phoebe thought fondly, joining in the applause. At least he'd made the effort. She admired him for that. Duncan's character is so amazingly different from his father's, she thought with surprise. Judging by his clothes, so was Brendan's. Conrad, though, looked to Phoebe to be just the sort of son she'd have expected Peter to have.

Conrad and his wife had turned up in time for the speeches, and both kissed Duncan before turning to be introduced.

'Phoebe, this is my brother C-C-Conrad. Conrad; Phoebe.'

He had all the family features, the large forehead, the thick fair hair, the blue eyes and the rather delicate straight nose, but he was much more thickset, almost with a beer gut; an indulger in over rich corporate lunches, Phoebe thought. His suit had clearly been specially tailored for him and had cost a lot. He had the careless air of one with wealth and authority. He was obviously a successful businessman.

'Hello,' he said. 'Glad to see old Duncan has had the sense to find himself a good wife at long last.'

'Phoebe, this is F-Fay,' Duncan said, curling his lip at his brother.

'Lovely to meet you, Phoebe! I hope you'll be very happy.' She was beautiful, Phoebe thought enviously, slim and blonde and confident. Duncan had told her that Fay was a businesswoman; the owner of an up-market catering firm which she had originally started single-handed, cooking cordon bleu dinner parties for the filthy rich. She bent forwards and brushed her scented cheek against Phoebe's. 'Isn't this a lovely day?' she said.

'In fact it's raining outside,' Conrad said.

'Phoebe knows what I mean.' Fay gave her a sisterly smile.

'Yes I do, and it is,' Phoebe said happily.

'How did you two meet?' Fay asked.

'Duncan rescued me from an Alsatian on Hadrian's Wall!' Phoebe said. 'He was on a walking holiday, and we both happened to be going along it in opposite directions, when this horrible dog just appeared and jumped at me, and Duncan rushed up and dragged it off!'

'How heroic!' Conrad said mockingly. 'You'll have got quite the wrong impression of him from that, I fear.'

'Do shut up, darling,' Fay said. 'I think it's a lovely story. But how did you see each other afterwards? It's such a long way from here to Somerset.'

'We didn't much,' Phoebe admitted. 'We talked every day on the phone. It cost Duncan a fortune!'

'But it was worth it, wasn't it?' Fay asked, turning to him.

'P-Probably,' Duncan said.

'Hey! That's a bit grudging!' Phoebe protested.

'Can I get you another drink?' Conrad asked them all and then, turning to his wife said, 'I take it you'll be on tonic water on the rocks today and for the next six months?'

9

'Please,' Fay said. 'Would you believe it,' she explained to Phoebe and Duncan, 'pregnant again at 40! The girls are horrified; they thought people of our age had given up sex long ago!'

'How old are your girls?' Phoebe enquired politely, but her mind was elsewhere.

'They're 18 and 17,' Fay said. 'They're sorry they couldn't be here today, but they're in the thick of exams. Oh, there's Hope. I suppose I ought to go and say good-day to the old witch, just to show willing!' She smiled brilliantly at Phoebe and moved off. Phoebe looked round. Duncan had gone to help Conrad with the drinks.

Sex, Phoebe was thinking, that's really the only fly in the ointment . . .   'M-M-More champagne?' Duncan said, reappearing.

'Cheers!'

'Cheers!' They clinked glasses.

Phoebe thought, It's just a question of practice. It'll be fine in no time at all. This is just the beginning of living happily ever after.

Chapter Two

First impressions could be deeply misleading, Duncan was later to think, and her name hadn't helped either. Would he ever have got involved with Phoebe if she'd been called something more appropriate, such as Sandra, or Maureen? He remembered the Phoebe he had first met; the ordinary youngish woman who was quite obviously apprehensive about the German shepherd dog which was approaching her at a run along the footpath. As it bounded nearer and leapt up at her in ebullient high spirits, she yelped from pure terror and put up her arms to defend herself. If anything, the dog seemed a bit put out, affronted even, but it went on jumping. It was clearly not savage in intent, but the woman looked so helpless and afraid that Duncan felt obliged to intervene.

'Get DOWN!' he shouted to the dog and ran over, grabbing it by the collar and forcing it to sit. The woman burst into tears and covered her face with her hands. 'It's all o-okay,' Duncan said. 'I've g-got it. It won't h-h-h . . .' He couldn't say the word 'hurt', and gave up, stroking the dog's head in silence and keeping it under control until its owner appeared rather huffily to claim it. Duncan watched it trotting away on a lead.

By now the woman had got herself together, had wiped her eyes and was blowing her nose. Duncan smiled at her and turned to resume his walk.

'Hang on,' she said. 'Don't disappear. I want to thank . . . You've just saved my life!'

'Well, I wouldn't go that f-far,' Duncan said modestly.

'But you did! Dogs always go for me; they know I'm scared. I got bitten once when I was a child, so I'm frightened of them, so they go for me. It's a vicious circle.' She smiled self-mockingly. 'Vicious is right,' she said. 'Did you see those teeth?'

Duncan, who had indeed observed the teeth and could see nothing remarkable in them, was nevertheless flattered to be cast in such a macho mould. He knew that she was

11

overdramatizing the incident, but it didn't displease him. Later, of course, when it had become known to all as The Big Rescue, it was far too late to disabuse anyone.

She seemed to him to be pleasant enough; an easy person to get on with. She asked if he minded if she walked back with him. She had lost her enthusiasm for walking alone, she said, and time was getting on anyway. He nodded, although really he preferred to be quiet and solitary.

'What's your name?' she asked.

'D-D-D . . .' he stammered, trying too hard.

'David?' she supplied helpfully.

'N-No.'

'Donald?'

'No.'

'Dennis?'

'NO! S-Stop it. Just wait a m-moment.'

'Sorry.' She really did look sorry.

'It's Duncan, Duncan M-Moon'.

'Duncan Moon, that's a good name. Mine's Phoebe.'

'How d'you do?' he said, and held out his hand. She looked disconcerted, but gave him hers to shake. It was hot and damp. He let go of it rather quickly, and thrust his own back into his pocket. They started walking.

'That's a huge rucksack,' Phoebe said. 'Are you doing the whole wall?'

'That's the i-idea.'

'I think this is the best bit. It's certainly the most photographed. Don't you think those crags are impressive?'

'Mmmm.' He did.

'Last time I was here, in May, the curlews were calling. It's my favourite sound. It's so lovely and empty and wild up here, isn't it? You can see for miles. I drive up and wander along the wall when I'm feeling gloomy, to pep myself up. Do you always walk alone?'

'Yes. I find it's e-easier.' He glanced sideways at her. The wind was blowing her hair into her eyes. It was thick, dark chestnut in colour and not quite straight, rather attractive actually. Her skin was very fair and inclined to freckles; the sort that didn't go brown in the sun.

'Why easier?' she asked.

'I don't know. I suppose I mean that I c-can go at my own p-pace and stop when I want to.'

'Where were you thinking of stopping tonight?'

'H-H-H . . .' He took a deep breath and tried again. '. . . Hexham.' He was grateful to her for waiting politely until he was able to get the word out. She seemed quite happy to do so, and not at all impatient. He warmed to her.

'But that's where I live!' She turned smiling to him. She had obviously just had an idea. 'Do you stay in hotels,' she asked, 'booked in advance?'

He shook his head. 'Bed and b-breakfast mostly, wherever I happen to end up.'

'Well then, why don't you stay tonight in my flat? Save money? I've got a spare sofa, and I could cook you supper.'

'Well, it's a very kind o-o-offer, but I . . .' He felt awkward.

'Please,' she said, 'I'd like you to.' Her eyes were freckly too; hazel. They looked hopeful and trusting, rather like those of Hickory, his mother's dog.

And so he had stayed for the evening and was pampered with convenience food, kept in the freezer for such emergencies, a bottle of supermarket wine, and music; mostly Billy Joel and Mozart. Duncan told her that his mother was a musician, played the viola and considered Wagner to be *bowel music*. She had laughed. She laughed easily. He began to relax, even to enjoy himself. She wasn't really fanciable – a bit overweight perhaps? – so he didn't feel that he had to prove anything. He found that he could be surprisingly comfortable in her company, but as the evening wore on, old anxieties began to surface in him. What did she want of him? Did she expect a performance in bed? Would he be able to get out of it without offending her? He found himself tensing up again.

At 10.30 she got to her feet, looking apologetic. 'I'm sorry,' she said. 'I'm whacked! I'm afraid I'll have to go to my bed. Will you be okay on the sofa?'

'Fine, thanks.'

'Goodnight then. Sleep well.' She went to the door.

' 'Night.' He tried to say 'thank you' but she had already gone. He breathed a sigh of relief.

13

In the morning she cooked him scrambled eggs and gave him real coffee. She was warm and friendly and undemanding. He found that he was loath to leave. I could get used to this sort of thing, he thought wryly.

'Will you give us a ring when you get home?' she asked, giving him her telephone number on a torn-off piece of paper. 'I'd like to know how you got on.'

'Surely.' He had no real intention of doing so, but he put the number in his pocket anyway, just to please her.

How he came to lose his keys, he never did know. He only discovered their loss when he arrived home at the end of his week off, and found that they were not in his pocket. He let himself into his cottage with the spare one under the big stone, and only as an afterthought did he find the crumpled number and ring Phoebe.

'Yes, I found them under the sofa.' She sounded delighted. 'Give us your address and I'll send them straight on.'

'Thank goodness for that,' he said. 'I can't think how they came to be there or why I didn't notice their absence straight-away.'

'Amazing!' Phoebe said.

'What is?'

'Do you realize, you haven't stammered at all, so far?'

'Yes.'

'I'm sorry, perhaps I shouldn't have mentioned it. It wasn't very tactful of me, was it?'

'It's okay. I don't mind.' He found that he really didn't mind.

'Have you noticed it before? Not stammering on the phone, I mean?'

'Sometimes, yes.'

'Does it bother you, stammering?'

'Yes, of course it does, but there doesn't seem to be much I can do about it. I've been to all sorts of so-called experts and got nowhere.'

'Perhaps you need practice,' Phoebe suggested. 'If you were to phone me on a regular basis, we could have long talks. It would be good therapy.'

He laughed, but the idea took hold of him and he began to look forward to hearing her voice. The telephone accentuated

14

her slight Geordie lilt and he discovered it to be rather endearing. She became a habit.

In October he found himself inviting her down for a weekend to see his cottage. He had only one bed and no sofa, so he had had to assume that they would sleep together in it, and prepare himself for the consequences. She was not totally unattractive in truth. That evening he drank some whisky to stiffen his resolve and later allowed himself to be cushioned upon her soft squidgy body, and made welcome inside it. He got the business over with as soon as possible and, after his brief spurt of pleasure, felt embarrassed and hoped she hadn't disliked it all too much. She appeared surprised rather than anything, but made no comment. He wondered how sexually experienced she was, and decided not to admit to her that he had been a virgin until he was thirty.

Now he had got that side of things started, he felt a lot better. It had been weighing on his mind ever since he met her (*the Englishman has sex on the brain – which is the wrong place*). She had obviously expected it of him; women usually did. He wondered sometimes what they got out of it. This weekend had been the crunch; something he had nerved himself up for. In the event, it hadn't proved so difficult after all. She was a nice sympathetic sort of girl, and she had made it easy for him.

From then on, they talked every day on the phone. Whenever she could, which wasn't often, Phoebe came down to Somerset for a weekend and did some tidying up and cleaning in the cottage. She said she liked doing it. She said it was very rewarding. Duncan thought that that sounded positively unnatural, but was happy that she should continue.

'I don't know how you manage without a washing machine,' she said one day. 'How on earth do you wash sheets?'

'L-Launderette in W-Weston-super-M-Mare' Duncan said, pretty sure that there was one there.

'What a drag to have to go all that way! I mean, I've got one and there's a launderette round the corner from my flat. It's still worth having one just for the convenience of it.'

Duncan, who had never felt this need, allowed a small wavelet of superiority to ripple over his ego. 'Mmmmmm,' he said.

'It seems daft my having one for just me,' Phoebe said.

15

'A bit un-un-uneconomic,' Duncan agreed. She gave him a long look. He thought her expression seemed a bit reproachful, but he couldn't think of anything he'd done to annoy her, so he forgot it.

At Easter, Phoebe took a week's leave from her job as Personal Secretary to a professor at Newcastle University, and drove down to Somerset. Duncan promised to take time off his work also, and they planned to build some kitchen units together. It was something which Duncan had meant to do for years. Once started, it didn't take nearly as long as he had feared. Phoebe was a great help, handing him tools, holding things steady, fetching wood from his shed and generally being encouraging. She made and brought him refreshments whenever he needed them, and was complimentary about his carpentry skills. She also seemed to approve of the cottage.

'I love this place,' she said, looking dreamily through the window. 'There are three daffodils out there! I wonder if there was a beautiful garden here once. It's got great potential, hasn't it? Why haven't you done something with it?'

'T-Too busy doing other p-people's,' Duncan said. He was lying on his back with his head under the sink, trying to fix an awkward support for the new draining board. His throat felt parched and full of dust.

'Phoebe,' he said, 'would you m-m-m-m-m . . .' He couldn't get it out. He drew breath to try again, but Phoebe burst in before he could.

'Oh Duncan!' she said, with a quiver of emotion in her voice. 'Yes, of course I'll marry you. Oh I've never felt so *happy*!'

Duncan, who had been trying to say 'Would you make me a cup of tea?', was so taken aback that he sat up abruptly and hit his head painfully on the sink above. By the time he had emerged, clutching it, and Phoebe had kissed it better, it was a bit late and too difficult to explain what he had really meant. Phoebe was looking positively radiant. He hadn't the heart to take the wind out of her sails, so he said nothing.

'I must phone my mum!' Phoebe said. 'She'll be over the moon. Joke! You must take me to meet your parents now, Duncan. Oh I'm that happy I don't know where to put myself!' She did a little dance round the kitchen.

16

'Let's have a c-cup of tea,' Duncan said, smiling in spite of himself at her enthusiasm. He was touched that the prospect of marriage to him would cause anyone to go into such raptures; touched and flattered. When he came to think of it, it did seem to be the sensible thing to do. They got on all right – no, more than that, he actually *liked* her. She was a good cook. She was cheerful. She seemed to care a lot for him. She could move into the cottage and life would go on as usual, but more comfortably. How could he go wrong?

And now here they were, at the wedding. It had gone rather well, Duncan thought. Phoebe was all got-up in a long dress, a sort of paleish colour with blue in it, and looking pretty good. They had acquired a whole tableful of presents; things he had never dreamt of owning. Would Phoebe ever actually use that wok? He was sure he never would. One or two of his employers as well as his family had made the effort to attend, to wish him well. It was all very pleasant. He felt he had done the right thing in getting married.

'What are you thinking?' Phoebe said, at his elbow.

He smiled down at her. 'What a g-good i-idea this is,' he said.

She slipped her arm through his and squeezed it. 'Good,' she said.

'Ah.' Duncan saw his half-brother approaching. 'You haven't met B-Brendan, have you?'

'Hi,' Brendan said. Close to, he looked even more suntanned and very fit. Phoebe admired his muscles. He's such a masculine sort of man, he can carry off that pansy shirt, she thought. His mouth was smiling at her, but his blue eyes looked curiously blank. 'I brought you some roses,' he said. 'Where the hell are they? Hang on, I think I left them in the cloakroom.' He turned and left them, elbowing his way through the guests with minimum apology.

'Who is his mother?' Phoebe whispered to Duncan. 'You never did tell me.'

'An actress f-friend of Father's. Died when he was f-fourteen. Don't m-mention it, will you? He gets a b-bit t-touchy about his o-o-origins.'

17

'Does your father have many *friends*?' Phoebe enquired, rather surprised.

'Who knows?' Duncan made a face.

'But how did your mother feel about adopting him? Surely –'

'Sssssh!' Duncan said. Brendan was coming back.

'Nicked,' he said. 'Can't trust anybody these days, can you? Never mind, it's the thought, and all that. Happy wedding.'

'Thank you,' Phoebe said, smiling at him. 'And thanks for coming. It's lovely to meet you. Are you between yachts just now?'

'Yeah, sort of. Off to the West Indies next week.'

'That sounds wonderful.'

'Mmm. We don't get much time for sightseeing, so it's not as wonderful as it might appear.'

'How long will you be away?'

'Six months, maybe more.'

'But what about your family? How do they manage?'

Brendan looked annoyed. 'Not a problem,' he said rather shortly. 'Must dash. Nice to see you, Dunc. Hang in there,' and he was gone.

'What did I say?' Phoebe appealed to Duncan. 'Did I upset him or something?'

'He doesn't have a f-family,' Duncan said, embarrassed.

Phoebe shrugged. 'So what? That doesn't explain why –'

'He's h-h-h-h . . . gay,' Duncan said, shortly.

'Bloody hell!' Phoebe said, going scarlet. 'You could have warned me; I feel a complete prat now!'

'It's n-not important,' Duncan said.

'Is there anything else you ought to tell me about your family to stop me from making a total fool of myself?'

'P-possibly,' Duncan said, 'but now's not the t-time.' He looked at his watch. 'Shouldn't we be g-going off soon?'

'I'll go and change,' Phoebe said. 'You ought to too. You can't go on a camping honeymoon in Norfolk in that smart suit!'

'You go f-first,' Duncan said. 'It won't take me long.'

When Phoebe came back some fifteen minutes later, wearing a simple cotton summer dress and looking more herself, she seemed puzzled and annoyed.

18

'I've just seen your mother,' she told Duncan.

'Oh?'

'Guess what she was stowing away in the boot of their car.'

'W-What?'

'Brendan's roses!'

Four years on, Peter's 'small favour' seemed odd to Phoebe. Why couldn't he ring Hope himself? And who was this Nancy Sedgemoor person who'd died? How should she break it to Hope? Was she an old friend? Would Hope be upset? Was that why Peter had chickened out? Phoebe felt uncomfortable. Should she wait until Duncan came home, and ask him? She sighed. What was the point? Duncan wouldn't be any help. He never told her anything; never *knew* anything, damn it! She dialled her in-laws' number before she could change her mind.

'Yes?' said Hope's voice. It was not an encouraging start.

'Er, hello, Hope. This is Phoebe. How are you?'

'I'm much as usual, but I do wish we didn't have this dreadful rain!'

'It's doing the gardens good, isn't it? Better than last month's drought.'

'It never knows when to stop. Was there something you wanted? . . . Only I'm in the middle of a quartet.'

'Well, no actually. I've got a message from Peter. He says he tried to call you several times, but you were out.'

'I haven't been out!'

'Oh well, I don't know . . .' Phoebe's voice faded away. This was going to be difficult.

'Well?' Hope sounded impatient.

'You know Nancy Sedgemoor?' Phoebe said in a rush.

'Yes, of course I do. Tiresome woman.'

'Um, well, she's . . . er . . . died.' There was silence at the other end of the phone. 'Are you there?' Phoebe said.

'Dead? Nancy?'

'Yes, I'm afraid so.'

'Did Peter say if he'd seen her?'

'He said he got there too late.'

'Hah!' Hope said, and it didn't sound to Phoebe like an expression of regret.

*

When Duncan came in that evening, Phoebe raised the subject with him.

'Mmmmm,' he said. He was standing by the electric kettle, waiting for it to boil, and in the meantime opening his mail, screwing up the envelopes and aiming them inexpertly at the wood basket.

'Please, Duncan,' Phoebe said. 'Don't just chuck them in there, they look so messy. Why can't you put them in the burnables bin like I do? Anyway, why did Hope react like that?'

'N-No idea,' Duncan said, pouring boiling water into the teapot.

'You must have some idea?' Phoebe said, frowning. 'Nancy Sedgemoor must have been quite close to your father, for her to have wanted to see him on her deathbed. It must have been really upsetting for Peter to have missed her by minutes like that. Hey!' A thought had struck her. Duncan didn't look up. 'Was she another of your father's *friends?*'

'NO!' Duncan said emphatically. 'Have some tea.' He handed her a mugful. They sat at the kitchen table opposite each other.

'No,' Phoebe said, sipping it reflectively, 'you're right, she can't have been. If she had, he would have sounded much more upset on the phone, wouldn't he?' Duncan didn't reply. Phoebe wished fervently that Duncan would just *talk* to her. He would speak when he was spoken to, certainly, but he never chatted. He never spontaneously brought up a subject and enlarged upon it. He never delighted her with unexpected thoughts, or (crazy optimistic idea) expressed his hopes or his fears . . . In the four years she had been with him, he had never yet confided in her. Phoebe felt that she had changed and become 'we'. Duncan was still stubbornly 'I'. She sighed. 'Did you ever meet her?' she asked.

'A f-few times, yes.'

'What was she like?'

'Nice e-enough.'

'No! Describe her to me. Was she tall/short? fair/dark? fat/thin? happy/sad? clever/stupid? warm/cold? posh/com-

20

mon? rich/poor?' Phoebe drew breath. 'I mean, what was she *like*?' She could hear herself sounding exasperated and she could see Duncan pulling up his drawbridge. His face took on a familiar mulish look and he refused to meet her eyes.

'Sh-She was g-grey when I knew her, and she w-was t-tallish and c-c-c-c-c . . .' He always stammered more at times like this. Phoebe clenched her hands into fists under the table, and willed him to get it out. '. . . Clever. She had a doctorate,' Duncan said eventually.

'What in?'

'I d-don't know.'

'Your mother said she was tiresome,' Phoebe probed.

'J-Just give it a rest, w-will you?' Duncan said, getting up and banging his mug of tea down.

'Where are you going?'

He didn't answer. Instead he said, 'T-Talking of Mother r-reminds me. She told me to t-tell you. This November the t-twenty-seventh is their G-Golden Wedding,' and he went out into the garden.

Hell! thought Phoebe. I suppose that means she's expecting us to do something about it.

Chapter Three

Duncan enjoyed his honeymoon in Norfolk in June of '87. They hired a dinghy on one of the secluded Broads where motorboats are not allowed, and they rowed out to a far bay through rafts of water lilies, towards a patch of clear brown water. Here they anchored and whilst Phoebe read a novel, Duncan got out his tin of questing maggots and his fishing rod and proceeded to fill his keepnet with coarse freshwater fish; bream and roach and the odd rudd.

'What do they taste like?' Phoebe asked.

'M-Mud and b-bones.'

'You mean you're going to all that trouble and we aren't going to eat any of them? What are you going to do with them then?'

'P-Put them back again.'

'What's the point?'

'S-S-skill!' Duncan smiled at her. She had got herself cozily curled up at the bow end of the boat, with her sleeping bag wrapped round her and an inflatable cushion behind her head. Her hair shone redly in the sun and the top strands lifted lazily in the gentle breeze. The water plopped at the sides of the boat, but otherwise all was quiet. They had brought sandwiches and a flask of coffee and a large umbrella in case of rain. What more could one want? Duncan thought contentedly. 'Good book?' he asked her.

'Very. It's all about how women feel and how people don't communicate with each other like they should, and about the crises that happen in their lives because of that. It's fascinating. You should read it.'

'D-Doesn't sound m-much like my sort of thing,' Duncan said.

'What is your sort of thing then?'

'I don't know – thrillers, w-war stories, b-biography . . .'

'Does emotion frighten you?' She had put her book down and

was staring straight at him. He felt as if she were challenging him to a contest; one in which he had no desire to engage. He avoided her eyes.

'What an o-odd qu-question!' he parried.

'So why don't you answer it?'

But his line tightened at that moment and he became fully occupied with landing another bream. Phoebe went back to her book and appeared once more to be absorbed in it. He wished she wouldn't suddenly come out with attacks like that. They were disconcerting. He didn't wish to discuss such things.

There was a sudden splash. Duncan looked up to see a large pale bird of prey emerging from the water only fifty yards away, with a dripping fish in its talons.

'Look!' he cried. 'An osprey!'

'What a marvellous sight! I've never seen one before,' Phoebe exclaimed, staring after it, before turning amazed eyes on him. 'Wasn't that a real treat? D'you reckon it's a good omen?'

'Omen?'

'For us! To see one on our honeymoon. It's got to be really lucky, don't you think?'

Duncan smiled at her. 'If it p-pleases you,' he said, patting her affectionately on the top of the head. He felt almost paternal towards her.

At the end of the day, it was always very pleasant to go back to the camp site and lie side by side in his tent, waiting for the kettle to boil on the camping gas stove. It had been warm and dry all day, but now he felt sweaty. The air seemed thick and the sky ominously yellow. Perhaps there was a storm in the offing.

'What's for supper?' he asked.

'Paella out of a packet and baked beans,' Phoebe said, rather apologetically, 'followed by tinned peaches and condensed milk, washed down with cider.'

It sounded disgustingly attractive to Duncan, rather like a dormitory midnight feast. It reminded him of some of the happier times in his school days, and he said so.

'Were you a boarder at a public school then?' Phoebe asked. 'Poor you. How old were you when you were sent there?'

'Seven.'

23

'But that's awful! It's really cruel. Did you hate it?'

'I g-got used to it.'

'Did all your brothers go too?'

'All except B-Brendan; he r-refused, and Herry. Herry went briefly, but he was e-e-expelled.'

'What for?'

'Some p-prank or another.'

Phoebe was surprised to find that she liked fishing, or rather that she was happy watching Duncan fish. The surroundings were so tranquil and beautiful. She enjoyed seeing the leaves of the white and yellow water lilies, flipping upwards in the breeze, the sentinel heron fishing from the distant bank, and an anxious brown mallard with her clockwork ducklings muttering along the water margins. The air smelled of damp woodwork and distant hay. Phoebe didn't like the actual catching of the fish or the process of disengaging them from the hook, but apart from that it was a restful and companionable way to spend time, and she was really enjoying her book. Then there was the osprey; what a thrill! Even Duncan, who didn't usually let himself go, had reacted excitedly to seeing that. He had been a bit condescending afterwards though, when she had said it was an omen. She was beginning to find that he could be quite patronizing at times, and old-fashioned; pompous even. Whoever used the word 'prank' nowadays? And he'd refused to enlarge upon it and tell her what Herry had actually done. No, she thought, I mustn't be so critical. It's just the difference in our backgrounds and upbringing, and after all, he is fourteen years older than me . . .

Phoebe wasn't going to let anything spoil this week. She twisted her new 18-carat-gold wedding ring round and round her finger and wondered whether Duncan would try to make love to her that night. The night before he had been put off by the proximity of some other campers, but today they had packed up and gone, and there were no others as close, so perhaps he would feel less inhibited. He surely wasn't ashamed of doing it, was he? They were married, after all! Phoebe would like to have discussed the subject with him, but she was discovering that he was surprisingly difficult to talk to, face to

24

face. Of course she had to make allowances; anyone who stammered as badly as he did would naturally avoid having to talk too much. It wasn't really surprising. She resolved to be kind to him, and more understanding.

The first rumble of thunder sounded as they finished washing up after supper. Heavy splashy drops of rain began falling, and campers all over the site hastily bundled their possessions under fly sheets or into vehicles, out of the wet. Phoebe and Duncan eased themselves naked into their double sleeping bag – two single ones zipped together – and lay uncomfortably entwined. The ground was hard under Phoebe's hip, but she suffered it in the interests of togetherness. The sound of individual drops falling onto the tent was soon overtaken by the steady drumming of heavy rain.

'I hope it won't leak,' Phoebe said apprehensively, looking at the ridge above her head. The tent had a built-in groundsheet, and the entrance was securely zipped up so, apart from that worry, it felt very safe and womb-like. It was still just light enough for her to see Duncan's chin. It was bristly and, like everything else, looked orange. She snuggled up tighter. Duncan's Adam's apple moved against her forehead rather jerkily but his voice sounded confident.

'It w-won't,' he said. 'I've used it in w-worse weather than this. G-Goodnight then. Sleep well.' He kissed the top of her head and disengaged himself from her, turning over and pummelling his pillow to make it comfortable. Within minutes he was asleep, and breathing regularly with a slight snore. Phoebe felt stranded in mid-air.

She lay awake with eyes wide in the increasing darkness, listening to the rain. She counted the seconds between the flashes of lightning and the answering growls of thunder, and heard the storm getting nearer and nearer. Now the thunder crashed almost simultaneously with the lightning. The storm was on top of them. During the flashes Phoebe could see Duncan's head and shoulders vividly illuminated. He didn't stir. He was fast asleep. Phoebe felt angry with him. How could he possibly sleep with such a racket going on? Why couldn't he be awake to share it with her? Why hadn't he wanted to make love? Didn't he fancy her after all? Had she annoyed him? This

25

week wasn't turning out quite as she'd hoped. Perhaps they should have been conventional and gone to a hotel; booked the honeymoon suite; spent the days in bed with champagne on ice. Duncan had said that that would be too expensive. Phoebe sighed. As soon as they got home, she would have to get herself a job . . . No, she wouldn't think about that now. She was on her honeymoon, for heaven's sake! She stared upwards. At least the tent wasn't leaking. Things could be worse.

What was that? Phoebe half sat up to listen to a thumping noise. Then she lay back smiling, grateful for her own relative comfort. It was some poor sod outside in the downpour, with a mallet, banging in tent pegs!

A fortnight after they got back from Norfolk, Phoebe met the famous Roderick Moon for the first time. She and Duncan were invited to go over to his parents' big house.

'Come for dinner tomorrow,' Hope said. It sounded to Phoebe more like a royal command. 'Rick's here for one night before he flies off to do a film in Madagascar.'

'Lovely,' Phoebe said. 'I'm so looking forward to seeing him in the flesh.' Yuk! she thought. Why did I say that? It sounds positively indecent.

'Poor Rick,' Hope said. 'Both his wives went mad, you know.'

'Oh,' Phoebe said. There didn't seem to be much else that she could say.

'Is Duncan there?'

With relief, Phoebe handed the phone to him. He said very little, but Phoebe noticed that he didn't stammer at all. It's magic, she thought, watching him with soft eyes. He was so calm and self-contained. Those were two of the things she loved about him. And he was so clever at making and doing things. He couldn't be made to conform, or rushed, but he took a real pride in getting things just right. He was a man out of his time really; he should have been a craftsman in the eighteenth century . . . She studied his profile with loving attention. She liked the straightness of his nose, the shape of his ears, the thickness of his untidy fair hair and even the fact that he was left-handed. He was her man; she was no longer second best. Duncan put the receiver down and smiled casually at her.

26

'How is she?' asked Phoebe, who hadn't had the opportunity to find out herself.

'She's got a-asparagus b-b-beetle,' Duncan said.

Phoebe quizzed Duncan about his youngest brother as they drove through the village the following evening. It was hard work. She managed to exhume a few bones of information, but no meat. His first wife had been 17 and pregnant when Rick married her, and they had subsequently had two boys. Her name was Poppy Schaffner and she was an American. They had got divorced after only three years. Poppy's parents had then got her into a sort of mental hospital in the States and Rick had got custody of the children. He had subsequently married Elenira, a Brazilian girl aged 16, who was beautiful but dumb, and who had killed herself after six months, with the baby she was carrying.

'How dreadful!' Phoebe exclaimed. 'But what about the children?'

'They have a r-resident n-nanny,' Duncan said.

'But they must be so confused and upset?' Phoebe said.

'They're n-not easy,' Duncan said.

'Will they be with him?'

'D-Doubt it. They st-stay in London while he's w-working.'

'How old are they now?'

'Um . . . t-ten and eight, I think.'

They turned into the drive down a green tunnel formed from an avenue of tall lime trees, and bumped over its stony surface towards the big house.

'Ten's a nice age,' Phoebe said, 'before the terrible teens.' A thought struck her. 'Why does Rick always marry such young girls? Can't he cope with real women?' The van slowed at a sharp bend in the drive, and the north side of the square grey house came into view.

'Ask him,' Duncan said. 'The-There he is.'

Rick had parked his silver sports car in the yard in front of them, below one of the many dark yews which overhung the stone outbuildings and gave the approach to the house a gloomy shut-in feel. He had just got out, and was pulling a bulky holdall from the passenger seat. He looked, Phoebe thought, even at a distance, very smooth; polished almost. He had the strong family

27

characteristics of the Moons, Phoebe already knew, but he was more like their father than the other brothers.

Duncan parked their old van next to Rick's car and Phoebe, who had bent down to do up one of her sandals, found Rick at her side, opening and holding the door wide for her to get out. She was surprised and not a little flattered at such an old-fashioned display of courtesy.

'Oh! Thanks,' she said. It sounded inadequate. She shuffled out rather awkwardly and smoothed down her dress.

'How d'you do?' he said. 'And not before time!' Without touching her, he ushered her towards the front door, calling over his shoulder to his brother.

'Hi, Dunc. I'm just kidnapping the little woman, okay?' He turned mischievous eyes onto Phoebe and winked in confident complicity. His eyes were very blue and took on a new intensity when he smiled. Phoebe had seen him several times on television and, although impressed by his acting, had been put off by his public image and quite expected to dislike the real man. She had been wrong; here in person he was charm itself. She glanced quickly behind her. Duncan was reaching into the back of their van for the bottle of wine they had brought.

'Don't worry about my big brother,' Rick said. 'He has you all the time, the lucky so-and-so. How are the parents, then? It's a long time since I've seen them.'

Phoebe's mind was a blank. After a pause, she said, 'Hope has asparagus beetle.'

'How shameful!' Rick said, roaring with laughter. 'I do hope it isn't catching.'

'Not personally,' Phoebe said hurriedly. 'I didn't mean . . .' She stopped, feeling foolish.

Rick was staring at the top of her head. 'I've always loved hair your colour,' he said, 'passionate red.'

Dinner was a formal affair with Peter very much in charge. A large joint of beef was brought in from the kitchen by Mrs B., the latest nonresident cook, and he set to with much flourishing of knife and steel to carve for everyone. Hope sat at the other end of the long polished table and stared out of the window at the evening garden. She was in one of her moods. Duncan sat

28

opposite Rick and Phoebe and in the space beside his chair, Hope's golden labrador, Hickory, sat, swishing her tail hopefully in an arc across the parquet floor, watching his every movement with liquid brown eyes.

'Madagascar!' Peter said to the world in general. 'I seem to remember that in the late nineteenth century its people had a violent insurrection. And against whom did they rise up in rebellion?' No one rose to his challenge, being too busy passing plates of meat down the table. 'Wretched woman,' Peter complained. 'Why must she overcook every damn thing? It should be *pink* in the middle; run *red* when cut! She needs a firm hand, my dear.' His wife's long thin hands twitched slightly on the table by her plate, but she went on looking out of the window. 'Well?' Peter demanded, looking all round him. 'Who were the evil oppressors? Why, the perfidious French, of course. Now what else do we know about Madagascar – apart from the fact that it's probably a most unsuitable place in which to make a film? Phoebe, what have you to tell us?'

Phoebe looked defensive. 'It has those little animals with stripy tails,' she said, 'ring-tailed something.'

'Lemurs,' supplied Rick, smiling.

'Yes.' Phoebe turned to him gratefully.

'Oh he won't see any of those,' Peter said, brushing the suggestion aside. 'No, what I'm interested in is the history and the economy of the place. Who knows what its population is? Ten million? Twenty million?'

'Twelve,' said Rick.

'And what's the source of their wealth?' Peter demanded, ignoring the interruption. 'Logging the rainforest – and squashing the lemurs, no doubt – but who can blame them if that's all they've got . . .' He went on talking, apparently unconcerned as to whether or not anyone was listening. Duncan nodded at him from time to time, and slipped Hickory sly savoury morsels, but really was watching in gloomy resignation as his brother continued to lay siege to Phoebe with his usual charming-the-pants-off-the-nearest-woman routine, which he always seemed incapable of resisting. Duncan could see that she was blushing with pleasure at his attentions and laughing enthusiastically at his jokes. Every so often she appeared to remember Duncan's

29

existence with a start, and at those times she would attempt to include him in their conversation. Duncan was not to be lured in so easily. He hoped if he was uncooperative that sooner or later his disapproval would register with his wife and she would have to stop hanging onto Rick's every word and pay proper attention to him. He heard Rick ask her about herself, and Phoebe telling the dog rescue story. He noticed his brother's sardonic glance in his direction and knew that he wasn't fooled by it. Then it was the proposal story.

'Duncan's so sweet,' Phoebe said, smiling briefly in his direction. 'He was too shy to ask me to marry him face to face, so he waited until he felt safe; lying in the cupboard under the kitchen sink with only his legs sticking out!'

'How romantic!' said Rick, drily.

'Well it was certainly different,' Phoebe said giggling. 'And when I said yes, he was so surprised he forgot where he was and sat up sudden like, and practically knocked himself out!' She laughed. Rick laughed with her. Peter was still talking about Madagascar. Hope was still looking out of the window. It occurred to Duncan that his marriage had not only been founded upon misunderstandings, but looked doomed to be burdened with them in perpetuity. He should have scotched them when he had had the chance at the time. Now it was impossible. Phoebe was talking about him with friendly mockery as though he were her property; something she had created herself. It made him uneasy. It was an aspect of marriage which he hadn't anticipated and didn't feel comfortable with – a kind of invasion.

'I proposed to your mother on one knee by the light of a flaming church,' Peter said, giving up the unequal struggle with Madagascar and attempting a takeover, 'during the Blitz.'

'You did no such thing!' Hope said, suddenly relinquishing her gaze on the garden, which was now too dark to see anyway. She faced her husband accusingly. 'It was in your mother's scullery. You were home on leave with a hernia!' She turned crossly to Duncan. 'I do wish you wouldn't encourage the dog, Duncan. It makes her such a pest.'

'She's always been g-greedy,' Duncan said mildly. 'Haven't

you, Hicky?' He rubbed her under her chin, and she closed her eyes in rapture.

'Your ma thinks she's in pup,' Peter said. 'She got out.'

'G-Great!' Duncan said. 'W-We'll have one, w-won't we, Phoebe?'

'Well, I . . .' Phoebe began, but they had all taken her acceptance for granted.

Phoebe got herself a job as secretary at a small theatre in the nearest little town. It wasn't the sort of job she was used to. It was mornings only and a lot less demanding than her Newcastle one, where she had had to master a lot of scientific jargon and zoological vocabulary. It didn't pay nearly as well either, but it suited her. In the early days of marriage she wanted time to devote to Duncan; time to sort out the cottage; time perhaps to conquer the garden. They had decided that they could live very cheaply. They had no mortgage to pay, as the cottage belonged to Hope and Peter. They were not intending to entertain or be entertained much, as Duncan didn't like social gatherings. Duncan didn't need smart clothes for work, and he could maintain and repair his van himself. Phoebe's car was an unnecessary expense to run, but worth quite a bit. They could use the money, so they decided to sell it. She could ride to work on a bicycle.

After the rush and busyness of the first few weeks, Phoebe began happily to wonder about the future. Duncan made nearly enough money, but it was irregular and uncertain. She would have to work whatever happened, maybe go full time if things got hard. So what about children? She and Duncan had never actually discussed them, but she assumed that he would be keen to have at least one.

'K-Kids?' he said, when she finally broached the subject. 'We're a b-bit old for that s-sort of nonsense, aren't we?' And the next time he came home it was with a small black labrador puppy which he handed to her with tenderness. 'F-Father says this one's g-got to g-go. He's already d-dug up Mother's b-best herbaceous b-border. They've called him Diggory. Father says he's H-Hickory's Diggory d-dog! Isn't he a little m-monster?' he bent over and pulled the silky ears delicately with a large hand,

31

and smiled up at her. 'Good ch-child s-s-s . . . substitute,' he remarked, and went to put the kettle on.

Diggory wriggled a bit in Phoebe's arms and chewed a finger exploratively with sharp little white teeth, then leapt up to lick her face enthusiastically, and she had to grab at him to stop him from falling. His fur was short and shiny and his paws were ridiculous. In spite of herself she relented. He was very charming. He was also a *fait accompli*.

Phoebe thought, This wasn't how I meant things to be.

Chapter Four

On 27 November 1991 the senior Moons' Golden Wedding party took place. Contrary to Phoebe's assumptions, it was not held in Somerset but in the Parliament Chamber of the Inner Temple in London, which was more accessible for friends, colleagues and most relations. Hope's quartet had borrowed another viola player for the occasion and, sitting on the platform, played elegant chamber music which was barely heard above the hubbub of conversation.

Clutching a glass of white wine, Phoebe wandered shyly amongst the throng of guests, marvelling that any couple could know so many people. She passed Peter holding court to a group of women, and hung about for a while on the edge, hoping to become included, but eventually gave up and moved on. She looked for Duncan and found him in earnest conversation with a purple hat, under which stood a sweet elderly woman half his height. He was bending low over it to catch what she was saying, and looked rather pleased with himself. Phoebe joined them and the old woman began the conversation all over again, to include her.

'Last time I saw Duncan, he was so high,' she said, putting out a veiny hand which quivered when horizontal. 'He must then have been about seven, but I knew him at once today. He was always such a sensitive boy and so clever at making things.'

'He still is,' Phoebe said proudly. 'He's just built a lovely pond for Hope and Peter, in their garden in Somerset. It's a really interesting shape!'

Duncan smiled and, excusing himself, moved on to talk to someone else. Phoebe started after him, but Purple Hat hadn't finished, and clutched Phoebe's arm confidentially.

'I see he still stammers badly,' she said. 'Such a pity. I blame his father, you know. Whatever poor Duncan tried to do, Peter would always top it; always had to have the last word; completely undermined the poor child's confidence. But stammering is quite unnecessary these days you know. Duncan could be cured if he wanted to be. I know a wonderful man . . .' She fumbled in a large bucket of a handbag. 'I'll give you his name . . .'

He could be cured if he wanted to be, Phoebe thought. Perhaps he doesn't want to be. Perhaps it's deliberate; a useful barrier to hide behind and a good excuse not to have to communicate.

All the brothers except Brendan were there, and all the next generation, from Fay's 3-year-old son up to her daughters of 21 and 22. When Phoebe left the woman in the purple hat, she came upon the intermediate group of teenage cousins lounging in a corner and tried to identify them. Only one was a girl. She must be Hereward and Becky's. One of the boys would be her brother – the one with the long hair? – and the dark one her half-brother. The other two lads were probably Rick's; they had immaculate haircuts and the public schoolboy's air of effortless superiority. Phoebe knew that they were called Roderick and Peter after their father and grandfather, but she didn't know which was which. She tried to engage them all in conversation but they shrugged their shoulders and answered only in mono-syllables looking embarrassed, which made Phoebe in turn feel awkward, as though she were speaking the wrong language. Perhaps, she thought, if I had children of my own, I'd learn how to talk to them. I'm thirty-five. There's still time. If only Duncan wasn't so against the idea . . .

'You're looking very solemn, Phoebe,' Becky said, appearing beside her through the crowd. She was dressed in her usual style which, to Phoebe, looked both eccentric and daring, with colours which were not supposed to go together but on her sister-in-law looked striking and unusual. She was said to buy all her clothes from jumble sales or Oxfam. She and Herry were not married, and one of her sons was the result of an on-and-off affair with an unpublished African poet. She was brash and confident and lived dangerously. She had long hair, down to her shoulders, which was already grey. She was forty and should have looked like mutton dressed as lamb, but she didn't. Phoebe felt a reluctant admiration for someone who apparently effortlessly flouted the rules of accepted behaviour and got away with it.

'So why the long face?' Becky asked.

'I was thinking about children,' Phoebe said.

'We'd always assumed that you didn't want any,' Becky said, without dissembling.

Phoebe found herself answering with the same directness. 'Oh I do,' she said, 'but Duncan isn't keen . . .'

'They hardly ever are,' Becky said, 'but they usually quite like them when they appear. I should go for it if I were you, before it's too late. You've only got one life after all.'

'But I've got a coil,' Phoebe said feebly.

'So have it taken out!'

'But wouldn't that be rather selfish?'

'Well, I don't know about you, but I'd rather be a touch selfish than a gloomy martyr. Hey, I'm sorry, that wasn't very kind, was it? I just think that good old Dunc could be a nice gentle sort of father. Why don't you try it and see?' She flashed her brilliant smile and moved on.

I'm old-fashioned, Phoebe thought, and not brave enough. I need to feel secure. Perhaps that's why I married Duncan; because he's even more of an old fogey than I am and he makes me feel safe. Dead safe, said a niggling voice inside her, *dead* safe.

Phoebe saw that Becky had rejoined Herry and that they were talking to Duncan. She remembered the first time that she had met them, three years before, and the surprise she had felt when Duncan had warned her beforehand.

'Herry's a b-bit of a sh-shit.' Such strong language from a normally mild Duncan! 'We've n-never g-got on very well.'

'Why?'

'He's e-e-egocentric and not very r-reliable.'

Phoebe's first impressions of Hereward were that he was casual, rather scruffy and had insolent brown eyes. He had, however, one overwhelmingly redeeming trait. He had held firmly onto her hand when they were introduced and later he'd stood between herself and Duncan with an arm over each of their shoulders. He was a toucher. Phoebe had thought, Oh I do wish Duncan was!

Now as she watched, Herry clapped Duncan on the back and they all laughed. Perhaps Duncan is a bit jealous of him, Phoebe wondered, even though most of his property speculations are dismal failures. He's so much more out-going. He probably enjoys life more. I wonder why he's wearing jeans to this do. You'd think he'd make more of an effort for such a special event.

Champagne was brought round on trays and the speeches started. Conrad, as the eldest son without a speech impediment, began. He said that the first fifty years of marriage were the worst, and then described in affectionate terms all the things that his parents had managed to achieve in spite of being married to one another. It was an urbane and witty speech. Phoebe was glad that Duncan had not been called upon to perform it. Stammering was certainly useful sometimes. She wondered how Hope and Peter had lasted together for so long. They didn't seem especially happy; Hope in particular. Phoebe had never seen them touch each other; never a casual hand on a shoulder, a light kiss on the back of a neck, or a teasing tweak of an ear. They appeared to be totally buttoned up. She couldn't tell if they even liked each other, and fifty years was a lifetime . . . Phoebe wondered how long she and Duncan would stay together. She was beginning to feel restless and broody. The cottage and garden were hard work and now rapidly losing their charm. Her job was dull. Duncan was dull. Phoebe had hoped for conversation, friendly arguments, some sort of mental stimulation; *any* form of stimulation. She had expected Duncan's well-educated family to be abuzz with ideas and challenges, but the successful ones were too busy, and the nonachievers too lazy, or so it seemed to Phoebe. The only one who did have ideas was Peter. He talked enthusiastically about anything and everything, but he used his quick mind and his wide superficial knowledge as a weapon, to seek out other people's weaknesses and reveal to them their inadequacies. It was never a friendly chat, always a duel. He didn't converse, he cross-examined. It was demoralizing.

Phoebe looked through the crowd at Peter as he made his speech. He was said to be very charming and irresistible to women. Phoebe couldn't see it herself. He'd never been charming to her. Perhaps it was because she wasn't pretty. Perhaps he was snooty about the way she spoke. Perhaps she wasn't good enough.

'Fifty years ago this month,' Peter was saying, 'Hitler's troops had invaded Russia and were beseiging Moscow. By the end of November 1941, things were desperate. The temperature had fallen to minus 40° centigrade, but the severe winter weather and the arrival of special troops from Siberia combined eventually to defeat the Hun. This month the news is not as desperate, but interesting in its own right. The oil-well fires in Kuwait have been extinguished ahead of schedule. Leningrad is to revert to being called St Petersburg. The JET laboratory at Culham has achieved a high-temperature nuclear fusion. A particularly good display of the aurora borealis was visible from Shetland to Bristol – but they told us about it after it had happened, which is no damn good. Terry Waite has been released from captivity in Beirut. Robert Maxwell has apparently died in very fishy circumstances. A vast iceberg 55 miles long and 35 miles wide, covered in penguins and with its own microclimate, has broken off from Antarctica and is drifting northwards into the shipping lanes. And there was a small tornado in a village near Cambridge. Bad as well as good news.'

Ten minutes into his speech and he hasn't so much as mentioned his wife yet, Phoebe thought.

'Fifty years is a long time,' Peter continued. 'How does anyone ever achieve it? In my case you may put it down to three parts inertia to one part an innate and reckless optimism. For in my book there is always hope,' Peter said, smiling, 'and for me, of course, Hope with a capital H!'

Hope's lips twitched obediently but without enthusiasm. Her grey eyes looked bleak. She must be so jarred off with jokes about her name, Phoebe thought, watching her as she stood beside her husband. Fifty years of marriage and he's still making them; worse still was that crack about inertia. That was unforgivable!

There were toasts at the end of the speech and cheers for the happy couple. Peter's Chambers (for whom, at 72, he was still working) presented them with an elegant stone plinth topped with a brass sundial. Phoebe thought that Peter suddenly looked very tired. She often found it difficult to remember that he was an elderly man; he was so vigorous and bombastic.

'*I wasted time and now doth time waste me,*' Rick quoted into her ear.

'True,' Phoebe said, turning to look at him. 'But Peter didn't really waste time, did he?'

'He should have been Lord Chancellor, or at the very least a judge,' Rick said, 'but he was too anti-establishment, too unreliable, too busy with other ploys. Now I think he wishes he had climbed the greasy pole.'

There was a sudden blinding flash and the clunk of a camera shutter. Phoebe hadn't noticed the presence of the press until that moment. 'Perhaps he'll be in the papers,' she said. 'That should please him.'

In the event, it was herself and Rick who featured the next day, under a small headline: *'HARVEST' MOON BUGS GREENS*.

'Actor Roderick Moon, seen here with a sister-in-law at his parents' Golden Wedding celebrations, spoke yesterday about his support for the destruction of the tropical rain forest by the people of Madagascar. "What else can they do?" he said. Moon (41) who starred in the controversial disaster movie *A Lemur Too Far*, made in Magadascar [sic] in 1988, spoke of the Malagasy's need to harvest whatever natural resources they had available. "After all, they've got to live, poor sods," he said . . .'

'Does he mean it?' Phoebe asked, pausing in her reading out loud, to question Duncan.

'I don't suppose he c-cares one way or the other. It's all p-publicity,' Duncan said.

Phoebe read on.

'The Worldwide Fund for Nature, Friends of the Earth and other environmental pressure groups who last week launched a campaign for a cessation of logging in Maddergascar [sic] were today critical of Mr Moon's comments. "The man's a complete air-head," their spokesperson said today.'

Phoebe giggled. 'So much for publicity,' she said. 'More like ridicule.'

'H-He thrives on it,' Duncan said. 'C-Column inches is what c-counts.'

'Well, I think it's all wrong,' Phoebe said. 'They say that the sea round Madagascar is all red with the soil that's been washed off the bare mountainsides, like blood.'

'Mmmm,' Duncan said, concentrating on eating his breakfast.

'Don't you care?' Phoebe put the paper down and picked up her toast and marmalade.

'Mmmm?'

'Doesn't it matter at all to you?'

Duncan sighed. 'There's n-not a lot either o-of us can d-do about it is there? I'd c-calm down if I were you.'

Later that night, soon after they had turned off the light to sleep, Phoebe lay in their bed next to Duncan, glad simply to have got the family party over and done with, and to have reached home safely without their van breaking down en route.

'Did you enjoy the Golden Wedding?' she asked him into the dark.

'I think it was a s-success,' Duncan said drowsily.

'Yes, but did you enjoy it?'

'What's the d-difference?'

'All the difference in the world,' Phoebe said. 'I want to know whether you personally enjoyed it, how you *felt* about it. Was it nice to see people you hadn't seen since your childhood? Did any of them tell you anything interesting? Are you surprised that your parents' marriage lasted so long? What are your impressions?' Duncan only grunted. Phoebe felt a familiar exasperation rise up and overpower her. She sat up and switched on her bedside lamp.

'Why won't you ever *talk* to me?' she demanded. 'Why can't we ever discuss things?'

Duncan turned over abruptly and shaded his screwed-up eyes with his hands. 'For G-God's sake,' he complained, 'I'm trying to s-sleep. Can't whatever it is w-wait until morning?'

Phoebe felt a desperate need to explain herself. 'I just want to share experiences with you,' she said, 'and mull them over. It really hurts me that you won't even meet me halfway. It's like going to the pictures on your own; when you come out, you're

39

dying to talk about the film to someone, and there's no one there. Life with you is like that all the time. It drives me *mad*! Please, Duncan, couldn't we just talk?' Duncan sighed, threw back the duvet and got out of bed. 'Where are you going?'

'For a piss.'

'Then can we talk?'

He turned to her irritably. 'Look, Phoebe, it's the middle of the b-b-bloody night. I'm tired. It's b-been a long day. I want to sleep. I d-don't understand why you're suddenly in such a s-state about nothing and I h-haven't the least i-i-idea what you're expecting me to s-say.' He left the room.

Phoebe heard him flushing the lavatory a few minutes later and then he reappeared. She was still sitting up in bed and hugging the duvet over her knees. While he was coming through the doorway she said, 'Duncan, if you're going to make a go of being married, you've got to adapt. You can't just go on in the same old way with no effort at all. I mean, if you weren't prepared for some changes, why on earth did you marry me in the first place?'

She looked up at him. His face was completely closed. Every panel of his armour was firmly in place and offered no possibility of infiltration; no chinks. He doesn't care, Phoebe thought. He doesn't give a shit!

'I'm going to s-sleep in the spare room,' he said, turning on his heel. 'I've got a l-l-lot on tomorrow and I can d-do without this.' He closed their bedroom door and she heard him go along the short landing and downstairs to the door at the bottom. He whistled for Diggory, and she heard the dog thunder enthusiastically up the stairs. Then the other bedroom door shut behind the two of them and there was silence.

He always runs away! Phoebe thought furiously. Why is he so feeble? Somehow or another we've got to talk. We've got to discuss our marriage, the future, babies . . . his whole attitude to life . . . even his stammer. There's so much that needs sorting out and he won't even *begin*. Perhaps I should go after him . . .

But she knew that by now he would be curled up in the spare bed with Diggory on his feet for warmth; Diggory, who was strictly not allowed on beds, who left great gobbets of mud, hair and spit on anything he touched, and who was soppily grateful for any human kindness. Already, in Duncan's mind, relief would have swept away momentary puzzlement and annoyance. He and Diggory would be blissfully asleep together.

And it was after midnight. And they had both got to go to work tomorrow. And it was, on the face of it, a stupid thing to argue over. Yes, it did appear trivial and unreasonable, but that wasn't the point, was it? It was only a symptom of the problems underneath. Surely any half-intelligent person could see that? Phoebe let out a long sigh and turned out the light. Then she lay on her back and tried to relax.

Why did he marry me? she wondered. More to the point, why did I marry him? She went through her reasons in an attempt to count her blessings. Duncan was gentle and unaggressive. He was clever at practical things. He was tall and good-looking and had a nice voice. He lived in a lovely part of the country. She had wanted the status of being properly married. She had wanted to belong to a large family. Duncan had clearly needed her. She had felt sorry for him. She loved him.

Phoebe turned over restlessly. It all seemed a bit inadequate; a bit thin? Why did anybody ever get married? Was it only worth it if you had a *grande passion*? What about love maturing into comfortable companionship? Wasn't that how it was supposed to go? Perhaps it took longer than four years? Certainly it wouldn't happen if only one partner worked at it . . . Somehow, she thought, we must talk. We always used to be able to, before we were married, so why not now? Then a brilliant idea struck her. Tomorrow evening she would go to the isolated public phone box at the other end of the village and *telephone* Duncan. Then he would be able to speak without stammering and everything would be a million times easier! And with that encouraging thought, she fell asleep.

Duncan answered the telephone sulkily. This is ridiculous, he thought, paying for the privilege of speaking to my own wife who has walked a quarter of a mile away from me just for that very purpose!

'Hello,' he said without enthusiasm.

'Duncan, this is like old times!' Phoebe said. Her north-eastern accent sounded more pronounced than usual. It irritated him. It emphasized his belief that he had married beneath him. It encouraged him to think that she was being unreasonable.

'It seems absurd to me,' he said.

'Please,' she said, 'just try it for my sake.'

'I'm here, aren't I?' There was a long pause at the other end.

'You're not making it very easy,' she said finally.

'Look,' Duncan said, 'if we're going to talk, let's talk. Silence at this moment is golden only for British Telecom.'

'Right.' He heard her take a deep breath. 'Well, first of all, I'm sorry about last night.'

'Forget it. It's not important.'

'Aren't you going to say you're sorry too?'

'For what?'

'For not even trying to understand me. For taking it for granted that I was wrong. For running away.'

'Look, Phoebe,' Duncan said, 'if we're just going to have a rehash of last night, then frankly this is a waste of time. I didn't understand then what all the fuss was about, and I'm not likely to now. Is that it?'

'*No!*' Phoebe sounded near to tears. 'Duncan, I want . . . a baby . . .' It was Duncan's turn to be silent. 'Well?' demanded Phoebe. 'For heaven's sake, say *something*.'

'But we've been through all that,' Duncan said. 'We decided that we're too old, we couldn't afford the expense, and we're fine as we are.'

'*You* decided that. *We* never even discussed it!'

'But you never told me this before we got married. You should have made it clear then. It's hardly fair to make such an issue of it now.'

'Well, I naturally assumed that you'd want at least one child. How was I to know –'

'You should never assume things about another human being,' Duncan said, conscious of having scored a point. 'We're all entitled to our own aspirations.'

'Don't be so bloody pompous!' shouted Phoebe. 'And as for not assuming . . . you assume things about me all the time! You assumed that life would go on unchanged after you married me, with no effort from you at all. You haven't even tried to be a proper husband. As soon as things get difficult, you rush off with Diggory.'

'You're surely not jealous of the dog?'

'Don't change the subject.' She was shouting even louder now. He held the receiver further from his ear and sighed heavily. 'Why can't we talk about having a baby? Why won't you even do me the courtesy of listening to what I've got to say?'

'I *am* listening,' Duncan said. 'I'm on the end of this bloody phone, doing precisely that.'

'Don't you fancy me any more?' Now she sounded as though she was actually crying.

'Of course I do,' Duncan said crossly. 'Now who's changing the subject?'

'So why do we only make love about once a month? Are you scared I'll get pregnant?'

'No, of course not.'

'Well, why?'

Duncan was caught off guard. 'I don't know . . . It's a normal enough frequency, isn't it?'

'*Normal?*' Phoebe seemed ready to explode. 'There's nothing normal about the way we make love. There's damn all at the beginning to get me into the mood, and then it's in and out in about two minutes flat, and that's it! If that's your idea of technique —'

'I didn't realize you had any complaints,' Duncan said stiffly. 'If it's so repugnant to you, perhaps we should dispense with it altogether.'

'What d'you mean, "dispense with it"? Don't you understand what I'm trying to say? I used to like sex. It used to be the high point of my life. But you don't seem to have the least idea of what it's all about! I've tried to teach you what works for me, but you never seem to remember it. Don't you care about how I feel? Don't you want to satisfy me?'

Duncan was overwhelmed by distaste for Phoebe, for himself, and for the whole sordid business of cohabiting. Another failure, he thought to himself. I failed as a son. I failed at college. I failed in the world of work and now I've failed as a husband. The knowledge was enough. There was no need to discuss it

43

further. 'I d-d-d-don't . . . know w-w-w . . .' he tried to say. Now
he was a failure at speaking too, even on his only safe recourse,
the telephone. He realized with relief that there was still a way
to escape. He put the receiver down.

Chapter Five

Phoebe walked home slowly from the phone box. It got dark at
4.30 these November days, and by eight o'clock was pitch-black.
When she got through the village, she felt in her pocket for a
torch and shone a comforting beam of light ahead of herself,
along the road and down their lane. Her brilliant idea hadn't
worked; worse than that, she had probably undermined Duncan's masculinity for all time. She hadn't meant to shout it all
out like that. She had intended to have a controlled polite
discussion. She had been so sure that everything could be sorted
out if it could only be talked through. She had never failed
before. Her sex life had always been more than satisfactory.
A picture of herself in bed with her teacher came to mind
and stayed there to taunt her. If only he hadn't been married to
someone else, then it would have been perfect. They were so
good together . . . It's not my fault, Phoebe thought. I'm good
at relationships. *It's not fair* . . .

She dawdled down the lane, shining her torch up into the
crown of a big oak tree in the hedge. A startled owl fell off one
of the branches and flew rapidly and silently away. The south-
east wind blew into her face and made her shiver.

I must have a baby, she thought. Time's running out. Becky's
right; Duncan would come round once he saw it. He's just got
no imagination, that's his problem. And that's not all, an inner
voice niggled her. What about the other things wrong with
him? She made a mental list of Duncan's failings. He was
old-fashioned and inclined to pomposity. He was a snob. He
was untidy. He didn't have a proper job and didn't earn a
regular income. He kept all his feelings to himself and wouldn't
talk. He had made no attempt to get to know her, let alone
understand her. He lived entirely in the present, with no
interest in the past or concern for the future. He didn't want
any children. He wasn't much interested in sex. He loved his
dog more than his wife.

Does he beat you? asked the voice of reason within her. Does he drink? Does he have affairs? Is he a closet gay, a criminal, a child abuser? No? Then what are you whingeing about? So he's not perfect; who is? How many women's husbands actually talk to them? He lets you live your own life without hindrance; just be grateful for that.

He's hindering the conception of my baby! Phoebe contradicted the voice. So don't tell him! Have your coil taken out and let it happen. Which voice said that; the voice of emotion or the voice of reason? Who cares? Phoebe thought. Whichever it is, it's right. She quickened her step. I'll get in, she thought and I'll apologize to him. I've been going about it all the wrong way. I've upset him, and I don't want to do that because in spite of everything I've just thought, I do love him and I don't want to live in an atmosphere of tension and accusation. I'll do it his way instead. And when I tell him I'm pregnant, it will be too late for him to do anything about it. And he'll be fine; he'll surprise himself. She got to the cottage filled with a resolve to do better. He wasn't in the kitchen.

'Duncan?' she called. No answer. '*Duncan?*' Oh God, she thought, he's walked out! She ran to the sitting room and flung open the door. Duncan was sitting at the telephone and listening. He flapped her away with one hand, frowning. Phoebe made an apologetic face and withdrew backwards, shutting the door quietly in front of her. She let out a great sigh of relief. How stupid I am, she told herself. Of course he hasn't walked out!

She looked in the cupboard where they kept drinks and tall groceries. There wasn't much there. She found a bottle of Drambuie with some eighth of an inch of liqueur at the bottom and uncorking it, raised it to her lips. It was hot and sweet. Duncan came in just as she was lowering the bottle. He frowned again. She put it down on the table.

'I'm sorry,' she said in a rush, 'I really am. You were right: the telephone idea was a nonstarter. Let's just be friends again.'

'Have you f-finished the whole b-bottle?' he asked.

'It was only the dregs. Please, Duncan.' He stood a few feet from her, irresolute. She held out her arms. 'Give us a hug,' she said. 'Am I forgiven?' He allowed himself to be embraced, awkward and still tense. She could hear his heart beating, and feel his breath on the top of her head. It wasn't much of a hug, but it was better than shouting. 'Who was on the phone?' she asked after a few minutes, drawing away from him so that she could see his face.

'Father.'

'How is he?'

'Fine.'

'What did he want?'

'Nothing.'

'So why . . .?'

'He's just heard that Nancy S-Sedgemoor has left him all her m-money and f-furniture and everything, in her w-will.'

'How amazing! Is it a lot?'

'Yes, a-a-apparently. Father thinks to d-distribute some of it amongst us s-sons.'

'But that's wonderful! When?'

'He wants us to go up to her f-flat in L-London and choose some s-stuff this weekend, t-t-tomorrow.'

Money! thought Phoebe. If it makes us not hard up, then Duncan won't be able to say that we can't afford a baby. It's an omen!

It was like being a licensed burglar, Phoebe thought, as she and Duncan went over Nancy Sedgemoor's flat. It produced in her a flood of conflicting emotions which were uncomfortable and unsuitable, yet exciting. They were allowed to take what they wanted, within reason. Peter and Hope had already had their pick and the other London-based sons had had theirs. Anything too big to carry off on the spot could be marked with a label, and rival claims would be put to family arbitration later.

The flat had large elegant rooms and had clearly been beautifully kept, but now its contents were covered in six months' dust, and the cut flowers and houseplants had died of neglect and showered the thick sea-green carpets with their shrivelled jetsam. Phoebe and Duncan were there on their own. They went from room to room, treading softly, almost reverently, as though in church. Phoebe was relieved to see that Duncan was in reasonable spirits, in spite of their row the day before. She was grateful for this distraction. She looked about the first room, the sitting room, with fascination tinged with unease.

This was someone's home. It was full of all her personal things. She had left it unexpectedly on the day she died, presumably unaware that she would never come back. She wouldn't have had time or opportunity to get rid of the things she didn't want other people to see. Here was no sanitized, expurgated version of Nancy Sedgemoor, carefully presented for posterity. Here was everything; unprotected and taken by surprise. Phoebe thought, How would I feel if I suddenly died? Would I mind people snooping through my things? She thought guiltily of the vibrator that her teacher had given her to console herself with when he had chosen to neglect her in favour of his wife. She had brought it to the cottage with her when she married Duncan and had hidden it, shamefacedly, at the bottom of her trunk, rolled up in a woollen vest. She now imagined unsympathetic strangers finding it and guffawing over it, and cringed at the thought. She resolved to get rid of it the moment they got home.

Nancy Sedgemoor hadn't had that chance. Everything here was left as it was, to be discovered, perhaps misinterpreted, sniggered over, and ultimately taken or rejected by her inheritors. And had she even realized who they might be? She had left the flat and its contents to Peter. Would she have thought of Peter's sons and their wives foraging through it? Could she at this very moment see them doing it? Phoebe looked up at the high ornamental ceiling as if searching for Nancy's spirit, wishing she could somehow gain her permission, and sorry that there was no way of receiving such a sanction. She wondered what sort of a woman she had been. What had she looked like? There were no photographs.

'This is a marvellous d-desk,' Duncan said, from the far window. 'I think we should p-put our moniker on it.' He bent down and blew the dust off its green leather top. Phoebe walked over to look. It was over four feet wide and made of a dark well-figured wood, polished to an antique shine. The fronts of the two pillars and all their drawers were asymmetrically convex, and the front of the central long drawer was gently concave, giving it a sinuous appearance. It looked grand and expensive. Duncan pulled open some of the deep drawers to show her. 'Lovely and s-smooth,' he demonstrated, 'beautifully made.'

Inside the drawers there were pens and pencils, elastic bands, heavy cream writing paper and envelopes, catalogues, press cuttings, old keys, bits of string . . . Phoebe wanted to look at them more closely, but didn't want Duncan to see her prying.

'It's gorgeous,' she said. 'Can we really have it?'

'If no one else b-bags it,' Duncan said. 'Father won't want it. He's g-got a huge d-desk of his own.'

'What's going to happen to the things no one wants?'

'I expect they'll get a firm in to c-clear the place,' Duncan said. 'They'll s-sell anything that's w-worth anything and p-probably burn the rest. Father says he's hoping to s-sell the flat as soon as possible.'

'It's a nice flat,' Phoebe said, 'but I'd hate to live in London. Let's look over everything first and decide what we like, and then go round later on and label our final choice.'

There were obvious gaps where things had already been taken; bright squares of wallpaper previously covered by paintings or mirrors, marks of castors on the carpet where chairs had stood, dust-free circles on table tops and window sills where bowls and ornaments had once been displayed. But there was still a great deal of furniture and it still felt like a home.

Phoebe left Duncan wandering round the sitting room, and went into the kitchen. The saucepans had all gone and so had the cooker. The floor stuck grittily to the soles of her shoes. Someone had spilt sugar on it and only partially cleaned it up. All the doors of the wall cupboards were open, revealing storage jars half full of raisins, lentils, macaroni . . . an open box of All-Bran, and a half-finished pot of dark marmalade with a grey crust. In the bread bin there was a loaf, hoary with mould. The flip-top bin stank. Phoebe grimaced. She didn't feel like delving too deeply here. Maybe just that cast-iron casserole, the sort she'd always wanted, the asparagus kettle and the electric toaster?

Phoebe found the spare bedroom to be lined with books. She was fascinated by their variety. A lot of them were academic texts on aspects of zoology, which she recognized from her university job in Newcastle. There was also a thesis and a row of bound periodicals, and boxes of reprints of scientific papers. Phoebe remembered Duncan telling her that Nancy Sedgemoor had a doctorate. She must have been a zoologist, Phoebe thought, and it gave her a feeling of fellowship with the dead woman; a kind of bond. She had obviously been very concerned about environmental issues too, judging from the numbers of books on that subject, and poetry . . . and music. Phoebe resolved to take as many of the best books that their van would carry, and looked forward with an intense pleasure that felt warm inside her, to reading them all. She wandered into Nancy's bedroom, smiling at the thought, but stopped short with a little cry of distress.

Someone had vandalized the room. All the drawers from the chest of drawers and the dressing table had been pulled out and roughly upended; their contents tipped recklessly onto the bed and floor, and then left in rifled, discarded heaps where they had dropped. The dust and detritus from years of use had trickled from the corners of the drawers and intermixed with them, smearing the pale pink bedspread and the cream-coloured carpet, and coating the tangled vests, the odd stockings and the long-legged thermal knickers. It was a desecration worse than all that had gone before, and Phoebe felt it keenly. She started to pick up things in an attempt to atone for it. She put the small bottle of eau de Cologne back on the dressing table and then gathered up more underclothes, face cream, handkerchiefs, a powder puff, safety pins, a packet of painkillers, an elastic bandage, hairpins, a magnifying glass, half a tube of ointment for haemorrhoids, earplugs, keys . . . She came upon a pair of false teeth half wrapped in a cloth but drew the line at touching them. What was the point? It wouldn't do any good now.

Who had done this? Phoebe found it hard to imagine how anyone could. Didn't it show an utter contempt for the dead woman? Or was it just an expression of confident certainty that there was no life after death; that the dead wouldn't know and couldn't care? Phoebe didn't believe in God, but she would never have acted so disrespectfully . . . just in case.

As she turned away from the defiled possessions, she saw

underneath a tin of athlete's foot powder something else dark blue. It was a passport. Phoebe bent quickly to pick it up. It was Nancy Sedgemoor's. It was more than ten years out of date and it contained the old-fashioned full description of the bearer. *Profession,* Phoebe read *University lecturer. Place and date of birth: London. 31.1.1921. Residence: England. Height: 5ft 7ins. Colour of eyes: Green. Colour of hair: Auburn. Special Peculiarities: None.* Underneath, her signature in black ink was bold and well formed. But it was the photograph opposite which riveted Phoebe's attention. She supposed that Nancy must have been in her late forties when it was taken. It had clearly been done in a studio. It was not the modern booth-produced caricature, but a proper black and white portrait of a striking face. She was handsome, Phoebe thought, and strong. The nose was long and straight, and the eyes wide set. The hair was probably already going grey. The mouth was full and slightly upturned at the corners; humorous? She was wearing no jewellery and her eyebrows were rather bushy. She didn't look particularly feminine, but she didn't look butch either, just intelligent.

Now Phoebe had seen her face, she felt she knew her; could imagine her here in her own flat. She had become a real person who would have had real feelings. She wouldn't have wept to see the mess Peter's family had made of her home. She would have been furious. Phoebe felt slightly better. Ghostly fury was easier to come to terms with than ghostly grief. She looked up towards the ceiling again and apologized out loud to Nancy's spirit.

'Who're you t-talking to?' Duncan asked, appearing in the doorway.

'No one.' Phoebe held the passport behind her back, out of his sight. Someone in Duncan's family had made this mess; someone who didn't give a damn about Nancy. Perhaps Duncan felt like that too? Phoebe felt estranged from the whole Moon family; more than that, she felt as if she wanted to protect Nancy from them all. 'I was just thinking aloud,' she said.

'G-God, what a shit h-heap!' Duncan said, looking about him.

Phoebe slipped the passport quickly into the two-ended muff-like pocket on the front of her sweatshirt. It just fitted, unseen. 'Who could have done it?' she asked him.

'A-A-Anyone,' Duncan said, without great interest. 'D-D'you want this d-dressing table?'

'I don't think it would go in our bedroom,' Phoebe said. 'It's too elegant. I'd love the little chest of drawers, though.'

'Have you b-been all round yet?'

'All except the bathroom.' Phoebe put her head round its door. It was a small room with an old, badly stained porcelain bath and a lavatory with a cistern high on the wall and a long chain. The bathmat was square and had a cheerful zigzag pattern round the edges. I'll have that, Phoebe thought, and bent down to pick it up. When she straightened up, however, she found herself gazing straight at a pathetic elderly nightgown which was hanging on the back of the door. It looked as though it were waiting for Nancy to come through at any moment and put it on. Tears came to Phoebe's eyes. Nancy had not been middle-aged and strong. She had been old and ill, maybe frightened, certainly lonely. Phoebe had a sudden vision of her mother in the future, perhaps in similar circumstances, and couldn't bear the thought.

She dropped the bathmat onto the floor again. She didn't want any part of the pillaging of this flat. Then she remembered Duncan saying that it would all be dispersed anyway, and sold or burnt. She might as well have what was going. She could look after it in Nancy's honour. She picked up the bathmat again, carefully avoiding the nightie, and went back into the sitting room, wiping her eyes on the back of her hand. Duncan was tying a label onto one of the brass drop handles of the desk.

They spent that night staying with Herry and Becky in their untidy rented rooms just round the corner from Nancy's flat. Over supper Phoebe described to Becky her shock at seeing the mess that had been made of Nancy's things.

'Mmmm,' Becky said. It obviously hadn't upset her in the least. 'I suppose it was a sort of mini revenge.'

'What on earth do you mean?' Phoebe asked. She glanced at Duncan. He was silent and looked moody. He clearly did not like this conversation at all.

'A small way of getting her own back,' Becky said.

'But who . . .?'

'Why, Hope, of course. Who else?'

Duncan felt gripped by depression, that familiar drowning
lassitude which deprived him of hope, of enterprise, and even of
introspection. He sat at Becky's table, ate little and said nothing.
As was often the case, his mood had been delayed in its onset;
had given him a day in which to hope that perhaps it wouldn't
appear after all. Perhaps he would be able to overcome the blow
to his esteem that his wife had dealt him. Perhaps he could
ignore it as ill-conceived, even malicious. Perhaps the fault lay
with her, not with him at all. But as usual it finally got him and
when it came, it was sudden and inexorable and weighed him
down like a thick layer of tar. There was nothing to be done but
endure until it decided to go away.

Duncan resented the conversation they were having. He felt
a fierce loyalty to his mother and hated her to be criticized in
any way. Of course Hope had tipped out those drawers –
although he wouldn't have admitted as much to Phoebe. Hope
was probably looking for evidence and it was the quickest way
to find it. It wasn't revenge or anything so melodramatic. She
wouldn't be so spiteful or so small-minded, Duncan was sure of
that. He couldn't however bring himself to say so. He didn't
want to have to explain. It would be all too difficult, and
anyway it was an unsuitable subject in front of Herry's three
children. He looked across at Phoebe. She was expressing
surprise and outrage. He considered her manner to be unnecessarily theatrical. His frown deepened.

Earlier that afternoon he had wondered if she was in some
way cheating him. He had gone into Nancy's spare room to
help her pack their chosen books into cardboard boxes, and she
had looked almost shifty, as though she didn't want him to see
something. She had declined his offer of help rather brusquely
and he had retired, hurt. Now he wondered whether he could
trust her. If you harboured a person under your roof, it was very
necessary that you should be able to, wasn't it? If you found you
couldn't, what then?

The teenage children seemed to him to be taking an imperti-
nent interest in matters which were none of their business, the
girl especially. Becky hadn't 'brought them up' at all, and Herry

didn't appear to care. Their table manners were revolting and their social graces nonexistent. And Phoebe wanted one? It was too much. He couldn't cope with the noise, the jockeying egos, his own unsettling suspicions, and the requirement that he be sociable. He got to his feet.

'Sorry,' he said. 'I'm g-going to b-bed.'

Phoebe was not surprised when Duncan abruptly left them in the middle of supper. He always retreated when depressed. She supposed that it was her fault. She shouldn't have told him that he was no good in bed. She saw Becky regarding her with sympathy and wondered if she could confide in her. Perhaps she would understand? Maybe Herry had similar problems?

Herry didn't look as though he had any problems at all. He was busy arm-wrestling his stepson and laughing at his own inevitable defeat. The brown muscular forearm of the boy was already stronger than Herry's and it easily pressed his arm down towards the table and held it there triumphantly, squashing a banana in the process, to the amusement of the other two.

'You can bloody well eat that now,' Becky said to him amiably.

'Gimme some cream and sugar and I will,' the boy grinned.

'Bollocks!' Herry said, separating the yellow skin and oozing pulp from the back of his hand. 'Get it down you!'

The boy made a great play of having to eat something totally disgusting with elaborate facial expressions including the rolling of his eyes, and with affectedly fastidious fingers. Phoebe laughed with the others. She liked the relaxed way that Becky and Herry dealt with their children. They were allowed more or less to do as they pleased and they seemed to have cheerful characters with no hang-ups. They lived in an absolute tip, she thought, looking around her at the things all over the floor, at the gaping cupboards and the crowded dusty surfaces, but they appeared to be happy. Herry rarely passed his partner without touching her lightly in greeting. His daughter often hung onto his shoulder to get his attention, and his sons beat him up in as many friendly physical ways as they could devise. They were like a pride of lions, apparently undisciplined and competitive in play, but actually a united and functioning co-operative.

Phoebe wondered how Becky had taught Herry to relax and be like that. Perhaps she hadn't had to?

Phoebe got her chance to talk to Becky alone later that evening when she had insisted upon washing up, Herry and the children having disappeared furtively like badgers at dawn.

'Leave them,' Becky said, gesturing at the supper things. 'One of the kids will do them in the morning.'

'No,' Phoebe said, running hot water into the greasy plastic bowl. 'I'd like to, really.' So Becky had dried up a few things to keep her company and put them away in an arbitrary fashion as though they didn't have fixed places in the kitchen, but went wherever they would fit that day. 'I'm sorry about Duncan,' Phoebe said. 'It wasn't that he didn't like the food, you know.'

'That's okay,' Becky said. 'He's like Hope sometimes, isn't he? I recognize the signs.'

'Why did Hope really do what she did?' Phoebe had been longing to discuss this further at supper but had been quelled, both by the look on Duncan's face and by the overeager interest of the children.

'She hated Nancy, or so I gather,' Becky said. 'She thought she'd behaved like a bitch. Perhaps she was just getting those feelings off her chest.'

'But what did Nancy *do*?'

'She had a long affair with Peter, years ago, and left her husband, I think. I did ask Herry once, but he was a bit vague about it.'

'But Duncan told me Nancy wasn't one of Peter's so-called friends,' Phoebe protested. 'And Peter wasn't a bit upset when Nancy died. I spoke to him on the phone that very day!'

'Peter never shows his emotions,' Becky said, 'and Duncan always protects Hope. You must have noticed that? He won't have a word spoken against her.'

'Duncan hardly speaks to me at all,' Phoebe said, 'not *properly*; not about the things that matter.' She suddenly found that her eyes were leaking. She went on washing up while the tears dripped down her nose and onto the foamy plates. 'He doesn't seem to have any feelings, and he won't even try to understand himself, let alone me.' She gave a little sob.

'Hey,' Becky said, 'don't get upset. Have a tissue.' She tore off a piece of kitchen paper towel and handed it to Phoebe. 'We all know that Duncan finds it physically difficult to say *anything*,' she said, 'and there's no point in trying to understand the Moons. They don't feel like we do. I don't believe in all that stuff about "finding" yourself anyway. Life's too short. You've just got to get on with it and enjoy the best bits.'

'You mean sex?' Phoebe asked, sniffing.

'Yeah, amongst others. Personally I prefer a really deep Badedas bath to sex, but the odd good fuck really bucks you up, know what I mean?'

Phoebe did. She remembered it well. Now she realized that it was no use trying to confide in Becky. Becky was one of those people who lived life on the surface, took what good things it offered and wasted no tears on might-have-beens. Phoebe blew her nose on the paper towel and wished that she hadn't tried to talk to her. The trouble was, who could she talk to? The people at work were too distant and offhand. The people in the village had known the Moons for years and years and would gossip. She spoke to her mother on the phone every week, but she didn't want to worry her. Wynne had been so relieved and delighted when they had got married. Phoebe's old friends in Hexham might understand, but she was reluctant to commit such thoughts to paper and confer on them the authority and permanence of the written word. Becky had been her best hope; someone in the family who was nearest to her in age and had a real chance of understanding, but she had failed her.

Phoebe glanced sideways at Becky to see if she was embarrassed or worse still, scornful, but Becky smiled at her encouragingly and patted her on the back.

'Time of the month?' she enquired sympathetically. 'It's a sod, isn't it? I'd get that coil out if I was you. Kids don't half take your mind off worrying on about the meaning of life!'

Duncan was asleep when Phoebe finally crept in beside him. She lay against his back, grateful for its warmth, and tried to think positively about the day. In the back of their van were boxes and boxes of lovely books which now belonged to them! Better still, underneath the books there were still better treasures, which she had found hidden at the back of the bookcases, behind the taller books; discoveries which she had surreptitiously stowed away to examine later. They were Nancy Sedgemoor's diaries, years and years of them, and a beautiful, really old book about animals and mythical beasts with illuminated pages. Phoebe wasn't sure why she had secretly taken these things and not showed them to Duncan. Perhaps it was part of her wish to protect Nancy from all the Moons. Perhaps it was misguided. Perhaps Nancy was a wicked immoral woman who deserved neither pity nor defence. Phoebe snuggled down comfortably against her husband and looked forward to the possibility of finding out.

Chapter Six

Hope was furious. She had celebrated her own triumphant survival when Nancy had died, but it had proved to be a fleeting victory. Then she had sunk again into her familiar quicksand of depression, blaming it as always upon her husband. Now she was very angry indeed. After the disposal of the will had been made known, Peter had offered her *Nancy's jewellery*! Had he no sensitivity at all? Hope had refused it contemptuously, sight unseen, and had been rewarded for the upholding of her principles later on by observing that the very small amount of jewellery that Nancy had owned, had in any case been of no great value. Peter had then extrapolated wildly beyond her expressed wishes and assumed that she had not wanted any of Nancy's money either. The man was off his head! He said he'd told all the boys that they would be getting a cut.

'Over my dead body,' Hope told him.

'They'll get it then anyway!' Peter said, looking pleased with himself.

'Well, you'll simply have to untell them,' Hope said, unsmiling. 'We can't just throw money around at this stage of our lives. What if we're ill? What if we need specialized care? Really, Peter, I do think you might have consulted me before you went about making rash promises like that. It's too bad of you!'

'It was left to *me*,' Peter observed sardonically, 'if you remember . . .'

'Conscience money!' Hope snorted. 'It's morally mine!'

'I had a case like that once,' Peter said, leaning back in his armchair and putting his feet up on the coffee table. 'The woman concerned just couldn't get it into her thick head that the law is not in any way concerned with morality. Whether the verdict is moral or not, simply doesn't come into it. The newspapers of the day bleated on a lot about "where was our famous British justice?"'. They should have known better.' Hope remained tight-lipped. Peter took a gulp of his pre-prandial gin and tonic. 'Before I forget,' he said, 'I'm away for a week from tomorrow. Got to go to Manchester.'

'A week?' Hope said. 'Don't you realize that it's Christmas in less than that time? A week yesterday to be precise.'

'Oh I'll be back by then.'

'But what about all the preparations; the ordering of the drinks, the getting in of supplies? I rely on you to help, as you very well know. I understood that it couldn't be helped last year, but this year you promised –'

'Couldn't you call upon Duncan and thingy?'

'Duncan's too vague, as you well know.'

'Well . . . but it would be an excellent chance for you to get to know the girl better. She could be just what you need; a daughter figure, on the spot. A little seasonal cooking together, sharing recipes, that sort of thing, and she'd grow on you in no time, you'd see.'

'I don't know why you persist with that ridiculous notion of yours,' Hope said crisply. 'Phoebe is no daughter of mine. I'm sure it's very necessary for Duncan to have a wife – I'm much relieved he has – but that's no reason for giving such a person the freedom of my house, let alone my kitchen. And anyway,' she gave him a look of triumph, 'Mrs B. would never countenance *me* in her precious domain, let alone someone like her.' She glanced at her watch. 'That reminds me; almost dinner time,' she said. 'Stew tonight, I believe.'

'Ah,' said Peter.

'What d'you mean, "ah"?'

'That was the other thing I've been meaning to tell you. It's no great loss, as I'm sure you'll quite soon come to realize for yourself. The woman is hopeless at cooking meat, as we all know; overdoes it quite horribly.'

'You don't mean . . . Mrs B. hasn't . . .?' Hope clutched convulsively at the arms of her chair.

'She's probably taken her own things and gone home by now,' Peter said smoothly. 'I'm sorry, my dear. I'm afraid she gave in her notice last night.'

59

'Peter's sloped off again and Mrs B.'s left, and I really am at my wits' end,' Hope said to Phoebe on the telephone. 'Christmas is ghastly at the best of times, but this year I just don't know how I'm going to face it . . .'

Phoebe, who had hoped to see as little as possible of her parents-in-law over the looming festive season, found herself volunteered to cook Christmas dinner for ten.

'I take it you can cook?' Hope asked her, dismissively, as if the times when Phoebe had entertained them to meals in her own house were of no account.

Phoebe wondered why she was being so gruff with her. Anyone would think that Hope's crisis was *her* fault! It wasn't the usual way people asked favours of each other, and if she hated asking so much – which she clearly did – then why do it? Phoebe supposed it probably was unreasonable to expect to find another cook at such short notice and over Christmas too, but there were such things as catering firms . . .

'Well enough,' she answered, feeling inadequate. 'I've never actually done Christmas dinner for so many, but –'

'We may be eleven,' Hope said, cutting in. 'Brendan still hasn't told me whether he'll be here or not. It is too bad of him; most discourteous.'

Phoebe, grateful that Hope's displeasure was temporarily diverted to somebody else, ventured a suggestion. 'Why not get Fay's company to help?'

'Good gracious me! Do you know how much these London firms cost? Quite out of the question!'

Why don't you do it yourself like a normal person? Phoebe wanted to ask. Instead she said, 'Well, what about Fay herself? She's a trained c –'

'Fay? How can Fay possibly do it? She's got young Jack to consider. A mother's place at Christmas is with her children, after all. That's why I thought of you.'

You tactless, selfish, bad-tempered old cow! Phoebe thought furiously.

'Well?' Hope demanded.

Phoebe took a deep breath and supposed she would have to

do what was expected of her with as good a grace as she could muster. 'Um . . . right,' she said, 'yes.'

Peter, sitting comfortably in the best seat on the shuttle to Manchester, stretched his legs, sipped his Famous Grouse, admired the bright castles of cumulus cloud which were visible from his aircraft window, and smiled to himself. He reckoned he'd handled things pretty well. He had managed to postpone this meeting until now, so that he could miss the dreary commercial acceleration towards Christmas. He wasn't good at that sort of thing anyway. He had never sent a Christmas card in his life. That was what wives were for; they actually enjoyed such exchanges.

Wives; Peter was relieved to get away from his at such a time. Hope always seemed particularly down at Christmas, unreasonably negative. Peter was glad to escape to a lighter atmosphere unpolluted by blame. He wondered if Mrs B. was making pejorative remarks about him in the village. It would be nothing new if so. The village would take it with its usual pinch of salt, he was sure. It was quite something when a woman like Mrs B. came out with such a ready put-down, though. He had had to admit a reluctant admiration for her when she had side-stepped him neatly and hissed 'Sexual harASSment!' through clenched teeth. Personally he would put the stress on the first syllable of harassment, not the second, but it was a common enough mistake. Education by television had a lot to answer for, he thought. Either way, he had been on to a winner. If she had acquiesced, it would have been a pleasant interlude. She had particularly nice teeth, when unclenched. But if she took offence, as she did, then there opened up the likelihood that a better cook could be employed, and also the possibility of manoeuvring Phoebe into Hope's home, hearth and good books; two birds with one stone!

Thinking of birds reminded him suddenly of Nancy. She had been such an avid observer of the natural world. Peter remembered her once or twice taking him out into the countryside, enthusing about it all and trying to teach him the names of things – which he had instantly filed in the out drawer of his memory. Peter preferred assignations to be held in comfort,

61

without ants or grass stains. To him the country looked pretty enough when the weather was good. It was quite pleasant to see it occasionally, but the actuality of it was inconvenient and messy. He had reluctantly yielded to Hope's pressure years ago when the boys were babies, to buy the house in Somerset, but he had always spent as little time there as possible.

Nancy and Hope actually had quite a lot in common! He'd never considered that fact before. He wished that Hope hadn't vented her feelings on Nancy's bedroom, but he supposed that it wasn't unreasonable under the circumstances; rather like being fought over. He smiled again, feeling rather smug. There was nothing in Nancy's flat that he had really wanted. He wasn't sentimental over things. He had all the material possessions he needed anyway. It was good sense to pass that sort of thing onto the next generation.

Christ! An irritating worm of half-remembered urgency had been eating away at the edge of his consciousness ever since he had heard that Nancy had died and left him everything. Now, suddenly, the nessage had got through.

'The bestiary!' he said aloud to himself. 'Whatever happened to the bloody bestiary?'

Phoebe was reading one of Nancy's diaries, picked out at random. She had decided from the beginning to ration her reading of them to make them last as long as possible. Earlier on she had spent a large part of the afternoon waiting for more than an hour in her doctor's surgery, in spite of their appointments system, and then finally, in a supremely undignified position and with some discomfort, she had had her intra-uterine coil removed. Next she felt she needed cheering up; a treat of some kind. These days she looked forward to reading the diaries as do avid readers who have newly discovered an author who really speaks to them. She felt like one who has just splurged all her money on a great heap of that special writer's books. On the rare occasions when she had money enough to buy several books at once, half the fun for Phoebe was to be gained while they were yet unread, in the happy anticipation of losing herself in the narrative and being transported elsewhere. The delicious tantalizing certainty of future satisfaction was, of course, even more acute if deliberately postponed, to be realized eventually little by little. However, this sort of iron control could not be managed indefinitely, and it always vied in Phoebe's thoughts with the shame-faced wish to be just a little ill, so that she could stay in bed and read nonstop all day.

She still hadn't told Duncan about the diaries and it seemed almost too late to do so, for she would now have to admit that she had taken them surreptitiously, and give an account of herself. She didn't really know why she had done it in the first place, so she couldn't possibly explain it to Duncan. Anyway, she thought, the diaries would make uncomfortable reading for him. They were all about Nancy's life and what she was thinking at the time; her hopes and fears and interests and ambitions. They were not Duncan's sort of thing at all. Phoebe had a good hour before he was likely to come home, so she had turfed Diggory out of the best armchair and curled herself up happily in his warm imprint, to read.

Saturday, 6 May – Weekend in the country. Pressure high and weather wonderful. Oaks in leaf and ash just starting. Apple blossom in cottage garden is in its full glory. At elevenses, as I watched, the nettles outside the kitchen window were smoking with pollen at each puff of wind. Mr Grave says I should assassinate them with Paraquat, but I need them as food plants for the butterflies, I tell him. His garden next door is always regimented in manicured blocks of bedding plants in summer. He favours garish colours which clash fiercely. He probably thinks I'm indolent, and resents all the weed seeds which drift his way! I suspect that he nips over the fence and murders things when we're in London. Tried cuckoo-calling this afternoon and got one to respond by flying directly over my head. Saw its stripes! Very hawk-like in flight. Did a lot of weeding. Hugh sat in the sun and burnt his shoulders – silly ass. Claude caught a grey squirrel and ate only its head – horrid cat! Cockchafer banging at the window p.m. A good day.

Phoebe read on rapidly until she came to a more personal bit.

Saturday, 10 June – At last! some time alone with P. He was in Suffolk last week, so we agreed to meet in Aldeburgh. Weather grey but dry, thank goodness. White Lion very comfortable. Only *just* remembered to use his name and take the label off my suitcase! He was late (of course) but we had most of the afternoon and eventually went for a walk along the beach. Sea quite rough. Fishing boats pulled high up the sloping shingle. Town crouched low behind them. Wonderful great expanse of sky. Walked north a little way, then south to the Martello tower, then down beside the estuary. Identified lovely yellow horned poppies, sea pea and hound's-tongue on beach and dittander, burr chervil, sea wormwood and mugwort amongst others on saltmarsh. Marvellous names! Pointed them out to P. who was really interested. Poor darling has always lived in towns and never had a chance to *see* the world around him. He thanked me for educating him! Beautiful sailing boat anchored on the River Alde. Felt like commandeering it and sailing away with P. over the grey horizon. He said, no use – he gets seasick – no soul! Good dinner p.m. P. told me hysterically funny stories, mostly about recent cases, and we laughed until we cried. I can't bear to think that it will be all over again tomorrow, until the next snatched spur-of-the-moment encounter. P. didn't bother to phone H. Perhaps things aren't good between them. I phoned Hugh. He sounded rather ratty, so I feel bad. It's only *one night*, for God's sake! and time is rushing by twice as fast as normal – too fast, as ever.

Things don't change, Phoebe thought with a pang. She looked at the date. Nancy must have been in her thirties then. Extra-marital affairs were the same in the fifties as, Phoebe had discovered to her cost, they were in the seventies; the only difference these days was that you didn't have to forge your lover's wife's name in the hotel register. Now no one cared who slept with whom as long as they paid the bill and didn't steal anything. She turned the page and read the rest of Nancy's illicit weekend.

Sunday, 11 June − Breakfast in bed: champagne and fresh orange juice − wickedly expensive! P. quite amazingly indefatigable. I shall remember him every time I sit down for weeks to come . . . not that I don't think about him all the time anyway. Will we ever be allowed to live together openly? I can't believe that we won't − it would be too cruel of the fates. Perhaps H. will die suddenly and after a decent (but short) interval I shall leave Hugh, and we . . . What rubbish! No one ever dies when you want them to, except in fiction. She'll probably go on for eternity, locked into her own private abyss. What a waste of life and passion! Poor darling P., I hope that the l. and p. I've shared with him this weekend will last him until next time − whenever that is.

The back door banged shut and Phoebe heard Duncan talking affectionately to an ecstatic Diggory, whose welcoming tail was beating a tattoo on the door of the dresser. Phoebe hastily leapt to her feet and slipped into the utility room. Once there, she put the current diary into its safe daytime hide-out. The rest of the diaries she kept in her old trunk under the bed. The one she was reading lived in the trunk at night, and by day in the one place which Phoebe knew would be completely safe from casual discovery by Duncan: inside the washing machine.

Fay braced her feet against the footwell of her husband's car as they drove on Christmas Eve, west down the M4 to Somerset. Conrad habitually drove too fast, and it always frightened her. She had told him that this was so on countless occasions, but he never seemed to remember. She knew that he considered himself to be a more than usually competent driver with super-fast reflexes, but she didn't share his confidence. In the back seat Jack strained against his seat belt and whined that he was bored. He was resting his chin on the life-sized pink plastic skull of the baby doll he had insisted on having for his birthday two weeks before, and from which he was now inseparable. Fay wished that her daughters had opted to come with them for Christmas at their grandparents' house, to help amuse

65

their little brother, but now that they were grown up it seemed that they had better things to do. She couldn't blame them. Given the choice she too would have gone elsewhere. The Moon sons were however very hot on family solidarity, even Brendan who might have been expected to stay away, would undoubtedly be there. Peter always made sure of that.

'I'm bored,' Jack said again, drumming his feet on the front of his seat.

'Only boring children get bored,' his father said crisply, without turning his head. 'Stop banging about and look out of the window. There's all sorts of interesting things going on out there.'

'What things?' Jack asked, disbelieving. Conrad didn't answer.

'Animals in the fields,' Fay said, turning to look at him. 'Big lorries on the road. Look, there's a man on a motorbike!'

'Where?' asked Jack, after a pause.

'Well, he's gone now, darling. You have to be quick and look straightaway or you'll miss things.'

'Don't like motorbikes. I want to get out.'

'We can't stop or we'll be late getting to Grandma's. Why don't you have a little sleep, and then the journey won't seem so long?'

'No!'

Conrad sighed. 'Contra-suggestible little bugger,' he muttered.

'Bugger,' said Jack happily. 'Bugger, bugger, bugger, bug –'

'Quiet!' said his father. He glanced at Fay. 'I'm sure the girls were never like this. They sat on the back seat and looked at picture books or drew things at his age. Why can't he be like them?'

'You expect too much of him,' Fay said, defending him as always. 'He's only just four, after all. Boys are often slower, and perhaps being left-handed doesn't help?'

'I was reading by three and a half,' Conrad said.

'Yes, dear, but you were a genius,' Fay said with heavy irony. 'Hope says that Duncan didn't read properly until he was seven.'

'Yes, and look where he's got in life! That's what I'm afraid of. I don't want my only son to end up with no qualifications as a jobbing bloody gardener!'

'Bloody,' Jack said. 'Bloody fucker. Bloody bugger –'

'Stop it!' his father interrupted. 'You shouldn't be using those words at your age.'

'You did,' Jack said stoutly. 'You said bloody gardener.'

'That's different. I'm grown up, so I can say what I like.'

'Snot fair,' Jack said, waving his doll above his head.

'Life isn't fair,' Conrad said, 'as you will doubtless find out one day.' He started to pull out from the middle lane to overtake, when a car which was already going past them at high speed, blasted him with its horn. Conrad swerved back and forth several times before regaining the centre of the middle lane.

'For heaven's sake, Con,' Fay said angrily, 'think what you're at! Didn't you see him coming?'

'Obviously not. Jack's flaming doll was in the way.'

Fay turned round again. 'Put your dolly down, love, you're stopping Daddy's view of what's behind us. You see that little mirror up there? Daddy looks in that and he can see through here and out of the back window, so then he knows when he can and when he can't go out into the fast lane.' Jack was silent. Fay thought he was looking rather pale. Perhaps I should have given him half a Kwell? She thought.

'I feel s . . .' Jack said, and vomited down the back of Conrad's seat.

An hour behind Fay and Conrad, Roderick Moon was driving his two sons and what seemed like a ton of luggage, in the same direction. He had a white Range Rover that he kept for occasions such as this, his sports car being too small and too special for grubby family use. The eldest boy (his namesake, Rod) now fourteen, was sitting in the front seat next to him, silent as usual. From time to time Rick glanced sideways at him. He was almost good-looking, he thought; only a mild outbreak of acne and lovely thick hair. What a pity he was so withdrawn and uncommunicative. He'd hardly spoken a word all journey, except to contradict his brother. Rick was sure that Rod did it on purpose to punish him for his frequent absences. It is also

67

possible that Rod, on the verge of manhood, was getting tired of basking in his father's reflected glory. This thought had, however, not yet occurred to Rick.

'. . . And the guy who shot the vampire wasn't exactly a baddie,' Pete, the younger boy said, from the back seat. He was going through the plot of a recent film he'd seen, at mind-numbing length. '. . . But the vampire wasn't really a vampire either, you see. He only sucked blood when there was no Coca-Cola available. He –'

'No he didn't,' Rod said with authority.

'Yes he *did*! And the guy that shot him was trying to kill the werewolf, but he missed because the vampire had just seen a can of Coke and made a grab for it and . . .'

'That was *before*,' Rod said scornfully.

'NO IT WASN'T! . . . And then the . . . now you've made me forget where I was!'

'Never mind,' Rick said. 'It sounded as though you'd got to the end anyway.' He wished Pete would just keep quiet, or at least learn to tell a tale half competently. At present estimation, he had all the makings of a prize bore. Body language seemed to be a complete mystery to him; even in its grossest form. People might yawn quite openly in the middle of his discourse, but Pete would ignore the signs and plough on grimly, oblivious. He must have inherited it from his mother, Rick thought. Poppy had never known when to stop either!

'Oh yes . . .' Pete said, gathering strength again. 'I remember now. The werewolf was only a werewolf after dark, and when the guy who wasn't a baddie really – remember I told you? – went and shot him, it was just at sunrise and the werewolf was changing back into a rhino, which is what he was in daytime, and the bullet was designed to kill werewolves not rhinos, and it bounced off the rhino's extra thick skin, because he wasn't a werewolf by the time it hit, you see, and ricco . . . ricco . . . bounced off again and hit the can of Coke and . . . No, that was later. Anyway then the –'

'Oh shut your head!' Rod said, turning to him irritably. 'You've got it totally arse about face, and it's boring Dad to infinity and back anyway.'

'It's not, is it, Dad?'

'Well, not quite as far as infinity,' Rick said absently, concentrating on passing a Mercedes.

Pete subsided into a sulk and began pulling at a bit of interior trim which was coming loose. A blessed silence took over. Rick wondered if everyone's sons niggled each other as much as his did. He wished he liked them both, or either of them, more. The main thing was, they were his and he had the custody of them. That was what mattered.

Earlier that day the boys had banded together in an unlikely alliance to protest about going all the way to Somerset to spend Christmas in that gloomy old house in the boring country, with their grandmother who was mad and their grandfather who was okay but not worth the long journey. Rick had read them a lecture on families and duty, and how it was only for three days so they needn't whine about it. It looked to him like being three days of hard work. He sighed. Then he remembered the expensive presents he'd got for them, all wrapped up in the boot of the Range Rover. They would be putty in his hands when they'd opened those!

Phoebe allowed herself a double ration of diary on Christmas Eve, knowing that there would be no chance to read much for the next few days. She had decided that she really must read them in chronological order, so she had started again, this time at the beginning in 1946. Not every day had an entry. Nancy appeared to write only when there was something that she considered worth saying. Phoebe felt a growing admiration for her, and an increasing sense of privilege at her own fortuitous opportunity to read the diaries. It made her feel as though she was being taken into Nancy's confidence, as though she were a special friend. She felt for her in her miseries, triumphed with her over her adversities, and identified strongly with her in her infrequent moments of joy. Phoebe had been there too. She knew how it felt, and knowing the end of the story lent it an added poignancy.

Phoebe assumed, of course, that Nancy's 'P.' and 'H.' were Peter and Hope, and it gave her a thrill of satisfaction to be allowed to spy on their early lives. Nowadays when she was with Peter and he outwitted her with his effortless verbal superiority,

69

there now remained within her the unshakeable confidence that he might be cocky, but he didn't know everything. There were things, very personal things, that she knew about him, *and he didn't know that she knew!* Similarly when Hope was sour and complaining, Phoebe now knew that she had been like that since 1951, if not before! It wasn't a special attitude she reserved for Phoebe, it was her strategy for responding to life in general.

Phoebe saw Peter through Nancy's eyes and took sides with him against Hope. She imagined him to have been even taller and more handsome then; crazy about Nancy, but trapped by honour in a dismal marriage. Nancy's own marriage to Hugh Sedgemoor had taken place when she was 25, in 1946, Phoebe discovered. Hugh had had a bad war and emerged from it with low self-esteem and boundless obstinacy. He had wanted to write thrillers, so after a very short uncommitted search, he had given up looking for work altogether and had been supported from then on by Nancy, who had a good career at the university and a flat of her own in London. He had never got published. Nancy seemed to Phoebe to be, in turns, fond of and exasperated by him. She couldn't decide which emotion had been the dominant one. It came across the pages as a rather uncomfortable and unsatisfactory marriage, similar to hers and Duncan's.

Saturday, 8 September 1951 – Party at S.'s house. Hugh too 'busy' as usual. Went alone. Met an extraordinarily mismatched couple, Peter and Hope Moon. She looked like death for most of the evening, barely spoke to anyone and obviously hated every minute. He, on the other hand, couldn't have been more charming. He has very intense blue eyes and a tremendous fund of funny stories. For some reason we seemed to hit it off at once. Felt rather guilty about his poor forlorn wife, but she made no effort whatsoever. I think I shall have to watch myself with P. Such men are dangerous! Hugh in a mood when I got home and didn't respond to my feelings of optimism and elation. As usual he took all the wind out of my sails and left me feeling irritable and unfairly deflated, then guilty as always. I'm truly sorry that so far he's failed to get published, hates his

70

lack of 'status' and can't bear to be quizzed about his 'job' at parties, but am I supposed to commit a sort of social suttee because of his hermit tendencies? To hell with that!

Poor Nancy, Phoebe thought, so full of life, so full of hope, but ultimately to die alone. She wondered what (if anything) Nancy would have done differently if she had been able to start again from 1951. That thought made Phoebe consider her own life. Would she have done things differently? Would she still have married Duncan, given the chance to do otherwise? It was too late for Nancy, but it wasn't too late for her. There were always options. They closed down and got smaller and smaller as you got older and older, but Phoebe wasn't even halfway through life yet. It was with that hopeful thought in mind, that she prepared to do battle with Christmas.

Chapter Seven

A twenty-two-pound turkey . . . Phoebe thought, going over her calculations again to make sure they were correct . . . at fifteen minutes a pound, equals five . . . and a half hours, plus a bit to be on the safe side, say six hours. Lunch for two o'clock, so turkey in at . . . eight, and the oven on to preheat at about half past seven. Right! She glanced around for a clock. There wasn't one in Hope's kitchen. There weren't enough working surfaces in Hope's kitchen either, and nothing was where it ought to be. There was no logic in the places where things were, so how could anyone be expected to perform to a high standard there? It was enough to drive a normal person mad, let alone a resentful daughter-in-law.

'Duncan!' Phoebe called. 'Can I borrow your watch?' No answer. Duncan *never* heard when she called, even if he was just at the end of their garden and she was at the back door. Phoebe often thought that even were she to play the bagpipes at full blast between screams, he would still be happily oblivious, pottering about absorbed in his own affairs, with his ears turned off. She was being unfair, she knew she was. No one in the other rooms of the big house would hear anyone calling in the kitchen. The walls were too thick; the distances too great. She went on with her mental list: chestnut stuffing already elegantly prepared by Fay. Forcemeat stuffing for the neck still to be done. Bread sauce to start. Christmas pudding waiting on its trivet all set to steam . . . sprouts and leeks could be done later. Spuds (two sorts) first, and parsnips, then carrots. Fay had brought her own home-made brandy butter. The clotted cream was in the fridge. We need some actual brandy later, Phoebe thought, to flame the pudding, and a sprig of holly with berries to go on top. Perhaps the boys could find me one.

'Did you shout? We were just out in the hall,' Fay said, coming in with a sulky-looking Jack, doll in hand. She looked harassed.

'I haven't got a watch,' Phoebe said. 'I was hoping to borrow Duncan's.'

'Have mine,' Fay said, slipping her hand through the gold bracelet and handing it to Phoebe.

'Are you sure?' Phoebe asked. 'It looks dangerously expensive. What if I splash it with gravy?'

'I want to watch TV!' Jack demanded in a shrill whine. It was clearly not the first time he had made his wishes known.

'Darling,' Fay said patiently, 'I told you just now, Granny hasn't got a telly this year. I'm very sorry but there it is.'

'She had one last week,' Phoebe said surprised, putting the watch on.

'She *says* it broke down the day before yesterday, so she got rid of it,' Fay said, pursing her lips sceptically. 'I think it's a plot to force the young to, quote, "do something more intelligent".'

'At Christmas?' Phoebe was scandalized.

'Wonderful timing as ever,' agreed Fay.

'NOW!' shouted Jack.

'How about opening some presents?' Phoebe suggested to him.

Fay frowned a warning. 'No,' she said, 'he's already opened all but the major ones. Hope seems to have a new rule this year, expounded at great length last night. She says that they shouldn't be opened until after lunch, because *presents are not the most important part of Christmas.*' She put on a Hope-like voice to convey her disgust.

'She hasn't suddenly got religion?' Phoebe asked.

'No, she's just being bloody-minded. It's a sort of power game with her; keeping us on tenterhooks until *she* gives us the go-ahead, and not before.'

'Terrific,' Phoebe said.

'I'm bored!' Jack said crossly.

'How about playing with some of the toys you got in your stocking?' Fay suggested, looking down and ruffling his hair affectionately, 'upstairs in your bedroom.'

'You come too!' Jack ordered, pulling at her hand.

'Just a minute and I will. I must just talk to your Auntie Phoebe first.' She looked up again. 'Have you got the bird in yet?'

73

'Already? It's...' Phoebe glanced at Fay's watch, '... only seven o'clock. God, I feel as though I've been here for hours, but it's only been one so far!'

'I don't know about you, but I always give a turkey a bit extra. It can sit in the oven and wait if it's done too soon, but if it's underdone, it's a disaster. Stop it, Jack! Mummy's coming now.'

'Right,' Phoebe said, turning the oven on. 'You're the expert. I'll get the brute stuffed straightaway then, and shove it in.'

'Are you sure you're all right?' Fay asked. 'I feel so guilty, letting you do most of the work. Please, Jack, don't keep on doing that! Sorry, Phoebe, I'd better go and amuse this tyrant.'

Phoebe smiled down at Jack. He gave her a cunning look and dragged his mother off in triumph. Mmmm, thought Phoebe, I shan't let mine order me about like that! She wondered, as she chopped onions, how long it would take her to become pregnant. They had only made love once (not very satisfactorily) since her coil came out, but you didn't have to have an orgasm to conceive, did you? Phoebe thought not. Her period was about due. Perhaps it wouldn't come? Perhaps it had already happened? If she started a baby now, it would be born at the end of... September. She smiled to herself at the thought.

'You look ch-cheerful,' Duncan observed, putting his head round the door. 'D-Domesticity o-obviously suits you.'

Phoebe smiled at him. If you only knew, she thought. But she said, 'Where is everyone? What are you all doing?'

'That's w-what I c-came to tell you. Rick's boys, C-Con and I are g-going over to our p-place for a walk and m-maybe to watch television for a while.'

'Oh do take Jack with you, will you? He's dying to see some telly, and it will gave Fay a rest.'

'Okay.'

'Where's Hope? And is Peter home yet?'

'F-Father's expected any time. Mother is s-still upstairs. Rick's p-probably still asleep.'

'Any sign of Brendan?'

'Not y-yet. S-See you.'

'Don't be late back, whatever happens,' Phoebe warned. 'Lunch at two o'clock sharp, or else!

74

Hope lurked behind her bedroom window at ten o'clock on Christmas morning playing, at the same time, her favourite piece of music. She was keeping a general lookout for a rogue heron which just recently had discovered the goldfish in their new garden pool, and had taken to picking them off, one by one. Hope was of the opinion that if she was able to frighten it off enough times, it would finally lose its nerve altogether. So far today there had been no sign of it, so in the meantime she played on. The melancholy sound of her viola escaped through the open window, but did nothing to intercept an unpleasant smell which had just started to waft inwards from the grey countryside outside. Hope wrinkled her nose in displeasure and put her bow down on the dressing table. She could hear the sound of farm machinery in the adjacent field and as she looked, a tractor towing a red tanker came into her view between the trees. It was spraying liquid slurry in a pale ginger fan from a jet at its back end.

'Well!' Hope exclaimed, shutting the window with a bang. 'Whatever next? Today of all days. The man has not one iota of consideration; none!' She picked up her bow and played something suitably strident to express her feelings.

There was still no sign of Peter. She was convinced that he did it on purpose to humiliate her in front of the family. She felt that she had always done her best and had remained at his side, preserving a united front and providing tactful disinformation on his behalf whenever necessary, for over fifty years! And this was the way he repaid her loyalty, by casual absences punctuated by offhand attendances. What sort of an example was that for the next generation? Had he no sense of duty? She frowned, concentrating on her music, and wringing out great splashes of emotion from an apparently arid source.

There was no need to go downstairs yet. She wouldn't eat breakfast today. Phoebe had promised to arrive at 6 a.m., so she would have things well in hand by now. She, Hope, had made her contribution by getting Duncan to pop her television up into the attic for the duration of the festive season. That would stop the wretched thing from dominating their lives! Hope

75

disapproved strongly of the modern habit of staying glued to the set throughout Christmas. In her day, people made their own amusement. They used their brains and their skills to entertain others. Today's children seemed to have no powers of concentration, no tenacity, no imagination.

Hope sighed. Rick's boys were either sullen or garrulous, but it wasn't their fault that they didn't have a mother. Conrad's boy was plain spoilt, which was Fay's fault because she was a working mother and felt permanently guilty. Herry's children were charming but totally out of control. They all needed some discipline. They were all much too self-centred!

Hope came to this conclusion with some satisfaction, drew a confident final chord and put her viola away in its case for the day. Tomorrow, she resolved, she would practise longer. Today she must do what was expected of her.

Fay heard Hope playing while she took Jack to the lavatory. It was a clear confident noise, which was at the same time wistful and powerfully emotive. She *must* have feelings, Fay thought, or she wouldn't be able to play so beautifully. She wouldn't be able to bring so much of herself to the music if there wasn't a deep source of passion within her to draw upon. So why does she hide it from the people who should most matter to her; her family? Why has she starved her sons of the emotional nourishment and empathy that every human being needs? Why has she taught them, by her own example, that feelings should be suppressed; so much so that she's rendered them incapable even of responding to emotion in others, let alone feeling it for themselves? The only thing she's given them all, Fay thought sadly, is a solid carapace of arrogance with which to contain and conceal the poor vestigial remnants of their humanity, and it is so watertight that hardly any primal instincts or enthusiasms ever leak out. No flutter of the heart is ever experienced by any of them, and the very lack of it makes them feel safe. They take no risks. They can never be violated or betrayed . . . Fay thought, I don't want Jack to grow up like that.

'I want my potty,' Jack said. His lower lip quivered.

'No, darling,' Fay said, coming back to reality suddenly. 'You stopped using your silly old potty ages ago, didn't you? Now you sit on the loo like all the rest of us do, to do poos. Show Mummy how grown up you can be, eh?' Jack burst into noisy tears. Oh God! Fay thought. Not this again! I hoped we'd got him over this one, at least. The bed-wetting was still a problem, yet everyone said he'd grow out of it eventually. But this business with the potty seemed never-ending and Conrad was so unsympathetic to him. It didn't help Jack if his Daddy constantly told him not to be a wimp. It just made things worse!

'Come on, Jacko,' Fay said encouragingly. 'There's no need to get all upset, darling. It's no big deal. I'll hold you and then you can't fall in. Okay?' Eventually, after much reluctance, Jack allowed his mother to suspend him above the lavatory. 'Put Dolly down a minute and hold onto the seat,' she said. 'It's all right, I've got you. There! Now you can go.' But he couldn't, or wouldn't. Fay eventually gave up. She resolved not to tell Conrad. He would only put more pressure on the boy. Lately, she had become concerned at his attitude which had been so different when their girls were at the same age. Why was he suddenly so disappointed in Jack? Why the hell did he have to let it *show* so much? Jack was crying again. The poor child seemed to be having a thoroughly unhappy Christmas. 'Never mind,' she consoled him. She helped him to pull his trousers up and then closed the lavatory seat and sat him on top of it. 'You can do a poo later. Now let's do your nose. Big blow? Good boy. Now let's go and see how Auntie Phoebe is getting on, eh?'

Phoebe was checking that the pudding was not boiling dry, as they went into the kitchen. She looked surprised to see Jack.

'Didn't he want to go?' she asked Fay.

'Where?'

'Over to ours to w-a-t-c-h the t-e-l-l-y?' Phoebe spelt it out.

Fay looked blank. 'I didn't know . . .' she began.

'Bloody Duncan!' exclaimed Phoebe. 'I *told* him to take Jack. I thought it would give you a break.'

'Is that where everyone is? I did wonder. That won't please Hope, will it?'

Phoebe smiled grimly. 'Serve her right,' she said.

'Are you doing okay?' Fay asked.

'So far. Why don't you take Jack anyway, and get me a nice sprig of holly for the pud while you're out?'

'Why not?' Fay said. 'Come on, Jacky.' She bent down to him. 'Let's go and find some prickly holly with lots of lovely red berries on it.'

'Boring,' Jack said scornfully.

'Are you all right?' Phoebe asked Fay. 'You look a bit frazzled.'

'The joys of unaccustomed full-time motherhood,' Fay said wryly, pulling Jack by the scruff of his neck towards the back door. 'You don't know how lucky you are!'

At one o'clock everything started happening together. As Phoebe was peeling Brussels sprouts, Fay came back alone to help her with last-minute things, and their mother-in-law made her first appearance. Hope was wearing a long black velvet skirt, and a silk blouse with a cameo at her neck. She looked very grand.

'Wouldn't you have thought that he would have had more consideration?' she demanded, as she swept into the kitchen and proceded to do a critical appraisal of Phoebe's progress so far.

Good afternoon, Hope, and a Merry Christmas to you too! Phoebe thought. Trust her to begin her day with a complaint. 'Who?' she asked.

'Why, Duckham, wretched man! Fancy spreading muck on Christmas Day. What have you used this for?' She said this last with such horror that Phoebe was paralysed in mid sprout. 'It smells of onions!' Hope said accusingly, brandishing a small wooden board.

'Yes,' Phoebe said, looking round. 'I chopped onions on it for the stuff —'

'*Never* cut up onions on *this* board!' Hope said. 'The smell persists for ever. Surely you should know better than that?'

A large black Bentley swished past the kitchen window at that moment, making for the front door. 'Peter!' Hope exclaimed. 'About time too!' She turned and walked swiftly out of the kitchen.

'It was the only bloody chopping board I could sodding well find!' Phoebe protested to Fay, after she had gone.

'What does she know?' Fay agreed. 'She never lifts a finger in here. Decent of the old man to put in an appearance, wouldn't you say? Now perhaps she'll be all graciousness and good cheer!' She flashed Phoebe an ironic smile.

Phoebe felt a growing feeling of solidarity with her sister-in-law. Until now she had thought of her as super-efficient and rather aloof. She had felt rather in awe of her seniority and envious of her achievements and good looks. She realized that she hardly knew her at all. Perhaps they might even become friends.

So far, it had been an easy journey down to Somerset, Peter thought. The Bentley was running sweetly as always. The weather was neutral; pressure was high and it was dull with a faint drizzle. He glanced sideways at his companion, who was still chattering away in that fresh unselfconscious manner which had no pretensions to any logical succession of ideas and, to his certain knowledge, was peculiar to young, very pretty girls. She was definitely no intellectual giant, but one could not have everything, and she was bright enough to regard him with obvious admiration, which was as it should be. She would without doubt enliven Christmas.

'I was expecting snow,' she said, in her amusing colonial accent, 'like on the Christmas cards, but it's just cold and grey. I reckon it's a swindle.'

'Anticyclonic gloom,' Peter said, agreeing. 'I don't suppose you get much of that in NZ?'

'Search me!' the girl said, giggling. 'If I knew what it was, I could tell you. One thing's for sure, I'm not in the least gloomy.' She gave him a dazzling smile and then frowned suddenly, changing tack with all the skill of a butterfly on a slalom course. 'You don't get all ponced up in the evenings, do you?' she asked, worried. 'Only I haven't got anything smart to wear. I never thought . . .'

'No,' Peter reassured her. 'We just come as we are.'

'We do that at home too,' she said, giggling anew, 'but my Dad has one unbreakable rule.'

'Yes?'

'Yeah. We can only come to the table in *dry* swimming cozzies.'

Peter had a wonderful vision of himself entering the crowded dining room at the big house and presenting her on a platter, resplendent in nothing but a brief bikini with acres of warm, smooth, suntanned, *edible* skin . . . as an alternative to the traditional flaming pudding perhaps?

'You've got a really wicked look on your face!' she exclaimed.

He smiled broadly. 'That's because I was having a really wicked thought,' he said, 'which was entirely of your making. Here we are.' He turned the car into his drive and they swept down the avenue between the limes. 'We'll go round to the front,' Peter said, 'then you'll see the house from its best side.'

'It's bloody *huge*!' the girl said, in awe, as they got out of the car. 'It's a mega mansion.'

'It's comfortable enough,' Peter agreed. 'Ah, here's my wife now. Hope, this is Thelma from New Zealand. The poor child had nowhere to go for Christmas, so I said I knew you'd be delighted to welcome her here.'

At five minutes to two, Phoebe was making the gravy. The turkey was sitting on its carving dish flanked by bacon and sausages in the warm oven. The roast potatoes and parsnips were keeping hot in a covered dish. The green vegetables were almost done. The bread sauce was ready. Any minute now, the exercise would be completed, and she could sit down and maybe even begin to enjoy the day. She glanced at Fay's watch. Spot on! she thought. Thank God for that!

'I'll go and call everyone, shall I?' Fay asked, coming in. 'I've laid the table and everything seems to be ready. You okay?'

'Fine,' Phoebe said, stirring as the gravy came to the boil. 'Finished now.' Fay came back again just as she was pouring it into the gravy boat.

'I don't think Duncan and the others can be back from yours,' she said. 'There's no sign of them.'

'Oh no!' Phoebe exclaimed crossly. 'I *said* two o'clock, for heaven's sake. The meal will spoil if it isn't eaten straightaway!'

'They're probably on their way,' Fay said optimistically. 'Guess what? Peter's done his usual trick and brought some unfortunate homeless person to share the festive pleasures of his hearth and home. Only, this year it's a young, good-looking girl, and she seems to be going down like a lead balloon with Hope.

You can cut the atmosphere in the drawing room with pinking shears!'

'Great!' Phoebe said sarcastically. 'That's guaranteed to improve Christmas! It's a good thing we cooked extra food, just in case, isn't it? Any sign of Brendan?'

'Not yet.'

'So, what shall we do?'

'Well there's no point in hanging on for Brendan, that's for sure.'

'I'll phone Duncan,' Phoebe said, putting the full gravy boat into the oven as well. 'Then I'll know for certain that they've already left.'

As she made for the telephone in the front hall, she passed Hope and then Peter and the girl on their way to the dining room. Hope was ahead of them. Her mouth was drawn in a tight line and her face was set hard. Phoebe was surprised to feel a small twinge of sympathy for her. It was a bit much of Peter!

'Ah!' Peter said, full of bonhomie. 'This is one of my daughters-in-law,' he gestured towards Phoebe. 'And this is Thelma.' He ushered the girl forwards proprietorially.

'Hi, daughter-in-law!' said Thelma. 'You look hot.'

'That's because I've been slaving over a hot stove all morning,' Phoebe said crisply, 'and my name's Phoebe. I'm sorry, I must telephone . . .' She dialled her own number with an impatient finger, watching as they disappeared into the dining room. The girl was wearing a tight sweater tucked into jeans, with a studded belt and high boots. She had long thick hair which lay like a swathe of hay on her shoulders and down her back. Her bottom looked pert. The telephone rang and rang. Good, thought Phoebe, they aren't there. They must be on their way. She was about to put the receiver down, when it was lifted at the other end.

'Hello?' Phoebe said.

'Hello, hello-ello, who's that?' It was Jack's voice.

Damn! she thought. 'Jack? This is your Auntie Phoebe. Will you fetch Uncle Duncan for me, please?'

'No,' Jack said with satisfaction.

'Please, Jacky? It's important. It's lunchtime.'

81

'I didn't do a poo,' Jack said earnestly. 'I didn't. I didn't.'

'No? well, never mind, but . . . Hello? Are you there?' There was a bumping noise and no reply. Jack had apparently put the phone down. Phoebe tried dialling again but got the engaged signal. It was off the hook. She put her receiver down and said, very loudly, 'SHIT!'

'And a happy Christmas to you in spite of that!' Rick said, coming down the stairs behind her. He was immaculately dressed and smelt of cologne. 'Where is everybody, and isn't it time for lunch?'

Phoebe turned a furious face to him. 'Yes it is! It's already spoiling and Conrad and Duncan and your boys are still watching the bloody television at our house, the selfish pigs, and the phone is off the hook, and I don't know what to do! I could kill the lot of them!'

'Fear not,' Rick said. 'I'll drive over there this instant and sweep them all up. We'll be back before you can say your dinner's in the dog!'

'Thanks,' Phoebe said with heartfelt relief. 'Thanks very much. Tell them if they're not back instantly, it will be!'

By twenty past two everyone was assembled round the long table in the dining room. Brendan had arrived on foot some five minutes earlier, all in black and sporting a dark felt hat with a wide brim. They were now outwardly all present and correct.

Inwardly, turmoil reigned. Phoebe had quarrelled with Duncan for being late, and was still fuming. Duncan was sulking. Rod and Pete had fought over which television channel to watch and were still niggling each other. Fay was cross with Conrad for trying to shame Jack away from his doll. Conrad knew that a boy with a doll was just asking for trouble, and felt justifiably aggrieved. Hope was furious with Peter for bringing that tarty parasite of a girl home without so much as a by-your-leave. Middle-aged male Ugandans down on their luck, or jobless young Swedish men stuck without a ticket home (like the year before and the one before that) she could understand and forgive, but this was outrageous! Thelma had decided that Brendan was extremely fanciable and was all excited; working out subtle ways in which to chat him up. Jack, who had woken that morning at 3 a.m. instead of his customary 5.30, was tired and fractious and clinging to his doll, refusing to put it down for lunch. Brendan, who had been hoping to spend Christmas with his lover, was feeling rejected and grumpy. Rick was thinking that Thelma looked like a useful distraction from family duties, and was on his mettle; assessing his chances, but feeling inhibited by the inconvenient presence of his two sons . . .

Peter, who had had his ego fed all morning, was the only member of the family comfortably in equilibrium.

Phoebe and Fay, refusing offers of help, began carrying in the turkey and all its trimmings.

'What!' Hope said. 'No consommé?'

Chapter Eight

'Medieval bestiaries,' Peter said, looking down the long table at his Christmas family assembly. He finished his mouthful of turkey and washed it down with wine. '. . . were produced in the twelfth and thirteenth century all in manuscript, with illustrations in colour; sometimes in gold. And why were they in manuscript, young Roderick?'

'Dunno,' Rod said, going pink with embarrassment.

'Because it was before printing was invented, of course! Amazing to relate, one fetched nearly three million in Sotheby's a year ago. Astonishing price.'

Phoebe tried to breathe some white wine by mistake, and choked. Rick banged her on the back and she retreated behind her napkin with streaming eyes and a hoarse apology.

'What's a bestiary?' Thelma asked. She looked at Brendan with wide eyes and giggled. 'Sounds rather rude to me.'

'It would,' Hope said. Brendan was silent.

'It's an ancient book of animals,' Rick supplied, 'birds, reptiles, fish and things, with some domestic ones and some imaginary fabled beasts, like unicorns.'

'With text,' Peter added. 'Usually of a cautionary nature.'

'An animal scrapbook with morals,' Conrad said, summing up. 'I doubt if many still survive today, unless perhaps abroad.'

'Wrong!' said his father. 'Ninety per cent of them are English and there are forty or fifty of them still extant.'

'You sound very sure,' Conrad said.

'I am.'

'How?'

'Education,' Peter said with satisfaction.

'Oh come on, Father,' Rick said. 'What's this leading up to?'

'Simply this,' Peter said, 'where is the bestiary which belonged to Nancy? It appears to have vanished without trace from the flat and no one has mentioned seeing it.'

'She probably flogged it,' Brendan said.

'I think not,' his father said. 'If she had, her estate would have been considerably larger.'

'How large was it?' young Pete asked innocently.

'Shut *up*!' his brother hissed. 'You're not supposed to ask things like that.'

'How do you know?'

'I just do.'

'I don't see –'

'*Quiet!*' Rick admonished them both. 'We'll doubtless all find out soon enough.'

'You'll find out after your father and I are dead,' Hope said firmly. 'Now this is a most unsuitable conversation. I'd be obliged if you would all talk about something else.'

'But,' Phoebe began, 'I thought –'

'N-Not now!' Duncan said sharply. She blushed uncomfortably scarlet.

There was an awkward silence. Pieces of turkey and vegetable were downed. Wine was sipped. Knives and forks clattered on plates.

Jack farted loudly and laughed delightedly. 'Big wind,' he said proudly. 'I can do another one.' His face grew dark as he clenched his tummy muscles in an effort to repeat his success.

'Be*have*,' Conrad told him sharply.

'I *am* being hayve,' Jack said virtuously.

'Oh that's great!' Thelma said with a little screech of laughter. 'Isn't that just cute? When I have children, I'm going to write down all their little sayings in a special book.' She looked across at Rick. 'Did you ever do that?'

'Sadly, no.' He smiled into her eyes.

'It's not too late,' Rod put in. 'Pete still says complustory instead of compulsory.'

'I do not!' Pete protested.

Hope intervened. 'I don't know why you two boys have to be so argumentative,' she said. 'Herry's children, your cousins, all get on together famously. It's only attention seeking. You'd get your fair share of attention without fighting each other, if you did but know, and it would be so much more pleasant for the rest of us.'

85

'My brothers and me fought all the time,' Thelma said, 'but we're the best of mates now.'

'More turkey?' Peter offered anyone, brandishing the carving knife. 'Brendan, finish the roast potatoes, there's a good lad. Stoke up with all the nourishment you can before the next voyage.'

'Voyage?' Thelma asked.

'He's a yachtsman,' Peter told her.

'Well, hello, sailor!' Thelma said delightedly. 'I've always fancied going on a big boat. You wouldn't like to give me a lift on yours, would you?'

Everyone started talking at once.

'What a shame Herry and Becky and the children couldn't be here this year,' Hope said. 'They're such a *united* family.'

'Jack,' Conrad said, 'try eating up those sprouts.'

'Driving in a sports car is far more stimulating than sailing,' Rick said to Thelma. 'You should give it a whirl.'

'It's the water I love,' she said. 'I feel dead uneasy if I'm away from the ocean too long, know what I mean?'

'One bite for Mummy . . .' Fay said encouragingly to Jack, '. . . and one for Dolly. Oh, now you've dropped it all down Dolly's front. That's no good, is it?'

'Now then,' Peter said to his grandsons, 'who knows who Ebenezer Scrooge is?'

'Right!' Conrad said. 'The doll's got to go. There's no way the boy can be taught even the rudiments of table manners with that ridiculous plastic baby in the way!'

'Modern education seems to me to be seriously deficient in the appreciation of the works of Charles Dickens,' Peter said. 'Nip into the study, young Pete, and fetch *A Christmas Carol*. It's in the bookcase on the left as I remember.'

'*Not now!*' Hope said. 'We're in the middle . . .'

Her voice was drowned out by piercing screams from Jack as his father pulled the doll from his limpet grasp and went out of the room with it, saying, 'Best place for this is in the dustbin, and that's where it will end up if he doesn't behave himself!'

Jack went purple in the face and threw his plate on the floor, lashing out with arms and legs in a paroxysm of rage.

'Oh, poor little mite!' Thelma exclaimed, before Jack totally precluded any further conversation with his loud roars of grief. Fay got to her feet jerkily, picked Jack up and holding him close, rushed from the room.

'Poor Jack,' Hope said. 'It's not his fault that he's a spoilt brat. I always say that a little benign neglect is a good idea. It doesn't do a child any favours if you concentrate on it too much. Becky's children have had to fend for themselves to a great extent, and they are all devoted to each other as a result. It's a pleasure to witness!' Rod and Pete started a scuffle over who should have the last quarter of an inch of wine from the last of the bottles. 'Boys!' Hope reprimanded them. 'You shouldn't be drinking at all. When I was a child, I was only allowed wine diluted with water.'

'But, Grandma,' Pete protested, 'I'm not a child. I'm twelve!'

Phoebe got up and started to clear away the empty dishes helped, unexpectedly, by Thelma and, after a nudge, by Duncan. She could barely contain herself. No one had so much as mentioned the food, let alone complimented her and Fay on their hours of preparation of it. She felt completely taken for granted. Where was everyone's Christmas spirit? Where was their generosity and family feeling? What was the point of it all? Even Rick hadn't paid her any of his usual attention. Duncan hadn't encouraged her or supported her at all.

'What's wrong with everyone?' she muttered to Duncan, as they heated up the brandy for the pudding.

'What d'you m-mean?' he asked, surprised. Phoebe gave up. She was convinced that Duncan had known all along that there was to be no sharing out of Nancy's money and had deliberately not told her. She felt cheated and resentful. She decided there and then that it would make no difference to her; she would still go ahead and get pregnant. She and Duncan would make ends meet somehow. If the worst came to the worst, she could always sell Nancy's bestiary – if that was really what she'd got. Surely it couldn't be worth all that much? Peter always exaggerated. Phoebe felt guilty and uneasy that she had taken it. Perhaps she ought to own up at once? She knew she would have to eventually, but at that moment she was too cross with all the Moons to consider doing so. It could wait. It would still be worth as much then as it was now. There was no rush. She felt tired. She had been conscious of the beginnings of a familiar dragging ache in her abdomen all afternoon. A September birth seemed unlikely after all. Sadness overtook her. She heard Conrad, Fay and Jack going back into the dining room again and Conrad admonishing Jack to be his age. Poor little chap, she thought. He's no age at all!

Phoebe poured the hot brandy over the Christmas pudding as Duncan held it on its special plate, and then set fire to it. The blue light danced and flickered over and around it as he bore it into the dining room in triumph and put it down on the table in front of Hope.

'Your f-flaming p-p-pudding, ma'am,' he said.

Even Jack forgot his tears in the excitement of the moment. 'The p-p-pudding's on f-fire!' he said.

There was a small hard silence.

'What did you say?' Fay asked.

'I s-said the p-pudding's on f-fire.'

'Stop it, Jack!' Conrad said sharply. 'It isn't funny to copy Uncle Duncan. He can't help talking like that, but you can.'

'No I c-c-can't.'

'Of course you can. You're just putting it on. You were talking perfectly normally just now. What's the matter with you?' Two more large tears slid out of Jack's eyes and splashed onto the tablecloth in front of him.

'That,' Fay said furiously, gathering him up and rushing out again, 'is the last straw!'

'Please excuse my family,' Conrad said, holding out his hands palm upwards to show his bafflement. 'I don't know what's got into them lately.'

'I think you were too hard on the child,' Brendan said. 'Try backing off a bit.'

'Oh I see,' Conrad said nastily. 'You're an expert on child care now, are you?'

Brendan gave him a furious look. 'I'm human,' he said, 'in case you've forgotten. That's the only qualification I need.'

'I think you'd make a lovely Daddy,' Thelma said stoutly. 'You're just the type.'

Phoebe caught Hope's eye as she started passing the bowls of Christmas pudding down the table, and intercepted her look of sardonic pleasure. Happy families, Phoebe thought. Happy bloody families!

The formal opening of the presents took place in the drawing room at four o'clock. Logs burnt in the big fireplace. The Christmas tree lights glowed amongst the spruce needles and tinsel. Hickory and Diggory lay against each other on the hearthrug, replete with leftovers and snoring gently. The hi-fi played quietly in the background, a tape of the *Messiah*. The presents, wrapped in gaudy paper with metallic bows and tags attached, were piled beneath the tree. Hope sat herself down in the best chair and prepared to direct the proceedings.

'Now then, Rod,' she said. 'You can sort out which present is for which of us. I suggest we open them one at a time, so that we can all enjoy each one. Who's first?'

'You are, Grandma,' Rod said diplomatically.

Phoebe watched as the presents emerged and the pile of torn-up wrapping paper and severed ribbon grew higher and higher. She felt no personal sense of anticipation. She had bought her own present from Duncan – a nightie – herself, to ensure that she actually got something. The year before Duncan had failed to think of anything suitable, and had given up.

Hope unwrapped her present from Peter. It was the same every year; a box of Black Magic. 'How nice,' she said. Phoebe had never seen her eat a chocolate, and was pretty sure she never did.

Thelma found that Peter had given her an identical box. 'I've got one too,' she announced. 'Yummy!' She reached over and gave him a kiss on his cheek. 'Thanks, Peter,' she said. 'Let's eat them now.' She tore off the Cellophane and opened the box, handing it round to everyone.

'Chocolate,' Hope said, 'is very bad for the complexion.'

'No worries,' Thelma said happily, biting an orange cream, popping it in and licking her fingers one by one. 'I can eat tons of the stuff and I never get spots.'

'Not like Rod,' Pete said with satisfaction. 'He only has to look –'

'When I was a girl,' Hope interrupted with authority, 'we

didn't gorge ourselves on sweet things the way children seem to today. I'm sure we were much healthier too. And d'you know, Herry always used to give his babies sultanas instead of sweets; so much better for their teeth, and they loved them!'

Rod unwrapped a Camcorder, gave a crow of delight and rushed to hug his father. '*Thanks*, Dad!' he said, beaming. 'It's just what I wanted.' Pete found that he had been given a Super Nintendo System, and joined in, loud in his praise. Rick gave each boy a mock punch, smiling broadly and winking at Thelma.

'What's the smaller boy got?' Peter enquired.

'It's a Nintendo console, Grandfather. It plugs into the TV and you play computer games on it. You must have heard of them? They're awesome. They cost an arm and a leg!'

Hope sniffed. 'We didn't go in for ridiculously expensive presents either,' she said. 'I remember being thrilled to be given–'

'A penny whistle,' Rick supplied. 'So you always say, Mother, but times have changed. Kids are more sophisticated these days.'

Phoebe felt a spasm of pain and instinctively clutched at her stomach. She looked round her, rather embarrassed. No one had noticed. She got to her feet and slipped quietly out of the room to find some Tampax. Her period had definitely come. She sat on the lavatory for a long time with her head in her hands. Her disappointment was unreasonable, but crushing nevertheless. It felt like the end of all her hopes. After a while she got up, washed her hands, pushed her hair into place and went into the kitchen to put a tray of mince pies into Hope's oven.

When Phoebe got back into the drawing room, she found it piled high with designer trainers, books, gadgets, clothes and toys. Jack, who had been subdued and had hardly spoken since lunchtime, was rushing around in a Batman costume and dragging his redeemed doll by one arm, behind him. Duncan had been given a sweater by Hope. It was a size too small, but Phoebe refrained from saying so. She opened her present from her mother-in-law, a set of headed notepaper and envelopes, and noticed at once that the postcode was wrong. She kept quiet about that too. Peter had dozed off under a layer of socks and handkerchiefs and a pair of Santa Claus boxer shorts. Brendan had disappeared altogether. Fay and Conrad were apparently not speaking to one another, and the heap of presents between them seemed to stand as a symbolic barrier to understanding and communication. Phoebe went over to Fay to thank her for her present of a bottle of perfume. 'Here's your watch back, too,' she said. 'I'd have been lost without it. I've got the mince pies warming up in the oven. How long do they take, d'you think?'

'I'll come and help carry them,' Fay said. She looked pale and tense.

'You all right?' Phoebe asked solicitously as they got to the kitchen.

Fay grimaced. 'Not really,' she said, 'but I expect I'll get over it.'

'Can I help?'

Fay turned a grateful face to her. 'Thanks,' she said, 'I'll be fine. It's just Christmas, but if Hope says another word about how wonderful Herry and Becky's children are, I swear I'll . . . strangle her!'

'I don't blame you. Why does she always do it?'

'Because she knows it teases? I'm damned if I know.'

'If you and Jack ever need a break,' Phoebe offered, 'you're always welcome at ours, you know.'

'You must come and see us too,' Fay said brightly.

So that's as far as it goes, Phoebe thought, disappointed. She won't let me in any further. She doesn't really need my help. They carried the mince pies and cream to the drawing room.

'Would you believe it?' Rick was saying, 'after all these years? She's staying with friends in Suffolk for the New Year, apparently, and wants the boys to join her.'

'Who?' Phoebe asked Duncan.

'P-P-Poppy.'

'Oh,' Phoebe exclaimed, 'it would be lovely for the boys to see their mother again! Does that mean that she's completely well now?'

'Doubt it,' Rick said drily.

'But they are going?'

'They seem to want to. God knows why. It fits in with my plans rather well, actually. I've got to be in Paris then.'

'How long is it since you've seen your mum?' Phoebe asked Rod.

'Ages,' he muttered, looking at the floor.

'It's *Batman* on TV at six,' Pete said quickly. 'I can't wait! And it's *Crocodile Dundee* two after that. They're the best films of the day! We can go over to your house again, can't we, Phoebe?'

'B-B-Batman!' Jack called, delighted.

'Well, I don't see why n –' Phoebe began, but Hope didn't let her finish.

'No more television,' she said crisply. 'You've all had quite enough already. You are after all supposed to be spending your Christmas with your grandfather and me. It would be churlish of you to rush off again; not at all the proper way to repay our hospitality! A mince pie would be very nice, thank you, Phoebe.'

Duncan was glad to get home on Christmas evening. He found the festive season exhausting, but it was good to see the family and the food had been excellent. He felt proud of his wife's efforts. Now he must take Diggory for a long-overdue but short walk, and then bed, the end of a good day! Phoebe seemed rather quiet. He presumed that she was tired. They opened the back door of their cottage and went in, preceded by the dog.

Phoebe gasped. 'What a mess!' she said, turning to him in dismay.

He glanced about him. The kitchen looked much as usual. He and the boys and Conrad had had the odd snack earlier that morning and hadn't got round to doing the washing up, and Diggory had killed a few newspapers, but that was no crisis, surely? Phoebe had gone on into the sitting room.

'Oh Duncan!' she wailed. 'There's muddy footprints all over the carpet and the sofa is covered in crumbs, and the furniture has all been dragged about anyhow and the cushions are all over the room! How could you let them wreck the place and not do anything about it? You were supposed to be in charge!'

'C-Come on,' Duncan said. 'It's n-n-n-not that bad.'

'And there's a stain on the carpet over here and it's all wet! What is it?'

'It's n-nothing. J-J-Jack knocked over a g-glass of R-R-R-R-Ribena. We m-mopped it all up.'

'You should have *washed* it all off straightaway! Now it's probably there for ever! Don't you have any common sense at all?'

'We'll c-clear up tomorrow. I'll h-help you, okay? Don't fuss.'

'Why is it that I can't trust you to do *anything* properly?' Phoebe asked him despairingly.

'I'll t-take D-D-Diggory out,' he said shortly. Why must she overdramatize everything? So the place looked a little lived in, so what? It was no big deal. Any half-competent housewife could put it to rights in a moment. He picked up his torch from the shelf and Diggory's lead from the hook beside the back door and withdrew thankfully into the darkness with the enthusiastic dog at his heels.

Phoebe took a deep breath and decided that she would indeed leave the clearing up until the next day. She was tired out. She went slowly upstairs and into the bathroom to clean her teeth, yawning and wiping her eyes with the backs of her hands. When she opened them again, the first thing she saw on the bathroom floor, between the lavatory and the bath, was a small pile of human faeces.

Jack! Phoebe thought, now understanding what he'd said to her on the phone at lunchtime. Oh no!

She went and found the coal shovel and got rid of the pile. Then she washed the shovel and scrubbed the wooden floor with a brush and disinfectant, before drying it off with a cloth. Thank goodness we haven't got a posh bathroom carpet! she thought. There was no sign of Duncan. It would be in character for him to stay out extra long, in the hope that she would be asleep by the time he returned. She washed out the cloth and hung it on the side of the bath to dry. Then she went into her bedroom.

She was tired, but felt too jangly to sleep. Alternate Christmases with the Moons had never come up to her naïve early expectations, but this one had been particularly miserable. Perhaps Nancy had had even worse times. Phoebe decided to risk reading one of the diaries before Duncan came back. She rummaged in her trunk and chose 1956, the year of her own birth and coincidentally the year when Nancy had been the age she was now: thirty-five.

Tuesday, 25 December – Skelpie Lodge, Scotland. Porridge for breakfast and then out for a marvellous walk in the snowy hills. Eleanor may be ten years older than me, but she's much fitter! Some friends of hers, Sandy and Muriel, came too. Sunny at first but cloudy later with more snow. Wore my new gaiters over knee-length socks and hiking boots – feet remarkably comfortable. Saw my first caper-caillie! It crashed down out of a pine tree as we walked underneath and flew off with a flurry of wings and a long glide to cover. Higher up there were ptarmigan, all white but for their tails, and flocks of snow buntings with big white patches on their wings – 3 ticks in one day! Hard walking over the heather and bogs, so we were exhausted and ravenous by the evening and did full justice to the hotel's Christmas dinner. P. phoned briefly – I miss him. Lovely to hear his voice (E. very supportive about him too) – good thing it was before I sampled the single malts! All sat round a huge fire and played games, did silly turns and sang songs accompanied by Sandy on the fiddle. Great hilarity. Bed very late.

Oh, Phoebe thought wistfully, why couldn't our Christmas have been like that? A great feeling of anticlimax engulfed her. She realized that she had had no fun at all during the day. There had been little joy or spontaneous affection displayed by anyone (except perhaps poor Thelma) and for Phoebe it had been just worry and hard work. No one had thanked her for her efforts, or shown any appreciation. No one had shown any interest in her at all, not even Duncan. Perhaps they all thought she hadn't done it very well. Tears prickled her eyes and she brushed them away. Maybe Duncan would say nice things to her when he got back.

The back door banged downstairs as Duncan came in with the dog. Phoebe pushed Nancy's diary into her trunk again and lay down, staring at the ceiling. After a few minutes Duncan came up the stairs and into the bedroom. He was rubbing his hands together to warm them up.

'You s-still awake?' he said. 'It's b-bloody c-cold out there.' He undressed quickly and got into bed beside her. ' 'Night,' he said, turning the light out and settling down for sleep.

Phoebe went on staring upwards, now into darkness. She thought, You selfish, thoughtless bastard! Why the hell did I ever marry you?

Chapter Nine

Duncan had now apparently gone off sex altogether. Phoebe blamed herself for accidentally saying too much, thereby undermining his confidence. But she blamed him for having such a pathetically low sex drive that he couldn't overcome such an unfortunate outburst on her part, and take it in his stride like any normal red-blooded male. To some men it would have been seen as a challenge! Why not to Duncan? Why couldn't he just *try*? His motto appeared to be: if at first you don't succeed, give up.

Nancy, after four years of marriage, had also had problems. Phoebe re-read the diary for 1950.

Wednesday, 19 April. Hugh is a cardboard replica (just like one of his own characters) it seems to me. He has no depth of feeling – no *ardour*. This is most disastrous when we're in bed. He can't seem to throw himself wholeheartedly into making love to me. It's as though he's afraid to lose control. I'm just the opposite. Unless I can give myself body and soul to it, it just doesn't work, and this is well-nigh impossible with Hugh. It's as though the cerebral part of him is standing there outside himself, uninvolved, watching the rest of him perform. His face wears an expression both sardonic and sheepish, as though the whole procedure were both ridiculous and unsuitable. It puts me off completely and stops me from feeling any desire at all. Then he ejaculates almost at once and I'm left unsatisfied, with feelings of worthlessness and anger. The crazy thing is that he thinks *I'm* frigid, when in fact the opposite is true! It's just that I can't bear to go through the whole unsatisfactory process, knowing that I'll end up wide awake, frustrated and cross, so I often reject his advances even though I'm *desperate* for a proper married life. What an absurd paradox! What should I do? It's not the sort of thing one can discuss.

*

It *is* the sort of thing people should discuss, Phoebe thought sadly, but it takes two to do it. Nancy had solved her problem by taking a lover, but I could never do that. It would be too confusing. I'd feel so torn, and if I got pregnant, it would be unthinkable not to know who the father was! I'd never put myself in that situation. But if I'm ever going to have a baby, I've somehow got to get Duncan interested again . . . There were things which Phoebe and her teacher had enjoyed together which had somehow never seemed appropriate with Duncan. She had considered that they would be beneath his dignity, and hadn't liked to suggest them, but perhaps desperate problems required desperate solutions.

Phoebe worried about this as she hoovered the cottage. Wynne, her mother, was coming down for a couple of days to see the New Year in. She would notice every particle of dust, every filament of cobweb, every hair of the dog . . . Which reminds me, Phoebe thought, I must get some gin in. Duncan was due back at lunchtime, so that Phoebe could borrow the van and meet her mother off the train. If there was time, she could buy some food first. She put the Hoover away and, with special care, made up a bed in the spare room. She was devoted to Wynne and always glad to see her. She wondered whether she might after all confide in her mother; maybe even discuss her own problems with sex? Wynne and Phoebe's father had got divorced twenty years before. Had Wynne had any sort of a sex life after that? Phoebe didn't know. She had lived alone ever since Phoebe had grown up and got a flat of her own. She had had men friends, of course, but Phoebe couldn't imagine her actually in bed with any of them. She had known about Phoebe's long affair with the teacher, whom she had liked, but they had never discussed it. Perhaps it was time they talked, woman to woman.

Duncan was late. Phoebe went downstairs to look at the clock in the kitchen. He should have been home a quarter of an hour ago. At this rate, Phoebe thought, there won't be time for any shopping. Why the hell can't he do as he promises? She opened the front door and looked up the lane; no sign of him. The air she breathed in was mild. There were gleams of sun in the grey

97

sky and the first signs of snowdrops by the wall, pushing up through the earth. The great tits were already singing their repetitive spring song. Phoebe thought, Why don't I feel full of anticipation for new beginnings too?

Duncan had spent the morning cutting up a fallen ash tree for a widow, and had been given a van load of firewood as well as cash in hand. He was feeling particularly pleased with himself. He closed the back doors by leaning hard against them, put his chainsaw in the passenger footwell, ushered Diggory onto the seat above and then got into the driving seat himself, and set off for home. Phoebe was waiting for him at the front door.

'You're late,' she said.

'P-Plenty of time,' Duncan said easily.

'No there isn't! I was going to do a major food shop on the way, and now there won't be time.'

'L-Look what we've g-got,' Duncan said proudly, opening the back doors of the van, 'and all f-for free!'

'Shit! Duncan, how the hell will I get Mum's bag in there with all that bloody wood?'

That's great, Duncan thought bitterly. We get free firewood and is she pleased? No, she fucking isn't! Whatever I do, she moans. It really pisses me off. 'It w-won't take long to u-u-unload,' he said sulkily.

'There isn't time,' Phoebe said. 'Just chuck some out and make enough space. I've got to go *now*.'

Duncan did. Then he watched her drive away in the van. He hoped that by the time she came back, she would be in a better temper. Wynne would cheer her up. She was a nice comfortable sort of a woman. Why couldn't Phoebe be more like her? Duncan couldn't imagine Wynne making the demands that her daughter did. Duncan was made to feel that he was always in the wrong these days. He always seemed to have disappointed Phoebe in some way, but he was never sure why. She looked hurt or reproachful at the drop of a hat. She sighed a lot. She clearly wasn't happy. What was he supposed to do about it? He would be content enough if only she'd leave him alone. There was nothing wrong with *him*. Why couldn't she just get on with life like everybody else? She kept saying that she wanted

98

encouragement; wanted him to talk to her. He *did* talk to her. Then she said she didn't want just 'pass the salt' sort of talk, but real *communication*. So, to get things started he'd asked her if she'd like a cup of tea, but she'd yelled at him and stormed out in a rage. It didn't make sense. It couldn't be the time of the month all the time; perhaps she was having an early menopause? Duncan hoped that Wynne would sort her out.

As Duncan changed out of his working clothes into something marginally cleaner, Phoebe brushed her hair and prepared to go downstairs to cook supper. She could hear her mother moving about in the other bedroom, unpacking things from her suitcase. She was looking well, Phoebe thought fondly, she seemed younger than her 55 years and full of confidence and optimism. Phoebe looked forward to having her on her own the next day, so that they could have a really good talk. She wished Duncan wasn't around that night, preventing them from doing it at once. She brushed her hair, trying to make it bend the way she wanted it, but it stuck out annoyingly and she gave up with an irritated exclamation.

'Damn!' she said. 'I should have washed it. It's a real mess!'

'Yes,' Duncan said, pulling on a sweater, 'it is r-rather.' Phoebe threw her brush on the floor. She looked furious. 'N-Now what?' he asked.

'Don't you know *anything*?' Phoebe demanded, keeping her voice low so that Wynne wouldn't hear. 'Didn't it occur to you that I might be wanting some reassurance? Couldn't you have said, "Nonsense, it looks fine"?'

'I was only a-a-a-agreeing with you.'

'Well, don't! I don't know why I ever bother to get dressed up; you never notice. You've never *ever* complimented me on my appearance. You've never said "You look nice" or "I like that dress". I feel bloody invisible when you're around. It makes me feel why the hell do I bother.' Duncan was silent. 'Well?' Phoebe demanded.

'You l-look all right n-now' he said reluctantly.

'I'm not talking about *now*. I'm not dressed up *now*, am I? I'm in my ordinary clothes. Can't you even see that? I'm talking about things in general, about Christmas, for example. I made a huge effort on Christmas night and did you say anything nice to me? Did you hell! I could have been wearing a couple of flour sacks with holes cut in them, for all the difference it made to you. You're my husband, Duncan. You're supposed to boost my confidence, make me feel appreciated, cared for. It surely isn't much to ask; just a handful of words at the right moment?'

Duncan sighed heavily. 'It's a b-b-bit late n-n-n-now,' he finally said.

'Damn right!' Phoebe said. 'You said it!' Duncan slid his feet into his slippers and made for the door. 'That's right,' Phoebe said, 'run away as usual!'

'I t-take it that you d-d-don't want to involve your m-m-mother in this d-discussion?' Duncan said.

'No, of course not.'

'W-W-Well then, I'll s-see you d-downstairs.' He went out. Phoebe heard Wynne coming out of her room at the same moment, and the two of them going downstairs together. She heard her mother saying, 'You've done so much to the cottage, Duncan. It's a real little gem, isn't it?' Then the door at the bottom of the stairs was closed and she was left to pull herself together.

She hadn't meant to have a row. She never did. When things happened to infuriate her she tried to keep them in, and told herself they were not important; that she'd get over it. Perhaps it was her own fault. Perhaps if she reacted at the time, then Duncan would learn. It was clearly no good bottling everything up and then releasing it in a flood at inopportune moments later on. Duncan didn't understand what was going on then. He had no intuition, no responsiveness; no capacity for abstract thought. If something couldn't be made sense of in immediate terms, then to him it was nonsense and better ignored.

It was always the wrong moment when it came to explanations, Phoebe thought. If you'd taken trouble to dress up and put your face on for an event, but went unnoticed by your husband and were feeling snubbed, hurt and low in confidence, how could you then say so without bursting into tears, wrecking your make-up, and rendering yourself incapable of carrying off the occasion with any sort of self-possession? Of course you couldn't. So it had to be contained, only to burst out at an

100

inappropriate time later on. Any intelligent man, Phoebe thought, ought to understand that; ought to be prepared to learn what to expect from his wife. No, it wasn't so much that Duncan was unwilling to make the effort. It was worse than that; he just didn't appreciate that there was any effort to be made. Phoebe sighed. It seemed hopeless. She took a deep breath and went downstairs.

Wynne was sitting in the kitchen talking to Duncan. Diggory was sitting on the floor next to her, resting his chin on her lap and angling his head rapturously so that her absently stroking hand landed on the desired part of his hard muzzle or on his soft scratchable ears. Duncan was making tea.

'Just think,' Wynne said, '1992 tomorrow! I wonder what that will bring?' Phoebe knew she was thinking about grandchildren.

'Who knows?' Duncan said. Phoebe knew he wasn't.

'I think Mum would like a drink, Duncan,' Phoebe said.

'Nearly r-ready,' Duncan said, watching the kettle.

'No, not tea, a proper drink. Here, let me . . .'

'I'll d-do it,' Duncan said firmly. 'Gin?'

'That would be lovely,' Wynne smiled. She turned to Phoebe as Duncan went to get the bottle from the next room. 'He's looking very fit, isn't he?' she said. 'I always forget what a good-looker he is, until I see him again. You're a lucky girl!'

'Yes,' Phoebe said.

The rest of the evening was fine, Duncan thought. Phoebe had cooked steak as a special treat and they had a bottle of red wine with it. Wynne chattered away cheerfully about nothing in particular, stopping every now and then for him to agree with her, so there was no need for him even to look at his wife. When he did glance in her direction half an hour later, she looked as though she'd got over her temper and was enjoying herself. Thank goodness for her mother! he thought.

'My trains did well,' Wynne was saying. 'The first was only ten minutes late, so I got the connection with no trouble at all. I'm glad I wasn't in the Severn Tunnel when those two trains went into each other though . . .'

'Yes,' Duncan said.

'D'you know, they had to wait five hours before they were rescued? I couldn't have stood that, all shut in. You'll never get me in that Channel Tunnel . . .'

'No,' Duncan said.

'I mean, that will be far worse. Just imagine being stuck in there!'

'Yes,' Duncan said.

'Mind you, I reckon as soon as it's finished the IRA will bomb it anyway. It will be such a tempting target, won't it? How will they resist?'

'Yes,' Duncan said.

'Unless they blow themselves up first, of course, like that couple did in St Albans in November. I thought at the time that it served them right, but when they said that the girl was only 18 and the man in his twenties, I was sorry for the poor thing. I expect she was led astray by him; didn't know what she was doing.'

'No,' Duncan agreed.

'You're very quiet, my pet.'

'I'm fine, Mum,' Phoebe said.

They ate fruit salad and cream for pudding and then went into the sitting room to watch television, ending up seeing the New Year in and laughing with Clive James.

'Here's to 1992,' Wynne said, raising her glass to Phoebe, 'and future happiness for us all. It's been a lovely evening. The food was delicious and your handsome husband is lovely to talk to. She raised her glass to Duncan as well. 'Happy New Year!'

'Yes,' Duncan said, tipping his own glass slightly in her direction. So he was lovely to talk to, was he! He liked Wynne. Perhaps she could knock some sense into her daughter. He caught Phoebe's eye, but couldn't interpret her expression. She clinked her glass with his.

'Happy 1992,' she said.

On New Year's Day Duncan went back to work. The weather in Somerset was grey and quite mild, so he was able to continue with the stone wall which he was building for a client in the village. Phoebe handed him his box of sandwiches and watched him turn the van and drive away up the lane. The following morning she would be back at her job too. It was not an inspiriting prospect. She went back into the kitchen. Wynne was still eating toast. Now, Phoebe thought, now we'll talk.

'How's Duncan's work going,' Wynne asked her, taking some marmalade, 'what with the recession and everything?'

'All right at the moment,' Phoebe said, 'but I don't know for how much longer. Luckily most people in the village have hung on to their jobs and can afford Duncan, but there's an increasing number of builders from further away who are getting on their bikes and competing with him for jobs. So far, thank goodness, folk would still rather have someone they know.'

'A man who does a reliable job,' Wynne agreed. 'Is this your own make? It's delicious.'

'I could always go back to work full time,' Phoebe said, 'if things get difficult.'

'Oh, I hope it won't come to that,' Wynne said. 'I expect your Duncan will see to it that it doesn't. I'm so glad you've got yourself such a good man, my pet. I used to worry about you so much in the bad old days.'

'Well,' Phoebe started, 'now that you mention –'

'I'm glad to have got you on your own, Phoebe,' Wynne interrupted, 'because I've got something to say. I would have said it earlier, but I wanted to speak to you first so you'd have time to think about it properly before telling Duncan about it.'

'Heavens!' Phoebe said. 'You make whatever it is sound very serious. Is it?'

Wynne's face looked suddenly anxious, almost pleading. She put down her toast and marmalade, took one of Phoebe's hands in both of hers and squeezed it. She seemed to be having difficulty in talking. A flush had begun at her neck and was travelling up her face to her greying hairline. She let go of Phoebe's hand and pulled at the collar of her woollen polo-necked jersey.

An unbreathing moment of dread took hold of Phoebe. 'What is it?' she asked urgently. 'You're not ill? You look so well . . .'

'No,' her mother said. 'It's nothing like that. It's good news . . .' She looked shy. 'I've got myself a new man,' she said in a rush. 'He's moving in with me next week.'

Phoebe saw her with new eyes. 'But . . .' she said, swallowing,

'. . . that's great! I'm really pleased for you.' She saw her mother relax and realized with surprise how tense she must have been.

'You don't mind?' Wynne asked.

'Of course not. Why should I?'

'I thought you might think . . . Oh, I don't know . . . that I was stupid or too old or something.'

Tears came to Phoebe's eyes. 'Of course not,' she said. 'You silly old thing. Come and give us a hug.' They came together by the table and embraced. The top of Wynne's head was level with Phoebe's chin. Phoebe could smell the scent her mother always used. She struggled with a conflict of emotions but was conscious above all of her mother's relief and love, as expressed in the surprising strength of her encircling arms.

'I think it's brilliant,' Phoebe said, into her hair. 'What's his name?'

'George,' Wynne said. 'Oh Phoebe, I was so worried you'd be upset. I can't tell you. And yet, just lately I've been so happy, the happiest I've ever been . . .'

I *am* glad, Phoebe thought. I truly am. I want her to be happy. But now I can't talk to her about my problems; it would spoil everything for her.

A new thought struck her. He'll be there, she thought, this unknown George, at the house in Hexham, all the time. It won't be an unconditionally welcoming place of refuge for me ever again.

The next day was Thursday. Phoebe got ready for work with reluctance. It was her mother's last day, and she resented having to leave her for a boring morning at the theatre office.

'Don't worry about me now,' Wynne said. 'Duncan's taking me round to his mum's house for coffee and a walk round their garden. I specially want to see that pond you told me so much about; I've a fancy for one myself.'

'If you're sure?' Phoebe said. 'See you at lunchtime then.'

She wheeled her bicycle out and walked it up the lane. The weather was grey and cool with a freshening westerly wind and spots of rain. She stepped in a puddle by mistake and mud slopped over the toes of her leather boots and crept messily up their insteps. She pulled up the hood of her kagoul with an irritated flick. I look a mess, she thought. In the old days in Newcastle she had dressed tidily for work, had driven herself there in her carefully polished car and, once there, had taken a pride in her job. And now? Was she 'letting herself go'? It seemed to be impossible to emerge from their lane in any sort of order, so she had given up trying to look smart. Few of her good clothes now fitted her anyway; she supposed she must have put on weight. Nowadays she went to work in jeans and sweatshirts. No one commented. It didn't seem to matter. She was only the secretary. Worse still, the work was boring and underpaid. The theatre was badly supported and its programme uninspiring.

Today, Phoebe remembered, was the beginning of four days of pantomime produced by the local amateur dramatic club. She was glad she had no involvement in it, other than answering the telephone and writing letters. The only possible excitement of the day might be a letter about a lawsuit against them, which an elderly woman was currently pursuing, over a plant tub she had tripped over in the dark on her way to the theatre from the car park the previous November. Never mind, Phoebe encouraged herself, only two days until the weekend!

At lunchtime Wynne enthused about the pond. 'Of course, it's much bigger than I'd need,' she said, 'but Duncan's built it ever so well, hasn't he? I only wish I lived nearer so he could make one for me too.'

'Well, you n-never know,' Duncan said, smiling.

'How was Hope?' Phoebe asked.

'Very charming, but I could see she was down, poor woman. Duncan warned me about her moods. Rick being burgled didn't help, I doubt. It would unsettle anyone.'

'Burgled?' Phoebe said. 'Rick?'

'Over Christmas, Hope said, but nothing obvious taken and no mess; most peculiar.'

'But why did he think he'd been burgled then?'

'There was a window broken in his basement and mud on his carpets,' Wynne said.

'Could have been his own boys,' Phoebe said.

'More than likely,' agreed Wynne.

105

An uncomfortable idea occurred to Phoebe. 'Does your man have any children?' she asked her mother.

'No,' Wynne said. 'His first wife couldn't.'

'Oh.' Good, Phoebe thought. At least it's only one person I've got to share you with.

'I'm sorry I can't stay, pet,' Wynne said, understanding. 'I'd love to be with you longer, but I've got to get back to work myself.'

'And back to George,' Phoebe said, teasing.

'That as well.' Wynne blushed like a girl. It seemed to Phoebe as if they had reversed their rôles, and she was now mother to Wynne. It felt odd and unsettling. It sent her a message, long overdue, but now coming through strongly. It was time to grow up. She was on her own.

Chapter Ten

In Nancy's Christmas entry for 1956, there had been no mention of Hugh. Phoebe was curious as to what exactly had caused their break-up. Was it a big event; the discovery of Nancy's affair with Peter? Was it an act of cruelty; the sudden death of love? She leafed backwards through the diary, looking for the moment when their marriage finally died.

Saturday, 7 July – at the cottage. Hugh insisted on working on his book today, even though it's the weekend. It doesn't seem to be going well and he's worrying at it like a monkey with its fist in a bottle. If he could just relax a bit, I'm sure the words would flow better. Actually it has suited my purpose very well. I seized the moment and packed a lot of my books into cardboard boxes and stowed them in the boot of my car. There's not much left in the cottage that belongs particularly to me now. I've been taking clothes and odd things over the last few months, whenever I've had the chance, and collecting them in the flat. I'm amazed that Hugh hasn't guessed my intentions. He still seems not to know about P. I shan't tell him. P.'s not the reason anyway. Hugh and I seem to have nothing in common any more. Our marriage has simply petered out (unintentional bad joke!) and we're already leading mostly separate lives. Hugh will be much better off without me. It will give him the chance to meet someone else and have the children he's always wanted. As for me? I shall be free to get on with my own life without being shackled by guilt and irritation and the crushing weight of Hugh's disappointed expectations. I'm not deceiving myself that P. will leave H. for me – after six years – why should he? But meetings will be easier, and I shall be able to put our on/off affair onto a more equal footing, and fit it in on my own terms. I've decided that I'm not good at marriage. I shall be much happier living on my own and having lover(s). The more I think of it, the more

I realize that I never really loved Hugh. I just felt sorry for him and he needed me. I now know that sympathy and need can very easily be confused with love. I wish I'd known it ten years ago. In fact our separation should be very easy. I shall make over this cottage to Hugh. He's much happier writing here than in London, and he's got the odd friend in the village who will help him. I shall send him enough money to keep him going for a year, and after that it will be up to him to earn his own living. I shall keep the flat (which was mine anyway) and pusskin Claude (ditto). Thank goodness I've got a well-paid job and capital which can finance all this. I know I'm fortunate. Now I've written all this down, it seems very logical and unanswerable. I hope Hugh will see it that way tomorrow.

Sunday, 8 July. A terrible day, made worse by uncaring wonderful weather. First Hugh tried to hit me, then he burst into tears and grovelled. I had to leave my darling Claude behind. When it came to it, I just couldn't leave Hugh totally bereft. I meant to explain things to him in an unemotional way, but it was hopeless. How could I ever have thought it possible? Just had to get in the car and go. Could hardly see for tears as I drove away. Never realized until today how much I love that little cat. Eleanor is staying with me for a few days, thank goodness. My beautiful, soft, silky, sociable, stout-hearted, wicked Claude, how shall I ever manage without you?

Nancy had clearly been crying as she wrote the last few sentences. The ink was smudged, and the paper distorted where the teardrops had dried. Phoebe was amazed that anyone could get so upset about an ordinary old cat. Perhaps Duncan felt like that about his dog. She knew that if she were ever to leave Duncan, it would be an absolute bonus to get shot of Diggory too! For the first time she felt out of tune with Nancy. Then she decided that Nancy's grief couldn't have been just because of the cat; it must have been the whole trauma of leaving her husband. It seemed that there had been no great drama to precipitate the end. It had just been a gradual wearing down

108

process which had no obvious trigger, just a weary inevitability. Phoebe wondered what Hugh had been like. Seen through Nancy's eyes, he came across as a total wimp. Nancy must have been unusually strong for her time. She hadn't been held back by convention; the marriage wasn't working to her satisfaction so she had dumped it. Phoebe doubted whether she herself would be so fearless, even though it was a million times easier in the nineties. People did it all the time.

'Anyway,' she said aloud, 'I don't want to. I still love Duncan . . . I think.'

Phoebe decided to make a big effort to overcome Duncan's lack of interest in her, and make things good between them again. She had to choose her moment carefully. At bedtime he was usually very tired and likely to fall asleep at once. It was no use waiting until then. He would complain that he needed his rest. She decided to make her move that evening when he came home from work and went upstairs to change out of his grubby clothes.

At half-past five she took the remains of the gin, some tonic and two glasses upstairs to the bathroom. She ran a hot bath, frothy with expensive bath oil which she had bought for the purpose. Then she went back down to the kitchen and waited. Five minutes later, when she heard the sound of Duncan's van in the lane, she nipped upstairs, threw all her clothes onto the floor, got into the bath and lay back luxuriously. She had left the door at the bottom of the stairs open, and she heard Duncan coming in through the back door. His first instinct was always to put the kettle on for tea. There was no need for that today!

'Duncan,' she called. No answer. '*Duncan!*' Still no answer. Bloody hell! Phoebe thought. I can't get out and drip all over everywhere just to get his attention. '*DUNCAN!*'

There was a rattle of claws on the wooden staircase as Diggory responded to her call, rushing helter-skelter up to the forbidden – and therefore extra desirable – upstairs, onto the landing, round the corner, through the open door of the bathroom and nearly into the bath itself. He slid to a halt on the previously white bathmat, got up on his back legs, put his forepaws on the rim of the bath and started drinking the bathwater with excessive enthusiasm, all the while looking at Phoebe good-humouredly with his soulful brown eyes.

Phoebe sat up abruptly, sloshing water and foam onto the floor at both ends of the bath. 'Stop it, you fool of a dog!' she said, laughing in spite of herself. 'Oh, just look at your paws; covered in mud as usual. Downstairs with you. *Basket!*'

'W-What's going on?' Duncan asked, appearing at the door.

'About time!' Phoebe said. 'I've been yelling myself hoarse. If I'd been drowning, I'd have gone down for the last time by now; lungs full of water and stone dead!' Duncan just looked puzzled. 'Please, Dunc, will you take your ridiculous dog downstairs and then come back up again?'

'Well, all right. If you s-say so. Digg! Come on!' They clumped down to the kitchen together.

Phoebe caught sight of herself in the mirror. She did not see the 'nymph in her bath' image which she had aspired to, but she felt there was still time to recover from this false start. She ran more hot water and swished it past her with her hands. Then she lay back, covering the parts of herself which were above the waterline with blobs of foam. She waited. She went on waiting. Duncan didn't come back. He had shut the door at the bottom of the stairs, so she was unable to hear what he was doing. It was no good shouting; she was stuck. Phoebe examined her hands. The skin on her fingers was starting to crinkle up like a washerwoman's. If he doesn't get a move on, she thought, my whole body will turn into a pink prune, and Plan A will be completely wrecked. Where the hell is he?

After an aeon or two, Duncan came back up. He was holding a mug of tea and inexpertly trying not to spill its contents. He put it down by her shoulder, next to the taps and made as if to go.

'C-Cup of tea for you. I'm going to g-get some firewood in,' he said.

'No,' Phoebe said. 'Don't go anywhere. Come and have a bath with me!'

Duncan looked taken aback. 'The-There isn't r-room,' he said.

'Of course there's room! Fitting in together is half the fun. Haven't you ever tried it?'

'No.'

'Well, before you do, pour us a gin and tonic each, and we can be really sinful.'

'It's t-too early for me,' Duncan said, noticing the bottles for the first time, with disapproval.

'Don't be so stuffy,' Phoebe said. 'Throw caution to the winds and live a little!'

'W-what's all this about?' Duncan asked suspiciously.

'It isn't *about* anything,' Phoebe said. 'It's just a fun idea. Go on, Dunc, just to please me?'

She succeeded in persuading him to take his clothes off and join her. He even poured her a drink, but refused to have one himself, electing to drink her tea instead. As he stepped awkwardly into the bath, Phoebe looked up at him with pride. He was a good figure of a man. His legs were long and muscular and a fine shape. His sleeping penis was also long, and his darker dangling scrotum looked vulnerable and endearingly ugly. He had enough hair on his chest to look masculine, but not so much that he became apelike. His shoulders were broad and his biceps looked as though they worked. His face wasn't especially macho, Phoebe thought. In fact it was a very mild face, almost vague, with absent blue eyes and scars where he had cut himself when shaving.

'There i-isn't room,' Duncan said again.

'Yes, there is. Go on, sit down facing me and then put one of your legs over mine and one under ... like that ... see? And then lie back. Now what do you think?'

Duncan looked embarrassed. 'I s-still think it's a bit c-cramped,' he said.

Phoebe attempted to pull one of his nipples with her toes. 'Relax,' she said. She applied soap to her foot and tried again, slithering over his chest and giggling. 'Lovely slidey stuff, soap,' she said.

'We're not going to g-get very c-clean like this,' Duncan said.

Phoebe stopped laughing. 'That's not really the point,' she said, 'but I'll wash you if you like.' She took hold of his foot and massaged it with soapy hands, running a finger between each toe in turn.

'Eeeek,' Duncan squealed. 'It t-t-tickles!'

Phoebe shifted her hips and slid porpoise-like as she extracted his other foot from underneath her. Another dollop of water slopped over the edge of the bath. Phoebe gave the second foot the same treatment. Then she placed it onto one of her breasts, all slippery with soap, and moved it about on the soft roundness.

'Nice?' she asked him.

'It s-still t-tickles.' He couldn't seem to let himself go, Phoebe saw. He was sitting there as if he had committed some social solecism whilst reluctantly attending a formal tea party. (*I'm so sorry, Mrs Cholmondely. I'm being bothered by a wasp.*) His penis, which under those conditions would be safely bundled up in his Y-fronts with no demands being made upon it, was now exposed, floating disconsolately out of its depth and getting more and more wrinkly and waterlogged. It looked both sulky and bashful, and it clearly had no intention of rising to the occasion.

Phoebe took a swig of gin. She was determined not to be beaten so easily.

'Stand up,' she said, getting to her feet. 'I'll do the rest of you.' Duncan stood up, spilling more water as he did so. They stood facing each other, steaming.

'G-Good thing we haven't g-got a c-carpet,' Duncan said. (*The rain has simply ruined my petunias, Mrs Cholmondely.*)

Phoebe ignored him. She rubbed more soap onto her hands and worked it to a creamy lather on his chest and belly. Then she put her arms round his waist and rubbed herself against him. His skin slid under hers and back again, unhindered in every direction, their bodies moving over each other with the effortless ease of skaters on ice, but hot and tactile and wonderfully delicious. Phoebe could feel her own blood responding. She put a hand on each of Duncan's buttocks and held him close, writhing against him. It was working! She could feel him beginning to take an interest.

112

She thought, if I'm not careful it will be all over in a couple of seconds, probably even before he gets inside! I must make him take it gently. She stopped moving and looked up at him. His expression had not changed.

'Let's get rinsed off and dried, and go to bed,' she suggested, smiling.

'Go on then. A-After you,' Duncan said. (*Another biscuit? After you, Mrs Cholmondely.*)

Phoebe sat down quickly in the bath and slooshed all the soap off herself. Duncan stood awkwardly, waiting for her to finish. He certainly had an erection, but he didn't look particularly proud of it. Phoebe almost expected him to whistle casually, as if disowning it. He ought to be wearing a T-shirt with the slogan 'That silly prick is not with me!' she thought, suppressing another giggle. She got out and dried herself and took her gin to bed, rewarding herself with a good gulp before stretching out under the duvet to await her man.

Duncan took a long time. He always took a long time. When he did appear, Phoebe realized at once that she would have to start all over again, this time with Plan B. This involved the use of Johnson's baby oil and her own capable hands. She bounced out of bed, smoothed the duvet over and invited Duncan to lie face downwards on top of it.

'What you need,' she said, 'is a relaxing massage.'

'What's that b-baby stuff f-for?' Duncan asked suspiciously.

'It helps the massage.'

'B-But won't it g-get all over the sheets?'

'And who washes the sheets? Me. So relax!'

'Is all this r-r-really n-necessary?' (*Please forgive me, Mrs Cholmondely, I have to rush off.*)

'Compulsory,' Phoebe said firmly.

Duncan suffered himself to be arranged in a prone position with his arms outstretched, his head on one side and his legs together. Phoebe climbed on top and sat astride him. She poured a little oil onto her palm and rubbed it between both her hands. Then she began the massage. She did Duncan's shoulders, his neck, his back, his waist, his thighs, his calves and his soles. She stroked his back with her pendant breasts. She caressed him with her lips.

Duncan lay like a log with his eyes shut. No groans of ecstasy escaped from his lips, not even a faint sigh of pleasure. After a while Phoebe decided to turn him over to assess the results of her labours.

'Roll over,' she said. He didn't move. 'Come on, Duncan,' she said. 'I'll do your front now.' He still didn't move. He was asleep. 'For God's sake!' Phoebe exclaimed. 'Haven't you got any bloody hormones?' In a rage, she climbed off the bed, administering a good slap to his behind as she passed. She started getting dressed.

'Ow!' Duncan said, blinking. He rolled over and sat up, looking confused. 'What t-time is it?'

'Half-past six.'

'What's the m-matter?'

'Oh, nothing worth mentioning.'

'Aren't we having any s-supper tonight then?' He smiled at her rather sheepishly. 'After all, a ch-chap can't be expected to p-perform on an empty stomach.'

'Don't worry,' Phoebe said furiously, 'I've given up expecting you to *perform* at all!'

Duncan had come home that day exhausted after a heavy day's work. He had managed to finish the wall and it looked good. His client had been pleased with it. Now all he wanted to do was to sit in front of the telly with his mug of tea, waiting for Phoebe to cook him his evening meal. He had earned it. He was slightly put out when she wasn't in the kitchen to greet him as usual. Then Diggory went haring up the stairs and Duncan had to follow him. Phoebe was sitting in a bath full of foam and rabbiting on about drowning. Duncan was confused. She usually had her bath in the evening.

She told him to go downstairs, so he had concluded that he'd better make his own tea as it was fairly obvious that Phoebe wasn't going to. Poor Phoebe, in spite of the camouflaging bubbles, she was not a pretty sight, he thought. A roll of flab hung round her middle and her tummy stuck out. Her hair was sticking out too, all wet round the edges. So he'd made the tea and taken hers up, and then she'd wanted him to drink gin instead, in the bath with her! At least she seemed to be in a good mood for a change, so he decided to humour her.

It was bloody uncomfortable. Thank goodness he didn't have the taps end – she must surely be burning her right ear? In his book, baths were things one took not more than once a week in order to get clean. That seemed an unlikely outcome of this one. Then she'd grabbed hold of his feet and started tickling them. It was worse than Chinese torture! When she started washing his chest, he reverted to his childhood instantly. He remembered his mother washing him in the same way. He couldn't visualize the exclusive first years when he had had the bath, and Hope, all to himself. He could only remember competing for her attention with Conrad, and later with Conrad and Hereward, and losing.

Then Phoebe had started cavorting about like a demented belly dancer and, taken by surprise, Duncan had begun to feel randy. But the image of his mother was still there, unavailable yet disapproving. He sat in the bath long after Phoebe had got out. The soap had killed the foam and left scummy green water which was rapidly cooling. It was obvious what Phoebe expected of him. He realized with a stab of petulance that he didn't like being manipulated in this way. He decided to get rid of his inconvenient erection by having a quick wank there and then. It didn't take long and it wasn't especially pleasurable, and as soon as he had done it he felt guilty. He pulled the plug and watched his precious semen whirl in a watery vortex down the drain. He didn't want Phoebe to know what he had done, so he realized he would have to co-operate in the charade of whatever it was she planned to do next, whilst knowing only too well what the outcome would be.

He discovered that he didn't particularly like massages either. He had no idea if Phoebe knew what she was doing or if it was all her own invention. Either way it did nothing for him. Then she began stroking him and he wondered if this was how

115

Diggory felt when he was stroked. It was nice; a comfortable sort of feeling. God, he was tired . . .

Next thing, Phoebe had spanked his bottom unnecessarily hard and was clearly in a hell of a huff. You can't bloody win with females, Duncan thought. You don't do what they want, and they get upset. You *do* do what they want and they still get furious. What was wrong with her? He'd had the damn bath. He'd let her pummel him about. She surely couldn't be as cross as that just because, at the last minute, he hadn't screwed her? That was nonsense. In spite of anything Phoebe herself might have said, Duncan had it on very good authority that decent women didn't like sex.

As Phoebe thumped down the stairs, the telephone started ringing. It was Fay.

'You know you said if Jack and I ever needed a break we could come to you?' she said, without preamble.

'Yes,' Phoebe agreed, feeling more cheerful all at once.

'Well, I know it's very short notice, but we're driving down to Cornwall on Friday to spend some time with my parents, and I wondered if we could perhaps stay with you overnight? Please say no if it's not convenient.'

'No, it would be great,' Phoebe said with enthusiasm. 'Stay the whole weekend, why don't you? We'd love to have you.'

'If you're sure?' Fay said.

'Positive,' Phoebe urged.

'You've nothing else fixed?'

'We never have anything else fixed!'

'Oh Phoebe, bless you. That does take a weight off my mind. We could have stayed in a hotel, of course, but it's not the same . . .' Her voice tailed off. She didn't sound like herself at all.

'Will Conrad be coming too?' Phoebe asked.

'No,' Fay said rather shortly.

'Is everything all right?'

'I'll tell you everything when I see you,' Fay said. 'Until Friday then, about sixish?'

'That's fine. I'll look forward to . . .' but Fay had gone.

How odd! Phoebe thought, replacing the receiver thoughtfully. There's obviously something wrong. I wonder what. Then she thought, Great! It won't be another difficult weekend on my own with Duncan. I'll have somebody nice to talk to!

Chapter Eleven

Fay had never felt so glad to get away. Conrad was impossible these days and it was having a disastrous effect on Jack. She had hoped that his stammering over Christmas was just a copycat thing, but he was still doing it. Perhaps it ran in families. Conrad strenuously denied this, saying it was just an affectation and the sooner the child snapped out of it, the better. Fay knew that this was nonsense.

It was for Jack's sake that she had decided to go to Cornwall; to see if he would be happier there with his doting grandparents. Her business would have to do without her for a while. Mid-January was a quiet time anyway. They would manage. Staying with Duncan and Phoebe had seemed a bonus, an opportunity to get to know Phoebe a little. Conrad had argued about this too.

'You're worried about the boy stammering, yet you're taking him to visit Duncan!' he'd said. 'You might as well take a first-time gambler to Las Vegas! It makes no sense at all.'

'It's only for a couple of days,' Fay said. 'It won't make any difference.'

'You think not? It's not something I'd risk.'

'He's your *brother*, Con!'

'So what? That doesn't make me want my son to take after him. Jack's at an impressionable age, Fay. Now is not the time.' Yes, Fay thought, he is impressionable and that's the trouble. He already knows he can't live up to his father's expectations, just like Duncan couldn't with Peter. Now's the time to get him away from Conrad, before he gets completely demoralized as well.

It was not an easy journey. Jack seemed to be incubating a bug and he was grumpy and argumentative. The weather, which had been just grey and cold in London, got gradually foggier as they drove westwards. Fay was glad finally to get off the M5, with only a twenty-minute drive to go, along country roads to Duncan's cottage.

Phoebe must have heard them coming, because she was waiting at the front door with her ready smile. She looked fatter, Fay thought, and it was time she had her hair cut properly, but her welcome was warm and genuine. Her kitchen was humid with the sharp citrus smell of marmalade, and ten newly capped jars of it were cooling on a pad of newspaper on the elm table.

'Don't touch!' Phoebe warned Jack. 'They're hot!'

'Ow!' Jack said, flapping his hand ostentatiously.

'You won't be told, will you?' Fay said, laughing.

'Where's D.D. Duncan?' Jack asked, scowling.

'Outside,' Phoebe said pointing, raising her eyebrows at Fay, 'in his shed in the garden.' Jack made for the back door. 'Yes, you go and find him. Good idea.' After he had gone out, she said, 'I assumed his stammer was only temporary.'

'So did we,' Fay said, sitting down by the kitchen table with a sigh, 'but it seems not.'

That weekend Phoebe thought that Fay appeared very tired. She had been looking forward to talking to her but discovered that conversation was all but impossible with a four-year-old child around. Jack demanded their full attention, and viewed any talk which excluded him as utter treachery on his mother's part. Only after he had gone noisily to bed in the spare room, was there an opportunity, but then Duncan was there too. It wasn't until after supper, late on Saturday evening, that there was a proper chance. Duncan went off to watch something on television and left Phoebe and Fay together in the kitchen, doing the washing up.

'You are lucky, Phoebe,' Fay said. 'It's so peaceful here. Not that it would suit me; I could hardly sleep last night, it was so quiet! No traffic sounds at all.'

'Except when there's an east wind,' Phoebe agreed. 'Then we sometimes hear lorries on the hill. But peaceful can equal dull, you know.'

'Does it in your case?'

'Sometimes, yes.'

'Doesn't your job provide any stimulus?'

Phoebe laughed. 'Not a lot,' she said, 'not like my old one in Newcastle; I really enjoyed that.'

'So why don't you look for one like it here?'

'No chance, unless it was in Bristol, and I haven't got a car any more.'

'No.'

Phoebe could see that Fay wasn't really listening. She was preoccupied, drying the same plate round and round again.

'What is it?' she asked. 'What's the matter?'

Fay grimaced. 'I'm leaving Conrad,' she said.

'What, for good?' Phoebe was taken aback.

'Yes.'

'But why? I mean, it's none of my business, but you always seem so good together, to have such a successful set-up, so . . . in control of things . . . I don't know . . .'

'It's because of Jack,' Fay said. 'I have to break the chain.'

'What d'you mean? What chain?'

'Those dreadful repressive attitudes which all the Moons seem to take in with their mother's milk, and which persist down the generations as an unbroken chain − the idea that feelings and emotions should be strangled at birth; that showing kindness or needing encouragement is a weakness; that sons are to be competed with; that sex is embarrassing; that love is only a word . . .' Fay's eyes brimmed.

'Oh Fay!' Phoebe said. She had tears in her own eyes now. 'I know just how you feel.' She wanted to comfort her sister-in-law, but her hands were wet with dishwater and she was afraid of spoiling Fay's elegant clothes. 'Duncan's just like that too!'

'I've had enough,' Fay said. 'I can bear it for myself − have done for years − but not for Jack. He's not yet five and already life's too hard for him.' She broke down completely and sobbed into the tea towel. Phoebe dried her hands on her jeans and put both arms round her, patting her back in sympathy, and weeping herself. They were standing like that when Duncan wandered into the kitchen in search of tea.

'Oh,' he said. He turned on his heel and went out again.

'See,' Phoebe sniffed, 'Duncan can't take emotion either.'

'Perhaps he was just being tactful,' Fay said, pulling away from her gently.

'Mmmm.'

They sat down at the kitchen table opposite one another. Phoebe found a box of tissues and they both wiped their eyes and blew their noses.

'I honestly believe,' Fay said, 'that *no* father is preferable to a bad father, from a child's point of view.'

'Maybe,' Phoebe said. 'My father always disapproved of me, and things were certainly easier after he left. But I did miss having a proper father figure, and I'm sure the lack of one screwed up my relationships with men later on.'

'I've got lots of friends who are men,' Fay said quickly. 'Jack won't lack male influences. I'll make sure of that.'

'What does Conrad say about all this?'

'He doesn't know yet. Don't tell anyone, especially Duncan.'

'But you're not leaving without telling him, surely?'

'Oh no. I plan to stay with my parents for a fortnight's holiday, then leave Jack with them for a week or two longer while I go back to London, tell Conrad and then move my stuff out.'

'Where to?'

'To a friend's flat in St John's Wood. She's abroad and she's renting it to me until I can find something permanent of my own.'

'Then what?'

'Then life goes on as usual. I continue running my business and Jack needn't go off to that bloody boarding school when he's seven.'

'That was Conrad's idea?'

'He wants him to "follow the family tradition". He's antediluvian!'

'Duncan's old-fashioned as well,' Phoebe said, 'but I think I probably am too. I really believe in marriage.' She said this half-apologetically, feeling sure that Fay would pour scorn on the idea. Fay surprisingly did not.

'Oh I believe in marriage,' she said. 'It's the obvious arrangement if you're going to have children. The danger comes when people – especially wives – expect all the wrong things of it.'

The kitchen door opened and Duncan came in. He looked relieved to see that neither of them was crying.

'C-C-Cup of tea?' he suggested, going to put the kettle on.

121

'Why not?' Fay said. 'Good idea.'

'Is everything a-a-all right?' Duncan asked tentatively.

'Fine,' Fay said at once. 'Just girl talk, you know.'

'Oh,' Duncan said, 'good.'

'It's lovely to get the chance of a good old natter,' Phoebe said, taking her cue from Fay. 'We've never really had that before.'

They sat round the table drinking tea. Fay asked Duncan about his work, and waited patiently for him to get all the words out. She seemed totally composed. Phoebe watched her in admiration. She was in her mid-forties but she was still beautiful and had kept her figure despite having had three children. Life alone would be easy for her, Phoebe suspected. She probably wouldn't be alone long anyway.

Duncan yawned and stretched. 'Well,' he said. 'I'm off to b-bed. I s-suppose you t-two will want to go on ch-chattering?'

'Yes. Don't wait for me,' Phoebe said. 'I'll creep in later.'

'Goodnight, Duncan,' Fay said. 'Sleep well.'

When he had gone, Phoebe got Fay to explain what she meant about the dangers of marriage.

'If wives are not careful,' Fay said thoughtfully, 'marriage can diminish them. It can stunt their personal development, weaken their friendships, undermine their self-assurance and bugger up their careers. I've seen it happen to so many of my friends.'

'I thought you were in favour of marriage?'

'I am.'

'But you're leaving anyway.'

Fay sighed. 'Because of Jack. He's my weak link. And to think that people have children on purpose to mend rocky marriages, and then are surprised when they have just the opposite effect!'

'You didn't do that?'

'Heavens no. Jack was a mistake. Don't get me wrong; I love him to death and wouldn't be without him for the world now he's here, but disagreements about his upbringing are the cause of our problems.'

They talked into the night, and when they had finished discussing Fay and Conrad, they started on Phoebe and Duncan. Phoebe discovered that she could unburden her problems in front of Fay, and she did so in a grateful flood.

'The way you tell it,' Fay said thoughtfully, 'it sounds as though your very identity depends upon Duncan. I think your expect too much from him. You can't get total fulfilment from just one person, you know – especially a man! It just isn't reasonable. Wouldn't it be better to have friends who could meet your different needs each in their own way?'

'But Duncan doesn't need any friends. He's self-sufficient.'

'I'm talking about *you*! You seem to have given up all your past life to submerge yourself, your whole character, into this magic "couple" idea. You've expected Duncan to do the same, and he hasn't, so now you feel hurt and resentful. I'm not surprised you do. I think you've started from the wrong premise altogether. Duncan is not your other half. He's a distinct, very different, but possibly complementary whole! He's got his own life sorted out to his satisfaction and he's getting on with it. I'm sure he expects you to do the same.'

'But what about the chain . . . all the things you were saying you didn't want Jack to be like? I thought you agreed with me that we all need love and support; that we can't go on without it?'

'I do, but you don't have to get it from Duncan. You could get it from a friend – from me, for example.' She put out her hand and rubbed Phoebe's arm.

'But it's –.'

'Not the same?' Phoebe nodded. 'I agree with you. It's not the same; it can be better!' Fay said. Phoebe was doubtful. 'You don't have to be part of a couple in order to be fulfilled, Phoebe. You're a complete person in your own right. You should value yourself; not wait for Duncan to do it for you. You deserve a job like your old one, which stretches you and gives you satisfaction, and friends who can boost your morale. You'd feel much more confident and you'd probably be a lot nicer to Duncan!'

'It sounds so easy, put like that,' Phoebe sighed, 'but I've never been particularly confident – that's my trouble. I desperately need to be approved of and I don't feel worth anything, unless I'm told I am.'

'And you expect Duncan to do the telling?'

'Well, yes. He's my husband. That's what he's for!'

'Then you'll always be let down,' Fay said firmly. 'Someone like Duncan is incapable of providing that sort of crutch. If that is truly what you need, then you've married the wrong man.'

'But I thought you were arguing that I should stay with Duncan and change myself,' Phoebe said, muddled. 'Now I don't know what to think!'

'I don't think you should take any notice of what I say at all,' Fay said ruefully. 'Advice on marriage from someone who's just about to leave their husband has to be more than a little suspect, don't you think? I was just thinking aloud really – trying to be dispassionate, I suppose.' Then she frowned. 'No, I'm talking crap,' she said. 'Or at the very least, I'm being disingenuous. That was all just theory. If I'm really honest, my marriage break-up isn't because of Jack. He's just the last straw. I thought I was proof against a lack of love and emotional reassurance – I've stood up against it for so long – but like you, I've been worn down. I suppose I've latched onto Jack's future as the perfect excuse; a more valid reason for leaving than just my own unhappiness.' She put her hand up to her face and pressed it over her mouth.

'Let's drink some gin,' Phoebe suggested.

'Great idea. Two large G and Ts. Any lemon?'

'No. I'm afraid they got used up in the marmalade.'

'No matter.' Phoebe got up to fetch the bottles. 'I do mean what I said about friendship, though,' Fay said. 'We can help each other.'

'Oh yes,' Phoebe said fervently. 'It's so wonderful to find someone who *understands*.' It was a tremendous relief, she thought, at last to find someone sympathetic to bare her soul to. Fay could offer a different viewpoint, could challenge her preconceptions without anger, could praise her good points and make allowances for her faults. She could, and did. By 2 a.m. the two women had got on to discussing the rest of the Moon family. Fay, who had been married to Conrad since 1968, was able to tell Phoebe all the family stories of the past twenty-four years, stories which Duncan could have shared with her, and more.

'I used to have terrible rows with Rick,' Fay said. 'For a time, we lived quite close to them and I saw what he was doing to those poor girls he married.'

'Hope told me that they were both mad.'

'They were perfectly normal before they married dear Roderick!'

'Did he beat them up? Surely not?'

'Nothing so obvious. I think it would be called "mental cruelty" these days. Rick wanted them for their looks, their youth and their biddableness. He didn't want to make any real commitment to them, and he didn't want any competition from them. He seemed to find it almost necessary to despise them. Then you see, he gave all of himself to his acting, and he's so superficial that there wasn't anything left underneath for his wives; no love, no support; same old story. I liked Poppy. She comes from a big, warm, demonstrative sort of family in the States. She naturally assumed that the Moons would be the same. She fought hard, but she caved in eventually. Poor Elenira didn't stand a chance. She didn't even speak English properly. He called her his "little Brazil nut" which, of course, she was in the end.'

'How did she do it?' Phoebe had often wondered.

'Jumped off Tower Bridge. She wasn't found for a week.' Fay shook her head. 'Poor unfortunate creature. He didn't deserve either of them and they most certainly didn't deserve him!'

'But Poppy is apparently all right now,' Phoebe said. 'Did the boys have a good New Year with her? Have you heard?'

'Really wonderful, so young Pete told me. Of course neither of them remembered her. Rod was three and Pete only one when she left them in . . . it must have been 1980 – heavens! Twelve years ago! But when they actually met her, Pete especially was absolutely delighted to find he had a real mum at last, and, of course, both boys are absolutely mad on all things American. They're longing to go and visit her there. I think Rod felt a bit resentful that she'd abandoned them, to start with, but she's obviously won him over. He's having the usual teenage

125

trouble with his dad at the moment, so it couldn't have come at a better time for him.'

'Or a worse time for Rick?'

'Yes. He's not best pleased. He refuses point-blank to let them go to the States, but he has grudgingly admitted that Poppy has a right to see them in London.'

'Another drink?' Phoebe offered.

'Yes, please!'

'So how about Peter and Hope?' Phoebe asked her. 'How do they stand each other?'

'I think they're very alike in some ways,' Fay said. 'They're both buttoned-up in emotional straitjackets. Perhaps if we were more like her, we'd get on better with our husbands!'

'No way!' Phoebe protested. 'So if she's well suited to Peter, why the great depressions?'

'He must be hell to live with. D'you know, when he's away he *never* phones her. She never knows where he is or when he's coming back. I'm sure that sort of thing can't help, and then there's her genes. It's an inherited thing, isn't it? Isn't Duncan the same?'

'Yes,' Phoebe agreed. Perhaps he shouldn't have children, she thought.

'Herry's different,' Fay said. 'I've always thought there was something odd about him. He doesn't seem to be part of my chain somehow.'

'And Brendan too?'

'Oh well, he's not Hope's, of course, and he was brought up in a completely different environment until he was 14. I've never been able to work out his and Hope's relationship. It seems to me that you'd have to be some sort of a saint to take in a bastard of your husband's – and a teenager at that! – and Hope's no saint, yet he's nearly always there at family gatherings, and she treats him the same as the others.'

'Perhaps she's grown fond of him.'

'She's not "fond" of anyone except herself!'

'When did Brendan tell the family he was gay?'

'A couple of years before your wedding. I think Peter was devastated at the time, although he was careful not to show it. Perhaps he's come to terms with it now, but obviously he must be very concerned about the possibility of AIDS. Who wouldn't be?'

'And Hope?'

'She was very calm. It didn't seem to bother her at all. It doesn't add up.' Fay shook her head. 'Weird family,' she said. It was three in the morning before the two women finally got to their beds. Phoebe was grateful that it was Fay and not herself who would have to cope with Jack's normal waking time of 5.30 a.m. There was a lot to be said for not having children!

On Sunday morning, they all went for a walk. Duncan strode ahead with Diggory, leaving the others far behind.

'I want D-D-Duncan to c-c-come b-back here!' Jack wailed unsuccessfully.

'He always does it,' Phoebe explained to Fay. 'I've given up going for walks with him because of it. He just gets impatient and I get knackered! I think we'll have to turn back soon anyway, if I'm to get the joint in.'

After a large roast lunch Fay and Jack prepared for their journey to Cornwall. Phoebe was sorry to see them go, but she had a lot of thinking to get on with. She felt a huge sense of relief. At last, she had found someone lovely to talk to. Her gratitude to Fay was enormous. She hugged her goodbye and kissed her on both cheeks.

'Come again whenever you like,' she said.

'Goodbye,' Fay said to them both. 'It's been so good to see you. Thanks so much.' She stretched up to give Duncan a kiss as well and he accepted it, but without bending down to make it easier for her.

'Bye,' he said.

'Give Uncle Duncan and Auntie Phoebe a kiss, Jack,' Fay suggested.

'No!' Jack said.

They drove away up the lane, Fay waving until they were round the corner and out of sight. Phoebe found that she had tears in her eyes.

'W-What's up?' Duncan asked.

Two tears overflowed. 'I'm just so pleased to have got to know her,' Phoebe said. 'She understands me.' She reached out and put both arms round Duncan's waist, resting her face against his chest. Duncan submitted to her embrace and, after a moment, put his arms round her too and held her.

'I'm g-g-glad s-someone does,' he said.

On Monday when Phoebe went to work, she found a letter on her desk, the contents of which were not altogether unwelcome.

Fay telephoned her in the evening from Cornwall to say they had arrived safely and that Jack had settled in well.

'How are you?' Fay asked her.

'Much better than I was. You've given me a lot to think about,' Phoebe said. 'I had a surprise at the theatre today. It's closing down! I've got a fortnight's notice.'

'Good! Now you can get a proper job.'

'I wish I could. There was something else I meant to say to you . . . about Jack's stammer. I'm convinced that Duncan doesn't have to stammer, you know. I think it's a useful screen for him to hide behind; a good excuse not to have to talk. Anyway, at the Golden Wedding do, I met an old lady in a purple hat and she gave me the address of some man in London who she says is an ace at curing stammers. Duncan pooh-poohed it, of course, but I've still got his address and I thought maybe you could take Jack to see him when you're both back?'

'It's well worth a try,' Fay said. 'Thanks.'

As soon as they had finished talking and Phoebe had put the phone down, it rang again. It was her mother.

'Phoebe pet,' she said, 'you remember my car?'

'The blue Polo? Of course I do.'

'It's four years old now but it's a good little runner. Would you like it?'

'*Yes!*' Phoebe said. 'I'd love it, but won't you –'

'George wants to buy me a new car next month,' Wynne said with satisfaction. 'It was his idea you should have the Polo. Shall I tell him it's yes?'

'Yes, please,' Phoebe said. 'That's really sweet of him and it couldn't have happened at a better time.'

Duncan was less enthusiastic when she told him. 'It'll be e-e-expensive to r-run,' he said.

'Well, I shall just have to get a better paid job then, shan't I?' As Phoebe said it, she realized that it might even be possible. Fay's influence was working already! There was great competition for every job these days, but someone had to win. She was experienced and well qualified. She could do it.

Fay telephoned her again two weeks later from her new flat in St John's Wood.

'How did Conrad react?' Phoebe asked.

'Badly. He refuses to believe I really mean it. Luckily he doesn't yet know where I've gone, so I've got a bit of a breather until he finds out.'

'You're still determined to divorce him?'

'Oh yes,' Fay said. 'Actually, Phoebe, I'm phoning about something else. Before we discussed our marriage, Con told me that Rick phoned him wanting to know if I had any contacts. Apparently Rick's housekeeper is having to have an operation and will be off work for a month or so. It wouldn't matter usually, but it's the boys' half term mid-February and Rick has to be away filming. Then I thought of you. You'll be out of work by then. I don't know how you'd feel about a week in London? Rick would pay you, of course, and we could spend some evenings together too maybe.'

'What would I have to do?' Phoebe was unsure.

'Look after his house, cook for the boys, wash their clothes and things, feed his cat.'

'I don't know,' Phoebe said. 'It's rather a responsibility and I hardly know the boys.'

'Rick's got a charming neighbour with children the same age. I'm sure she'd help and advise, and it's only for one week. Think about it. I'll see how much money I can screw out of Rick! He can afford it, after all. It'll be worth it to him not to have to spend time interviewing and vetting total strangers.'

'The money would be useful,' Phoebe agreed, 'and it would be great to see you as well . . .'

'Duncan could manage on his own for a week, couldn't he?'
'Oh yes, easily.'
'There you are then!'

Chapter Twelve

'Here,' Rick said, standing in his high-tech basement kitchen, 'is the microwave. The dishwasher is under here. The freezer is full of stuff – help yourself. The sink has its own disposal unit – don't put any spoons down it! The ceramic hob is here, of course, and the oven in the wall over there. Airing cupboard by the door with sheets and towels and stuff. Right?'

'I don't know how to use a microwave, or a dishwasher or a disposal thing,' Phoebe said apologetically. 'We don't have them at home, you see.'

'Oh, don't worry. The boys will show you,' Rick said easily. 'The washer/dryer is through there, and this is where the water turns off if there's a flood or anything.' Phoebe followed him obediently up to the ground floor of his house, wondering what she had let herself in for. 'The central heating control switch is here,' Rick went on. 'It's fully automatic, so just leave it as it is. Downstairs john in there. The burglar alarm in the hall here has to be inactivated as soon as you come in, by keying in the right code. Memorize it if you can.' He scribbled five numbers onto his telephone pad, tore the top sheet off and handed it to her. 'Again, the boys will show you.'

'Is it new?' Phoebe asked, remembering his burglary.

'Yes,' Rick said. 'Better late than never.'

'Did your burglar take anything?'

'Apparently not. Nothing I could find anyway. It was clearly my lucky day.'

'It couldn't have been the boys?' Phoebe asked.

'No. They're quite definite about that. Anyway, they've both got keys. Dining room here. My study in there.' They went upstairs to the first floor. 'Drawing room in here,' Rick said, standing aside to let her precede him, 'with views to the square.' The room was large with a high ceiling and tall windows flanked by long expensive curtains.

'Daffodils already!' Phoebe said, looking out into the dusk. 'What a lovely garden.'

'There's a key to the gate on a hook in the kitchen,' Rick said. 'It's residents only, so there's no dog shit, thank God!' The carpets here, as everywhere, were thick and the furniture was large and opulent. There were abstract paintings on the walls, Phoebe saw, but no books. The whole house had no individuality that she could feel. It was more like an impersonal up-market hotel. 'The TV and video are in the couch-potato room over there,' Rick said, 'where the boys are now. My bedroom is next door, in here. I thought you could sleep here as it's the most comfortable bed.'

'A four-poster!' Phoebe exclaimed. She wondered how many people had sat in it with Rick, drinking champagne afterwards. Perhaps he wasn't much good in bed either.

'My bathroom is through here,' Rick said, opening a communicating door. A fan purred into life. Phoebe saw a lavatory, bath, shower and bidet with a matching blue carpet and gold taps galore. They were marked F and C. 'French,' Rick explained, 'and the fools of builders put them in the wrong way round, so C now stands for cold (not *chaud*) and F stands for effing hot.'

Rick led the way back through his bedroom, out onto the landing again and up the last flight of stairs to the top floor. 'Another bathroom up here and the two boys' rooms,' he said, indicating the three closed doors. One had a poster on it, underneath a PETER nameplate, which said: *DANGER – Teenager in Residence!* The other had a neat hand-painted sign nailed to it, which read: *Rod's Studio. Keep Out.* 'If you're very privileged, you'll be invited into one or both of those dens,' Rick said. 'I've no idea what sort of a state they're in. I never go in.' He turned and led the way downstairs again. 'That's about it, I think,' he said. 'Have I covered everything?'

'More or less. Um . . . what sort of things do Rod and Pete like to eat?'

'Oh they eat anything and everything,' Rick said; no help at all.

'And do you have any particular rules that I should see about?'

132

Rick laughed. 'What a quaint idea,' he said. 'Don't let them murder each other and don't give them any money – apart from that, no.'

'What about a phone number, in case I need to contact you?'

'Tricky,' Rick said. 'I'm likely to be all over the place. I can give you one, but only use it *in extremis*, okay. They don't like being bothered with social calls.' He took a pen from his inside pocket and wrote a London telephone number on Phoebe's proffered piece of paper. 'Oh yes, and the cat,' he said. 'He only eats the special stuff in the larder. He has to have those biscuit things too, and fresh water. He likes to sit on shoulders and he bites a lot, but only in fun.'

'Oh.' Phoebe had forgotten the cat. 'What's his name?'

'Geronimo. Sorry this is all rather a rush,' Rick said, 'but I have to catch the damn plane. Now, you've got enough cash?'

'More than enough, thanks.'

'And there's nothing else you need?'

'Well . . . I don't . . .'

'Good. That's it then.'

The taxi driver announced himself by ringing the doorbell. Rick nipped upstairs to get his bag and say goodbye to his sons. Phoebe was surprised that they didn't bother to come down-stairs to see their father off. It was something she would have insisted upon.

'I'll be off then,' Rick said. 'Have fun in the big city.' He smiled his famous smile and ran lightly down the steps to his cab. Phoebe watched him climb in and waved as he drove off in it. He didn't turn round or wave back. He hadn't thanked her for helping him out either, Phoebe thought.

She closed the front door and wondered what to do next. She felt out of her depth in this shrine to conspicuous consumption; a real country cousin. She climbed the stairs to the first floor and put her head cautiously round the door of the television room. Rod was lying on the small sofa with his back to her. He was resting his boots on one of its arms, and his head on the other. Pete was sitting on the carpet, hugging a leather pouffe. Both were intent on watching the television, and both ignored her. Phoebe looked at it too. A menacing robot with a knife was about to do something very nasty to an already bloody half-naked black girl. The music rose in a crescendo. The shot zoomed in on the girl's terrified eyes. Phoebe looked away hurriedly.

'Hello,' she said. 'Is there anything —'

'SSSHHH!' Rod said imperiously, without taking his eyes from the screen.

Phoebe withdrew. Were they allowed to watch such stuff? Rick hadn't said. She hadn't liked to confront them so early on. Tomorrow would do. She decided to unpack her things instead, and carried her suitcase up to the master bedroom. She stood briefly at the window and looked out at the typical London square with its elitist garden behind the locked gate. All was illuminated by the sodium glare of the streetlamps. The other houses were like Rick's, tall, thin and cream painted with red burglar alarm boxes. Their basements were protected from the street by iron railings. Their front doors displayed shiny brass furniture and some had entry phones. They had stone steps leading up to them, and pillars. The cars parked beside the pavement were all less than two years old. In one parking space there was a builder's skip which was full of perfectly acceptable furniture. Phoebe wished Duncan were with her. He would have gone out and scavenged a lot of useful things from it! Here, in this part of London, there were no vagrants or homeless people with or without cardboard boxes, but there was plastic and paper litter everywhere, and many of the paving stones were cracked and uneven. Unsmiling people walked past without greeting each other. In the distance she could hear the two-tone sound of a police siren. In spite of its wealth, the area seemed threatening and unfriendly to Phoebe; the epitome of pride before its fall? The cottage in Somerset was enormously attractive in contrast. I don't belong here, Phoebe thought. Thank goodness it's only a week.

She opened her suitcase and took out the clothes which needed hanging up. All the wardrobes turned out to be full, and she could only find two spare coathangers. She compromised by hanging several things on each one. She took her nightie over to the bed with a view to putting it under the pillow until later on. The bottom sheet was grey with dirt! Phoebe recoiled in disgust. Then she pulled the duvet back for a proper look. It was not only grey, it had *stains* on it.

'Yuk!' Phoebe exclaimed. 'How could Rick leave them like this, knowing I was coming?' She went down to the airing cupboard in the basement and found herself some clean linen and a towel. Then she carried them up two flights of stairs and remade the bed. She realized she was very hungry indeed. It must be time for supper.

She went downstairs again. At this rate, she thought, I'll get enough exercise anyhow. Rod was on the telephone in the hall as she passed.

'Tomorrow,' he said. 'Great. No, we won't forget them. Yes, I'll tell her. Okay. See you.'

What shall I cook? Phoebe thought. Something easy. She found a large deep-pan pizza in the fridge and decided to cheer it up with some added vegetables and a few black olives. There was no shortage of fresh food. Rick had seen to that, at least. When it was almost ready, Rod ambled in.

'That was Poppy, just now,' he said. 'She's taking us out for the day on Saturday, tomorrow. She told me to tell you.'

'Oh . . .' Phoebe said. Rick hadn't briefed her on this possibility, but then she remembered Fay mentioning it.

'She's calling for us at ten.'

'Right.' Phoebe looked forward to meeting her. 'Will you tell Pete supper's ready?' she asked. Rod nodded and went.

The table in the kitchen was small, but big enough, Phoebe reckoned. She didn't feel like going to all the trouble of laying the formal table upstairs in the dining room. By the time both boys turned up, Phoebe had cut the pizza into thirds and was making a start on hers.

'Only one problem,' Pete said, sitting down beside her, 'I'm allergic to mushrooms and Rod hates tomatoes.'

'But your father bought both the tomatoes and the mushrooms. I naturally thought . . .' Phoebe said, exasperated. 'Why would he do that?'

'Dunno,' Rod said, scraping his chair over the floor.

'Well, *he* likes them both,' Pete said, as though that were a perfectly rational explanation.

'But he surely knows you don't?'

'Doubt it,' Pete said. 'He doesn't know much.'

'Well, just leave the bits you don't like,' Phoebe said. She was beginning to wish she hadn't taken on this job at all. She examined the faces of the two boys as they all ate. Rod was single-mindedly wolfing his food and looking neither to right nor left. He was even more spotty than at Christmas. His nose was coarsening into its adult form and there were dark hairs on his upper lip. His hormones were clearly working overtime. He looked sulky and self-conscious. He could be a good-looking young man, Phoebe thought, if he would learn some charm from his dad. Pete was more disposed to be sociable. His voice had not yet broken, and he still had a baby face and the unabashed self-centred candour of childhood. If anything, he would be even better-looking than Rod eventually.

'Last time I ate mushrooms,' Pete said, 'I was sick ten times. It was brown with orange bits in it.'

'Shut up!' Rod said.

'Don't waste them,' Phoebe said. 'I'll eat them.' She held out her plate and Pete, after a moment's hesitation, shovelled his mushrooms onto it.

'You might get AIDS,' he said. 'You can catch it from spit.'

'You can not!' Rod said.

'Yes, you can. Spit's a bodily fluid, isn't it?'

'Well, yes,' Phoebe said, 'but it's blood contact that's dangerous, and you have to be infected with HIV in the first place.'

'Who says I'm not?'

'Well, it's unlikely,' Phoebe explained. 'It's passed on from one person to another when they sleep together . . .'

'I know a lot about sex,' Pete said with authority.

Rod's ears flamed. He gulped down the last of his pizza and stood up abruptly. 'Garbage!' he hissed at his brother.

'Have you had enough to eat?' Phoebe asked him anxiously.

'Yeah.'

'Sure?'

Rod picked an apple and three clementines from the fruit-bowl, nodded, and went out. Phoebe heard him clumping upstairs. He was still wearing those unnecessary boots.

'I do,' persisted Pete.

'Good,' Phoebe said, hoping this would shut him up.

'Don't you want to know how I know?'

'How?' She was resigned.

'From videos,' Pete said triumphantly, 'sex 'n' violence.'

'Are you allowed to watch such rubbish?'

''Course,' Pete said scornfully. 'Everybody does.'

'Doesn't your father mind?'

'He's never here.'

'I expect your mother will have something to say about it?' Pete suddenly looked shifty and shut up. 'Rod tells me you're going out with her tomorrow,' Phoebe continued. 'What will you be doing?'

'Dunno.' It might have been Rod sitting there. Phoebe realized she'd made a tactical error. Pete swallowed the last of his pizza, rooted in a drawer for a bar of chocolate and made for the door.

'What are you going to do now?' Phoebe asked him.

'Watch the TV,' Pete said. 'There's an ace film on. You should come too.'

'Don't you or Rod ever read books?' Phoebe asked.

'Nah. I'm going to invent computer games and Rod's going to be a film director and boss brainless actors about. Who needs books? They're history.'

Phoebe woke next morning with a start and wondered, for a full second, where she was. When she remembered, it was without pleasure. Rick's clock radio told her that it was 7.30. She switched it on, got the *Today* programme and lay back for a while, smiling at Brian Redhead and wondering what Macclesfield was really like. She wished someone would bring her a morning cup of tea in bed. Fat chance! At eight o'clock, reluctantly, she got up and had a shower in the beautiful blue bathroom. Then she put on her clothes; unaccustomed tights and a skirt and her best shoes. She made up her face carefully in front of one of Rick's many mirrors. She brushed her hair into shape and glued it in place with hairspray, and having thus

137

polished her self-confidence to its highest attainable shine, she emerged to deal with the business of getting breakfast.

Pete was in the kitchen already, demolishing a cheese and marmalade sandwich.

'Are you having cereals,' Phoebe asked him, 'or an egg or anything?'

'No,' Pete said, with his mouth full. 'This is what I always have.' He was eating it standing up, and he waved it about as he spoke. Phoebe made herself a pot of tea and some toast. She didn't expect Rod to be around for some time yet, so she was surprised when he wandered nonchalantly in at nine o'clock. His slicked-back hair was wet as though he too had had a shower.

'Didn't expect to see you up and about so early,' Phoebe said to him pleasantly.

'Mmmm,' Rod said, wandering over towards the bread bin and elbowing Pete out of his way.

'He usually sleeps until lunchtime,' Pete said, 'but today's diff – OW! What did you do that for?' He appealed to Phoebe: 'He kicked me!'

'To stop you gabbing on,' Rod said. He was holding his younger brother's arm tightly, too tightly by the look on Pete's face. 'I got up because *she's* here, okay?'

'But that's what I was going to say,' Pete said, aggrieved. 'I wasn't going to tell . . .'

'SHUT UP!' Rod said.

'What are you having for breakfast, Rod?' Phoebe asked, hoping to distract them. She wondered if they ever called a truce.

'This'll do,' Rod said, catching sight of her toast, and sitting down. 'Marmite! Pete!'

Pete opened a cupboard, got the pot of Marmite out and threw it sulkily at his brother. Rod caught it, just.

'Look,' Phoebe said, 'could we forget all this aggressive stuff while I'm here? It's not something I'm used to, and I don't like it.'

'Don't worry about it,' Rod said, not looking at her.

'It's normal,' Pete told her.

138

Phoebe sighed. 'What will you be doing today, Rod?' she asked.

'Sports,' Rod said.

'Yeah,' Pete said. 'We go to this massive leisure centre and they have everything there, even a dry ski slope. I'm going to swim and ski and lift weights and –'

'You couldn't lift a freeze-dried toad!' Rod said scornfully.

'I wouldn't want to!' retorted Pete.

'Sounds like a great place,' Phoebe said quickly. 'I love swimming too.'

'You can't come today!' Pete said urgently.

Rod gave his brother a warning look. 'He means we don't know our mother very well yet . . .' he explained.

'No, of course not,' Phoebe said at once. 'I didn't mean today.'

There was a silence whilst they chewed their breakfast. Rod poured himself half a pint of orange juice from the fridge and downed it like beer.

'Right,' he said, wiping his mouth with the back of his hand. 'Things to do. Come on, Pete.' Then they got up and went out together. So far, Phoebe thought as she washed up the breakfast things, I haven't exactly got through to those two boys. I wonder what it takes?

At ten past ten the front doorbell rang. Phoebe was in her bedroom looking in her handbag for Fay's telephone number. The boys had been closeted upstairs in their rooms since breakfast, but at the sound of the bell they exploded downstairs. Phoebe walked down after them and found them in the front hall with two enormous bags and a large attractive woman dressed entirely in red.

'Well, hi!' the red woman said, beaming. 'You must be Phoebe. I've heard so much about you. I'm real glad to meet with you at last. I'm Poppy, these guys' mom.'

'It's lovely to meet you too,' Phoebe said. Poppy wasn't a bit as she had imagined. She was fat and cheerful and outgoing, with not a hint of neurosis. She didn't look or act anything like the lathlike bimbo whom Fay had described to her.

'Not like you expected, huh?'

'Well . . .' Phoebe struggled for the right words. 'I knew you were good-looking, but . . .'

'That's neat! You Brits are so damn polite; real classy! Put it this way – I weighed 98 pounds only; I was *thin*, and I was so screwed up. Now I'm liberated from male-oriented sex-rôle stereotyping and I'm great!'

'You certainly are,' Phoebe said in admiration. 'Good for you!'

'Are we going then?' Rod said, shuffling impatiently.

'Sure thing, honey. Have you-all got everything you need now?'

'Yep,' Rod and Pete said together. They picked up their bags and heaved each one casually over a shoulder. The bags looked heavy.

'What *have* you got in there?' Phoebe teased. 'Several kitchen sinks?'

'Sports kit,' Poppy said, smiling widely. 'Kids have every damn thing nowadays, don't they just?'

Phoebe smiled back. 'It seems so,' she said.

'Well, I guess we'll hit the road then,' Poppy said.

'What time will you be back?' Phoebe asked.

'Hard to say – 8 p.m., maybe later. Don't you worry about a thing, Phoebe. These guys are safe with me.'

'Right.' Phoebe watched them as they went down the steps to the waiting taxi. 'Have a nice day!' she found herself calling after them.

Pete opened his window and shouted something as they drove off. It sounded suspiciously like, 'Missing you already!'

Phoebe was talking to Fay on the telephone. 'Is Jack back yet?'

'No,' Fay said. 'He's doing so well in Cornwall, I decided to leave him for an extra week. I'm driving down to get him next weekend. I could give you a lift home then?'

'Great idea.'

'Why don't you come round this afternoon and see this amazing flat?'

'I'd love to, but I must be back by eight,' Phoebe said. 'That's when the boys are due home. They've gone out for the day with their mother.'

'I didn't know Poppy was over here again?'

'I thought you said she often was?'

'No.'

'Oh.' A small unease stabbed Phoebe briefly, but she sat on it firmly.

'I'll run you home in good time,' Fay said. 'Shall I collect you as well?'

'No, I'll be fine. I'll come by tube. OW! Gerrof!' Phoebe found herself unexpectedly engaged in an undignified tussle with a sudden brown cat which had been intent on sitting on her shoulders and had, in the process, dug his claws painfully into her back.

'What's the matter?'

'It's Rick's cat. It's the first time I've seen him and he's just leapt at me from behind. Ouch!'

'Like a leopard up a tree,' Fay said, laughing. 'He's an up-market beast, you know, pedigree chocolate Burmese and all that. See you about three then?'

'Lovely,' Phoebe said, rubbing her shoulder. ' 'Bye.' She put the receiver down and regarded Geronimo with disapproval. He was certainly very handsome, with clear green eyes in a dark brown face, and short sleek fur which changed colour in subtle gradations from pale coffee round his shoulders and neck to a deeper brown on his back and tail. He was sitting on the carpet in a rejected huff and as she watched him, began a little paw washing in an affectedly unconcerned manner.

'You may be a snooty pedigree,' she told him reprovingly, 'but your manners are pure mongrel.' Geronimo got up slowly, wound himself round Phoebe's legs and began nipping her ankles in a confident but entirely friendly manner.

'Mind my tights!' It occurred to Phoebe that he might be hungry. They went downstairs to the kitchen together, Geronimo leading the way with his tail in the air. Phoebe opened a tin for him and he sniffed at his bowl disdainfully for several seconds before condescending to eat what she had put out for him. How different from dear Diggory who would eat the bowl as well if he could; Phoebe thought, warming to him. She wondered where he had been all this time. Where had he slept, with the boys? Phoebe had been reading more of Nancy's diary the previous night before she went to sleep. Nancy had been desolate without her cat for months after she had left home. She wrote about him a lot, remembering his funny ways and his irritating habits, now rendered charming by their enforced absence and the passage of time. Phoebe discovered that he had been called Claude as a joke because, as a kitten, he made Nancy feel well and truly clawed whenever she engaged him in jollification. Phoebe wondered if Claude had been a Burmese too.

There was a double clang from the back door and Phoebe saw that Geronimo had left the house via a cat-flap. He was free to come and go as he wished. She understood that all she had to do was to provide food and keep a warm house. Geronimo did not require any further service of her. She realized that in fact she could have done with his company that morning. Perhaps this was the edge that cats had over dogs; they were able to play hard to get until you were well and truly hooked.

Phoebe looked about her for something to do to kill the morning until it was time to go to Fay's. She collected up the dirty bed linen, put it into the washing machine with some soap powder and turned it on. Then she watched for a while as it went round and round. She hoped she had done the right thing in letting the boys go out with Poppy . . .

Chapter Thirteen

Fay was amused at Phoebe's reaction to her borrowed flat.

'It's amazing,' Phoebe exclaimed, fingering the tapestries on the walls and nervously avoiding the collection of tall Chinese vases on the floor. 'It's so full of *things*! It's overpowering. Whatever will you do with them when Jack comes? Won't they all get broken?'

'I'm planning to move all the breakables into the study and lock the door,' Fay said. 'It's a collector's paradise, isn't it? Have a good nose round if you like.' She watched Phoebe as she walked round the sitting room. She was touched by her childlike curiosity. Phoebe was not blasé. She had no false airs of sophistication; she was open and charming. Fay thought of the owner of the flat, her friend, who had so recently proved to be a collector of people as well as of things. She felt a stab of grief, tempered by a quick anger. I will not wallow, she told herself fiercely. Phoebe's here now, and she's so totally different, she'll help me to get over her. She's a good, kind person. More than that, she's got beautiful chestnut hair, lovely speckled hazel eyes and that wonderful almost translucent skin. Perhaps she and I . . .? No, Fay thought. It's too soon.

'Your friend must be very trusting,' Phoebe said, 'to let you have this place when there's so much of her precious stuff about. She must be a very special friend?'

'Yes,' Fay said.

They had tea together and talked, mostly about Conrad and then Duncan. Phoebe was easy to talk to and generous in her attitudes, Fay thought. It was too bad that she had chosen to marry such a cold fish as Duncan. It was a waste of all that zest and enthusiasm. Perhaps she should encourage her to leave him? On the whole, Fay thought not. It was up to Phoebe. She herself was in no position to hand out advice!

*

Phoebe had enjoyed her visit to Fay's flat, and regretted the need to get back to Rick's unwelcoming house. The time had gone by too quickly and she found that she was loath to relinquish her sister-in-law's company. Fay drove her back in the dark through the crowded streets of London, dodging taxis, changing lanes expertly and apparently impervious to the blatant discourtesy and carelessly dangerous behaviour of the other road users.

'Everyone in London is so *aggressive*,' Phoebe complained. 'It's all V-signs and blaring horns. Whatever happened to good manners?'

'Another victim of high-pressure living?' Fay suggested. 'It doesn't bother me. I suppose I take it for granted.'

When they got to Rick's house, Phoebe remembered the burglar alarm with apprehension. She wasn't confident of doing the right thing by it.

'Will you come in with me,' she asked Fay, 'and show me how to press those damn buttons?'

Fay laughed. 'I envy you,' she said. 'It's obviously a different world in Somerset!'

'Stay until the boys get back, and eat with us?' Phoebe urged. 'There's loads of instant food.'

'Well . . . okay, thanks.'

They made themselves at home in Rick's drawing room, taking off their shoes and both curling up on the two plushy sofas, facing each other across the highly polished coffee table.

'Have a drink?' Phoebe suggested.

'Just tonic water for me,' Fay said. 'I've got to drive home.'

Phoebe padded across the carpet in her stockinged feet to the drinks cupboard, poured herself a generous glass and handed Fay hers. 'What's the time?'

'Eight o'clock already!'

'The boys should be home any time now,' Phoebe said, without enthusiasm.

'Don't you like them?'

'They're a bit hard going, aren't they? I'm not good at talking to them. Perhaps it's because I haven't any of my own.'

'Is that something you're sad about?'

'I don't know.' Phoebe surprised herself by discovering that she really did not know. 'If you'd asked me that only three months ago, I'd have said yes, without a shadow of a doubt, but now I'm not so sure.'

By half-past eight Rod and Pete had still not appeared and Phoebe and Fay were hungry. They decided to go ahead with their supper anyway.

'We can always bung the boys' food into the microwave when they arrive,' Fay said.

'Magic,' Phoebe said. 'Duncan doesn't believe in convenience food, in spite of the fact that it's never him who's inconvenienced!'

By 9.30 Phoebe was beginning to get restless. 'They ought to be home,' she said. 'Wherever can they be? The leisure centre must surely be closed by now? You will stay until they get back, won't you?'

'I'll stay,' Fay said. 'But has it occurred to you that they may have gone somewhere else entirely?'

'Oh God!' Phoebe said, allowing her unease to surface in a burst of realization. 'You think she's abducted them! You think she's taken them to America, don't you? I thought those bags were too big for sports kit. I should have said so. I should have made them open them!'

'Steady on!' Fay said. 'I wouldn't say abducted exactly. I'm sure the boys would be more than willing to go to the States.'

'But, whatever will I say to Rick? If it's true, it's all my fault!'

'How can it be?' Fay said reasonably. 'How could you have stopped them? They're not babes in arms.'

By midnight the boys had still not returned, and Phoebe, who had been fortifying herself with gin, was tipsily convinced of her worst fears.

'I should have guessed,' she said. 'Pete nearly let the cat out of the bag this morning, but Rod squashed him. I thought it was just their usual niggling. I should have known then.' Another thought struck her. 'Poppy said I shouldn't worry. She said

145

"These guys are safe with me." I didn't realize what she meant. I'm so *stupid*.' She burst into tears. 'How am I going to tell Rick?' she wailed.

'I'll tell him,' Fay said.

'We must phone the police!' Phoebe cried, struggling out of the depths of the sofa.

'No,' Fay said. 'What could they do? She's their mother. She's within her rights.'

'But Rick has custody. She's probably not allowed to take them abroad!'

'Is that fair? She's their mother and it's illegal for her to entertain her own children at home?'

'Well . . . but she did desert them.'

'She was ill. Do you think she should be punished for that forever? You saw her, did she look like a wicked person to you?'

'No,' Phoebe agreed, 'but we must do something. I feel so responsible.' Tears ran down her face.

'Look, Phoebe, don't get all het up. This may be no big deal. She may well have taken them to the States. She may equally well send them home again after they've had a good holiday there. Either way, there's not a lot we can do. They're probably halfway across the Atlantic by now. It's a job for Rick's lawyers.'

'But we should phone Rick,' Phoebe said, sniffing.

'Not tonight,' Fay said. 'Let's wait until tomorrow morning at least.' She took a linen handkerchief out of her pocket and stooped over Phoebe, gently wiping her eyes with it. 'Maybe it's not such a tragedy,' she said.

'Another breaking of the chain, you mean?'

'I fear it's too late for that,' Fay said. 'Those boys are too old. Their characters will have been set in stone by now. But in a way, yes, I suppose it may be. Come on, let me help you up to bed.' She put an arm round Phoebe's waist and walked with her upstairs.

'Don't go home,' Phoebe said. 'I can't bear the thought of being here on my own.' She felt quite overcome by guilt and by gin, so she was barely conscious of Fay helping her out of her clothes, pulling her nightie on over her head and easing her under the duvet in the four-poster. And when Fay herself got into the other side of the bed and snuggled up to her back, it was the most comforting thing in the world. Phoebe slept.

The telephone rang on Fay's side of the bed at 7 a.m. She groaned and fumbled for the bedside light, before sitting up properly and picking up the receiver. It was Rick.

'Fay? What are you doing there?' he said. He sounded curt.

'Looking after Phoebe,' Fay said. 'We were going to phone you this morning. We think Poppy –'

'She's only fucking well taken the boys to America!' Rick interrupted furiously. 'I've just been woken by my morning call and a bloody fax from her from New York! What the hell happened? How could Phoebe have let them go? I can't believe it! Is she there? I want to speak to her.'

'Yes, but she's very upset, Rick. It's not her fault. Both Poppy and the boys deceived her. How was she to know?'

'Any sentient being could have worked it out, surely? It doesn't take a doctorate in anthropology, just a tiny measure of common sense, or is that too much to ask?'

'That's not fair, Rick.' Fay glanced sideways at Phoebe. She was awake and looking up at her with startled eyes. Her hair was spread out on the pillow around her face. She looked like Botticelli's Venus. 'Rick wants a word,' Fay said to her. 'The boys *are* in the States.'

'Oh God!' Phoebe said. She sat up jerkily and took the receiver from her. 'I'm so, so sorry . . .' she began.

Fay slipped out of bed and covered her nakedness with Rick's dressing-gown from the back of the door. It smelt of his cologne. She wondered if Phoebe was embarrassed by nudity? Fay had put the nightdress on her the night before, just in case. It had been like dressing a child. Sweet! thought Fay. Phoebe was still apologizing. Fay left her to it and went downstairs to make some tea.

When Fay came back into the bedroom, Phoebe had put on a sweater over her nightie and was sitting up in bed with the duvet bunched defensively round her. So she is shy, Fay thought, smiling at her encouragingly.

'That was awful,' Phoebe said.

'Well at least we know what's what now,' Fay said, putting down the tray.

'It explains Rick's burglary too. Apparently it was Poppy's current boyfriend. He took her marriage and divorce certificates and the boys' birth certificates to get passports for them. That's why nothing else was taken. Poppy told him where they were kept.'

'How do you know?'

'Rick said it was all in the fax. It sounds as though Poppy wanted him to know how clever she'd been.'

'Oh, I see.' Fay poured two mugs of tea and put them down next to the telephone. Then she got back into bed and handed one across to Phoebe. 'Tea.'

'Thanks.' Phoebe looked sideways at Fay. 'I don't remember going to bed last night,' she said. 'Was I totally plastered?'

'Pretty much,' Fay said cheerfully.

'I mean, did I do anything embarrassing?'

'Now let me see . . .' Fay saw Phoebe's anxious face and relented. 'Nothing at all,' she reassured her.

'Thank you for staying.'

'It was a pleasure.' Fay decided to explain herself in case Phoebe was wondering about her presence there. 'The other beds in the house looked rather foetid, so I didn't think you'd mind me sharing this one,' she said. She hadn't looked at any other beds, but it seemed a fair guess.

'No,' Phoebe blushed. 'It's odd to be in bed with another woman,' she said. 'I never have been before. What would people think!'

'That we were lesbians?'

'No, that's daft, isn't it? No one who looks as good as you could possibly be one of them.'

Phoebe drank a second cup of tea, sitting in the four-poster bed next to Fay. The events of the day before played and replayed themselves in her head like a never-ending loop of muzak. She felt punch-drunk. She didn't know what to do next. Rick had been so furious on the telephone, so scathing. He hadn't seemed at all relieved that the boys were safe. She said as much to Fay.

148

'No, well, I don't think he loves them the way I love my children, for instance. It's more a sort of pride of ownership, and now they've been stolen from him by someone he particularly despises. I think that's what makes him so angry.'

'I can't bear people being angry with me,' Phoebe said. She felt near to tears again.

'You poor creature,' Fay said kindly, patting her arm. 'You're very thin-skinned, aren't you?'

'Wouldn't you be upset?' Phoebe demanded.

'Not if I knew it wasn't my fault. I'd be angry back. You should try it.'

'I'm not strong-minded like you,' Phoebe said.

'You could be, if you were determined to be,' Fay said briskly. 'Positive thinking and all that. More tea?'

'No,' Phoebe said, 'thank you. I must get myself together and decide what to do next. I suppose there's no point my staying here now, unless Poppy brings the boys back.'

'Rick didn't say?'

'Apparently there was nothing in the fax about their coming back.'

'I should think it's unlikely then.'

'So I'd better go home. Oh!' Phoebe stopped, distressed.

'What?'

'I forgot to phone Duncan last night! I phoned on Friday night, but last night in all the fuss about the boys, I forgot.'

'Well, he knows Rick's number. He could have phoned you if he was worried,' Fay said reasonably. 'So he probably isn't.'

'Oh,' said Phoebe, 'yes.'

'Look, Phoebe,' Fay said, 'you're all in a state. Don't rush off today. Spend it with me and go home tomorrow when you feel better, yes?'

'But what about the cat?' Phoebe said inconsequentially, 'I can't go away anyway, and leave him!'

'We'll pop next door and ask the neighbour to feed him until Rick gets back,' Fay said. 'That's all he needs.'

'But . . .?'

'Just say you'll stay and spend today with me,' Fay said.

Phoebe let out a long sigh. 'All right,' she said, and because

149

this didn't sound very gracious, she turned and kissed Fay on her cheek. 'Thanks,' she said.

In Somerset, Sunday was a bright cold day. Hope and Peter drank their morning coffee in the dining room, where Peter deflected all Hope's verbal assaults on him with imperturbable urbanity. They had had this conversation many times before.

'You said you would retire last year,' Hope said accusingly to her husband. 'You said it the year before too, but you never do. I hardly ever see you!'

'You're seeing me now,' Peter said mildly. 'I'm home for this weekend in the country, aren't I?'

'You're 73 this year,' Hope went on. 'Other men stop and look after their wives well before they get to 70! Why can't you?'

'You've got the capable Mrs White to look after you now,' Peter said. 'She does it so much better than I could.'

'She's just the housekeeper!' Hope said. 'It's not the same thing at all. But that's irrelevant, as you well know. It's just a red herring. So I ask you again – when are you going to retire? And I want a sensible answer this time.'

'I can't possibly stop earning money,' Peter said, quite untroubled by her tone of voice. 'We wouldn't either of us last long on our pensions.'

'What nonsense!' Hope said. 'You've got plenty of money. *I've* got plenty of money. It's just an excuse. You're a tiresome selfish old man!'

'I'll retire at 80,' Peter said unabashed, 'or when I'm too old to work, whichever comes first. That's a promise. Will that please you?'

'It will be a bit late then!' Hope said. 'You won't be worth spending time with, once you're too old to work!'

'I'm always worth spending time with,' Peter said cheerfully. 'Now, will you accompany me for a short walk to inspect the goldfish?'

'I most certainly shall not!' Hope said. She knew that Peter would do exactly as he pleased. He always had. He never admitted it, and he always won.

'There may also be a daffodil out,' Peter said encouragingly, 'green shoots to identify, slugs to murder.'

'If you're determined to change the subject,' Hope said crossly, 'you'll just have to inspect things on your own. I'm sorry, but there it is. Put a coat and scarf on; it's cold.'

She watched him through the French windows as he went down the garden path a few minutes later. He was not wearing the suggested coat. Obstinate old fool, she muttered to herself. His arthritis was apparently not so acute at the moment, because he was walking with his stick quite briskly. Neither of us is really old yet, Hope thought. We can still do what we want. We've still got our full complement of marbles. There's still time for us to be together, and yet even now after all these years, he refuses to make the effort. She set her face in determination. I shall not let him see that it upsets me, she said to herself. I shan't give him the satisfaction!

'What would you like to do?' Fay had asked Phoebe in Rick's flat, after they had had breakfast, and Phoebe had packed her things, and they had made arrangements for the feeding of the cat.

'I've always wanted to go down the Thames in a riverboat to Greenwich,' Phoebe suggested.

'Ye-es,' Fay said, 'but not in February, I think. It would be too bloody cold. We'll do it in the summer. Now, how well do you know London?'

'Not at all,' Phoebe confessed.

'Right then . . . I know, I'll drive you round on a scenic tour, we'll eat lunch at a little bistro I know, and then we'll spend the afternoon at the Tate. It opens at two o'clock on Sundays. Will that do?'

'Lovely,' agreed Phoebe. Fay thought she would probably have agreed to anything, just so long as she was not called upon to make any decisions.

Now, as they sat together on a bench in the Clore Gallery admiring the Turners and resting their feet, she was glad she had decided for them both. Phoebe was relaxed again and enjoying herself. She was loud in her praise of the paintings and full of awe at their size and their grandeur.

151

'I love that one,' Phoebe said, 'the castle with the cow in front and the sunlight on the water. And that canal one with the sailing ship and the cathedral in the distance. I'm really glad I didn't go straight home, Fay. I'd hate to have missed this.'

'Good,' Fay said, smiling at her. When the gallery closed at 5.30 they went to her flat. 'Let's stay in this evening,' she said. 'I'll cook us something later on and we'll have a good bottle of wine.'

'That would be great,' Phoebe said. 'I'm exhausted. No gin, though, I've gone right off it!'

Fay put the gas fire on and they lazed in front of it. Phoebe finally got too hot and took off her sweater, revealing a baggy T-shirt. Fay fetched a family photograph album from one of the stack of cardboard boxes in the bedroom, which contained all her personal things, and showed Phoebe pictures of her daughters. Phoebe said all the right things as if by instinct as she turned the pages, and Fay felt more than usually at ease in her company. Phoebe was avid for family stories, so she talked to her about how she and Conrad had met and more about the senior Moons in the old days.

'Did you ever meet Nancy Sedgemoor?' Phoebe asked her.

'I did once, at our wedding in 1968. She was pretty alarming as I remember, very bright, didn't suffer fools gladly. I rather admired her. Why?'

'Just wondered,' Phoebe said. She was lying on her stomach on the rug between Fay and the fire, with her chin cupped in her hands supported by her elbows. Her eyelashes were long and curled up at their ends, Fay noticed looking down from the sofa. The glow from the fire showed up the fine blonde hairs on Phoebe's arms and the red highlights in her thick hair. Fay wanted very much to reach down and stroke her head, but she did not.

Later on, she went into the kitchen to cook supper, and Phoebe went at the same time into the hall to telephone Duncan.

'There's no answer,' Phoebe said, appearing at the kitchen door moments later. 'He must be home by now, it's dark.' When she tried again a quarter of an hour later, he was still not answering and Phoebe began to look worried.

'Try Hope,' Fay suggested, beating egg yolks into a white sauce.

'I try not to phone her if I can help it,' Phoebe said, 'she's always so rude. But it looks as though I'll have to.' She went to do it.

Fay added grated cheese, and salt and pepper, whisked egg whites and folded them in, and then poured the mixture into a deep round dish before putting it carefully into the oven.

'No answer there either,' Phoebe said coming in again and looking more worried. 'I kept dialling. I even got them to test the line. It's very odd. They hardly ever go out in the evening and Duncan never does. I hope there's nothing wrong.'

'Perhaps Duncan will phone you?'

'He can't phone here, can he? He hasn't got the number.'

'Oh no, of course not. I keep forgetting that I'm not legit these days. Look,' Fay offered, 'do you want to go back to Rick's house after we've eaten, in case Duncan is trying to get in touch?'

'No,' Phoebe said at once. 'I'd much rather stay here. It's probably nothing to worry about. I'll try again later, or I'll ring first thing tomorrow. He's bound to be there then. What are you cooking?'

'Surprise!' Fay said.

It turned out to be a perfect cheese soufflé, and Phoebe ate it with gusto. 'It's so nice to have such an appreciative person to eat one's food,' Fay said, pleased.

'It's absolutely delicious,' Phoebe said, between mouthfuls. 'Aren't men lucky? I wish I could have a wife who looked after me half as well as you do!'

Could be arranged, Fay thought with a wry smile. She wished she could tell Phoebe everything.

'What?' Phoebe asked.

'I didn't say anything. Have some more salad?'

Fay watched her covertly as she ate. The urge just to touch Phoebe's bare arm teased her resolve with a dangerous new excitement. Fay felt that if she got too close to her, it would jump the gap like an electric arc and declare its existence to the

153

world. It is too soon, Fay thought. More importantly, I don't want to risk alienating Phoebe. She's too valuable as a friend. So don't screw it up! she admonished herself, but the frisson remained. Fay was amazed that Phoebe seemed not to sense the tension in her. To Fay it made the air between them heavy with a kind of unfolding potency which promised limitless possibilities for happiness. She recognized with a pang that this was exactly how she had felt the last time she had fallen in love.

Chapter Fourteen

On Sunday, when Peter had gone down the garden towards the pond, it was more to get away from Hope's nagging than actually to inspect anything. He had no interest in the emerging bulbs which were now declaring themselves all over the garden. He positively disliked daffodils, and he was much too squeamish to squash a slug. He knew full well that if he invited Hope to accompany him, she would refuse. Women were so predictable! he thought amusedly. It was just as well really; how else would a fellow cope with them at all?

It was colder than he had expected. He wished he had put on the coat and scarf which Hope had advised, but it was too late now. Going back to the house at this point would only give her a moral victory. He pressed on. The pond was out of sight from the major part of the garden, behind a series of clipped yew hedges which separated the lawn from the roses, the herb garden from the herbaceous borders, and the annuals and nursery patch from the kitchen garden. It was all visible from the upstairs rooms, laid out like an architect's coloured plan, with paths and pergolas and several urns, but outside on the ground one could wander from one green-bounded area to the next without knowing in advance what delightful surprise awaited.

Peter liked the formality of it, even though the subtleties of horticultural design evaded him. It was Hope's domain and he was happy to leave its evolution to her. The pond, though, was a different kettle of fish altogether. It had been his idea. Bother! Peter thought. Why didn't I get Duncan to build it in a huge kettle shape? It could have been an excellent spot test for visitors as well as a jolly good in-joke. Under his instruction, Duncan had worked hard on that pond. He encouraged frogspawn in it, each year, and had placed boulders in the shallows for young froglets to haul out onto. He had planted it with special weeds, and had stocked and restocked it with carp of various colours and fancy fin shapes. Peter was hoping to train them to come to be fed at the sound of a little handbell, but since he was rarely at home it seemed an unlikely achievement. In any case, he didn't want the bother of doing it himself; he just liked the idea. Perhaps, he thought, I could get the girl – Duncan's wife – to come over once a day and do it? Then she and Hope would be bound to meet more often. Good idea! He rounded the corner past the last hedge smiling inwardly.

There was a heron standing there at the water's edge, a few yards away. It was as bold as could be, with one of his best fish in its beak! His smile vanished.

'Hi!' he shouted, keeping his eyes on the bird and starting forwards at an awkward run, waving his stick in the air. The heron had started to swallow the fish head first and took off while the golden tail was still waving from the side of its tightly clamped yellow beak. It lumbered into the air over his head with slow beats of its wide grey wings, leaving its long legs trailing out behind it.

Peter, thinking to teach it a lesson it would not forget in a hurry, lunged at it with his stick as it passed, but he was unaware that he was so close to the edge, or that the mud at the shallow margins of the pond was so treacherous. As the bird sailed away unscathed with the fish now safely in its gullet, and its head settled comfortably back between its shoulders, it uttered a harsh gutteral '*Fraaaarnk!*' at the ridiculous old man below.

Peter didn't hear it. His feet had slipped from under him, throwing him forwards into the pond. He fell wildly with flailing arms and struck his head on one of the frog boulders, which rendered him instantly unconscious. As he lay there senseless, black tadpoles began to nudge at his ears and wriggle through his thick white hair, and the first draught of cold green water was drawn irresistibly into his lungs.

When Duncan woke up the following morning, he still felt wiped out. A heavy load was weighing down his spirits before he had even opened his eyes, and it took him several seconds before he remembered with a shock of wakefulness, what had happened the day before. He looked around him. He was in his old room at the big house with the William Morris curtains and the threadbare Persian carpet. He had stayed the night to keep his mother company, although he didn't know what to do about her, so he felt he probably wasn't much help. Mrs White, the new housekeeper, had much more idea than he did. She had stayed overtime and made Hope take the sedative the doctor had left for her. Then she had put her to bed with hot milk and sympathy, and had unplugged the telephone on her bedside table to make sure that she wasn't disturbed. Duncan had put his head cautiously round the door much later on and had found her asleep. Mrs White had been very kind to Duncan as well, as though he were a weeping small boy. In fact he hadn't cried. He just felt bemused and unbelieving and extraordinarily tired. Sleep had been a welcome escape and he had embraced it eagerly.

Now he was awake again and found himself unwilling to face up to the day ahead. Work was clearly out of the question. I need something to make the day normal; to give it some structure, he thought. I don't know where to begin. He didn't want to be ordered about. He just wanted a breathing space to get his thoughts together. He recognized, with uncharacteristic insight, that it was Phoebe he wanted. He needed her! He hadn't realized before how much he relied upon her to be there. And where the hell was she? He'd tried over and over again to ring Rick's house the night before, and there was no reply. Perhaps she had taken the boys out. But they'd hardly still be out at midnight, surely? He couldn't for the life of him think where she might be. How could she be missing at a time like this, he thought resentfully, just when there's so much to cope with?

He became aware that there was a telephone ringing now, downstairs. He leapt out of bed and ran down, three stairs at a time, to answer it. It was Phoebe.

'Oh, *Duncan*,' she said, all in a rush, 'I'm *so* glad to speak to you. Wherever have you been? I was so worried.' Then without waiting for his answer, she told him the whole story of Poppy and the boys and how bad she had felt, and still felt about it. 'And I was so afraid you'd be phoning Rick's house,' she said, 'and I'm here with Fay, you see. Well, I just couldn't stand Rick's house on my own, and she's been so kind to me. Anyway, I'll tell you the whole story when I see you. I'm coming straight home today. Can you meet the train at Bristol Parkway? Duncan?' He couldn't speak. 'Duncan, are you still there? Are you all right? What's the matter?'

'It's Father,' Duncan said with an effort. 'He's had an a-a-a-accident.'

'Oh no!' Phoebe said. 'What's happened? Is he all right?'

'No,' Duncan said. A great tidal wave of emotion swept in and engulfed him, all unprepared. 'He's dead,' he managed to say, and burst into noisy tears.

Phoebe enjoyed train journeys as a rule. They were a good excuse to buy a paperback, a newspaper and a packet of prawn sandwiches, and to divide one's time between reading, watching the countryside, eating and doing the easy crossword. If you were lucky you didn't get crowds of screaming children or zombies with over-loud Walkmans. Very occasionally you even came across someone who was fun to talk to.

Today she did none of those things. Instead she stared blankly out of the window as the long line of the Berkshire Downs went past on the skyline, and worried about Duncan. She had never known him to break down before. She had even begun to wonder if he *had* any feelings. When they had heard officially two weeks before, that Conrad and Fay were to split up, he had been completely unmoved. He hadn't even wanted to discuss it. But now he was desperately unhappy and not only was she not there to look after him, but she had gone on and on about her own problems, when he . . . Phoebe bit her lip. She willed the train to double its speed. She needed to be there *now*!

Phoebe wondered how Hope was taking her husband's sudden death. Would she be devastated? Would she show she was human after all? Phoebe herself felt no particular grief at Peter's departure. He had never been nice to her. She had thought him a selfish show-off. She was glad of this now; she would be able to care for Duncan so much better if her own emotions were not involved as well. She wondered how the other sons would react to the news. Would Hereward be as upset as Duncan? Would Rick abandon his film? Would Brendan fly home from his boat? Would Fay now feel she had to go and comfort Conrad?

Fay. Phoebe began to think about her too. She was the only good thing around at the moment, it seemed. She was so supportive, so easy, so intuitive. Thank God for Fay, Phoebe thought, she's the best. She's the sort of person you can be totally relaxed with. You don't need to put on an act; she takes you as you are.

Phoebe had spent a second night in another double bed with Fay. The friend's flat had only had one bed, so there hadn't been any choice. Phoebe hadn't minded at all. It had taken her back to her childhood, years before, when she had stayed at a schoolfriend's house and they had slept, giggling together, in a huge bed. This had the same quality of conspiratorial fun about it. It was simply friendship, Phoebe thought, warm, comforting and entirely innocent. Sex did not come into it, although these days it seemed to have to come into everything (with Duncan as the notable exception). True, Phoebe had been taken aback that first morning when Fay had got out of bed quite unselfconscious and stark naked. Phoebe had never seen an adult female body other than her own, apart from unreal ones on television, and she couldn't help looking at Fay's with envy. She could quite understand why artists liked to paint them. At the time, she was busy grovelling on the phone to Rick, but she still noticed that Fay's pubic hair was only a fraction darker than her head hair, which made her a natural blonde. Then she had realized that she was staring and had got all confused and embarrassed and turned away, redoubling her apologies to Rick. Luckily Fay had gone out at that point to make tea, and by the time she came back Phoebe had covered herself up so that Fay wouldn't see how fat and unattractive Phoebe was in comparison to herself.

The next night Fay had found herself a nightshirt and wore that in bed, so there wasn't a hint of awkwardness between them. Phoebe marvelled at how easy this friendship was, and how ridiculous that no one would believe it. Women in the past used to have very close relationships and no one sniggered about them, she thought. She sighed. The next few weeks were going to be difficult, but Phoebe felt buoyed up by Fay's help and encouragement. The main thing was that Duncan, at last, really seemed to need her. Perhaps, Phoebe thought, Peter's death will bring us closer together. She hoped so.

When the train arrived at Bristol Parkway Phoebe got out and looked about for Duncan. He wasn't there. She carried her bag up the stairs and over the bridge, and it wasn't until she was going down the other side that she saw him coming up towards her. He looked exactly the same as usual. Phoebe didn't know what she had expected but she was surprised that he looked so untouched. There hadn't been space to give him a hug, because of all the other people on the stairs, so they did without, and Duncan carried Phoebe's bag to the car park. He looked perfectly under control, Phoebe saw. As they drove down the motorway towards home she didn't like to question him too deeply about his father's death in case he broke down again and crashed the van into something, but she did find out that Peter had fallen and been drowned in the pond, and that he had been lying there for some hours in the cold, before Hope had found him.

'How is Hope?' Phoebe asked.

'She's a-all right n-now,' Duncan said. 'It was a t-terrible shock of c-course.'

'It would be.' Phoebe patted his knee in sympathy. 'I'm so sorry I was away,' she said, 'just at the wrong moment.'

'Not your f-fault,' Duncan said.

'Did you miss me?'

'You've only been away a c-c-couple of d-days,' Duncan said.

Three days after Peter's death, Hope began to feel more like herself. It was the shock, of course, which had upset everything. Once she had got over that, she felt she could cope. After the first night she had refused all offers of help, insisting that she was perfectly all right and would in fact *prefer* to be alone. Duncan called in every day, of course, and Phoebe.

Hope was sure that Phoebe meant well, but she didn't feel much like talking to her. Phoebe had read somewhere, she said,

160

that it was a good thing to talk about a deceased person to the bereaved relatives, and that the worst thing possible was to avoid mentioning them as if they had never existed. That was all very well, Hope thought, but she had spent the last fifty years existing with Peter, and that was quite enough thank you. So she said merely, 'Not just at the moment, Phoebe, if you don't mind.'

Phoebe had blushed and said, 'No, of course not. How silly of me!'

Hope had been relieved when Phoebe had told her about the car she was going to have and had suggested tentatively that she was thinking of going up to Northumberland to fetch it.

'I'd like to have it as soon as possible,' Phoebe explained, 'because it will be such a help in looking for another job. I'll only be away for one night. You don't think that now is the wrong time to be going away? Perhaps, I should wait until after the funeral.'

'Oh, I should go now,' Hope said at once. 'There's got to be an inquest, of course, before any funeral; plenty of time.'

'That's what Duncan said. I thought he'd need me to be here, but apparently not.' She sounded piqued. Hope wondered whether theirs was a happy marriage, though she wouldn't have dreamt of asking.

'Duncan's like me,' she said briskly, 'quite used to being solitary.'

So Phoebe had gone up to Newcastle on the train and wouldn't be visiting her for two days. Duncan had resumed his usual working routine, and Hope found herself temporarily unencumbered by anxieties or responsibilities, apart from answering letters of condolence. Duncan and Phoebe between them had informed all the friends and relatives. The will would have to be sorted out, but there would be time for that after the funeral. She would have to give up the flat in The Temple, of course, and all the furniture there would have to be found a new home, but again not yet.

Odd, Hope thought guiltily, the main thing that I always worried about was where Peter *was*, and what was he was doing. Now I know he's safely at the undertakers, I don't need to worry any more. She felt like a lifer scenting freedom.

*

Duncan had suffered over the years from his relationship with his father, but he had never consciously thought about it or tried to exorcise its demons. Before Peter died, he had always rather assumed that sometime in the future – when his father was no longer around to be disappointed in him – he, Duncan, would be off the hook and free to become himself at last. As a consequence, he was quite unprepared for the despair he now felt. It was far worse that his usual self-castigation or his habitual depressions. It was a final, irrevocable, feeling of failure. Duncan had always admired his father, but he knew he had never come up to his expectations. He had never tried to confide in him. He had no idea how his mind worked. He should have made an effort to talk to him. He should have discussed the traumas he had endured at his hands, and then perhaps he might have understood them.

Perhaps after all his father *had* valued him; had loved him, even. Now it was too late. He would never know. The tangle at the heart of his stifled emotions would never be unsnarled and nothing would ever be resolved. Duncan himself could not analyse this inner misery. It did not even form itself into coherent sentences. It just festered inside his head, inarticulate, hopeless and utterly consuming.

He was glad that Phoebe was away for a couple of days. She would keep asking him to try and talk about what was bothering him. She said she understood, of course, that he was upset by his father's death, but that it would help him to get it off his chest and start to grieve properly. She didn't seem to realize how impossible this was. She kept badgering him . . .

Why, Duncan asked himself, did Peter have to die such a pointless death? The newspapers were full of it: *QC DROWNS IN FOOT OF WATER*. Duncan read the obituary in *The Times*, written by a fellow barrister, and was amazed by it. There was so much he hadn't known of his father. It was like reading about a stranger. What had clearly begun as a brilliant career, somehow hadn't quite made it, as though he had got so far and

162

then run out of steam. Had he glimpsed how hollow ambition may be and decided not to pursue it after all? Or had he tried and failed? Either way, it was of no consequence now, but why had he died so ignominiously? Why couldn't he have gone out with dignity?

I wish I'd never built the bloody pond! Duncan raged. If I hadn't, then he would still be alive. He, who never cried, found tears seeping from his eyes again and oozing between his fingers.

Phoebe drove back to Somerset from Northumberland in her new car. It was a cold day but the sun was shining and her mood was light and open. It was quite the newest car she had ever owned and it was very smooth to drive. She wondered how she had managed to do without one for so long. Cars were so much more than just transport; they represented independence and freedom. I shouldn't really have accepted it, Phoebe thought. Now I'm just like everybody else, burning up the earth's nonrenewable resources and polluting its environment. She smiled ruefully and then put her foot down hard on the accelerator and zipped past a line of lorries. Nancy had worried about the world's ecology and the future of the planet. She had written about it in her diaries often. If Nancy were my age now, Phoebe wondered, would she refuse to run a car? Would she take a stand on it on a matter of principle? Or would she be like me and think, Yes, there should be a reduction in the number of cars on Britain's roads, but not *mine*, not just yet anyway ... .? Phoebe had aired this dilemma to George, her mother's new man, and he had pooh-poohed it.

'You don't want to take any notice of those environmentalists,' he said. 'Doom and gloom merchants, the lot of them! There's no way society is going to go backwards. It'll be through technology that we sort ourselves out, you mark my words. If we've got problems in the future then science will see us right. It always has, and I reckon it always will.'

'Will it cope with the greenhouse effect?' Phoebe had asked.

George snorted. 'Three hot summers and they call it global

163

warming! Why, not so long since they were warning us about another ice age coming soon. They want to make up their tiny minds!'

Phoebe warmed to George. He was just the right mixture of bigot and optimist. He would suit Wynne down to the ground. He was nothing to look at; late middle-aged, fattish and bald, but he was sincere in his regard for her mother and clearly anxious not to alienate her daughter. Phoebe had been pleased to witness their closeness and glad they seemed so happy. She had also felt annoyed, and it struck her only now as she travelled southwards, why this was. She was jealous! Her mother had got herself a man who had opinions and didn't mind expressing them. He *talked* to her. He had every intention of looking after her. Phoebe was unconditionally glad for Wynne, but she wanted her own man to do the same.

She realized that she hadn't thought of Duncan for over twenty-four hours. Her heart sank at the prospect of going home to him and having to cope with his moods. She had done everything she could think of to help him, but he resolutely refused to confide in her. She felt left out, superfluous and hurt.

I need to be needed, she thought, and he doesn't need me at all. He's never said he loves me – not once! Phoebe invented a scene in her head where Duncan rushed out to greet her with open arms when she got home, saying that he'd missed her so much and he'd never realized before how essential she was to him . . . She felt tears rising in her eyes and sniffed them back crossly. There was nothing to be done about that particular problem. If someone didn't tell you they loved you, then that was that. You couldn't risk asking them if they did, because if they said 'no', then everything collapsed into hopelessness, and if they said 'yes', then you wondered why they hadn't thought to say so themselves, so you didn't believe them. You couldn't win. By the time she did arrive at home, she was tired. It had been a long journey. No one was at the door to meet her, and when she found Duncan sitting at the kitchen table he did not greet her with any obvious enthusiasm.

'Are you all right?' she asked him.

'Not r-really,' Duncan said. 'We've just f-found the w-will. Father's left all his m-money to b-bloody B-B-B-Brendan!'

Chapter Fifteen

The following Sunday Phoebe knew she was ill. Her throat was dry, her nose streaming, her temperature was up and her very bones ached.

'Go to b-bed then,' Duncan said.

'I think I'll have to. I'm sure I caught it from someone on the train. People shouldn't travel on public transport when they're infectious, should they? Selfish pigs!' Phoebe said. 'I'm sorry. Will you be okay?'

Duncan nodded. 'What about b-breakfast?' he asked.

'There's bacon and eggs in the fridge for you. Could you bring me up some toast and a glass of orange juice?'

'Right.'

As soon as Phoebe had climbed into bed and sunk her head and shoulders onto a pile of cool pillows, she knew she had done the right thing. She really was ill. She really was justified in staying in bed, even though there was so much to be done. The cottage needed hoovering. There were piles of dirty washing and a basket full of ironing. Duncan would need cake for his packed lunches the following week. They were nearly out of dog biscuits . . . It's no good, she thought, Duncan will have to cope.

Outside it was raining, a steady drizzle. Phoebe pulled the duvet comfortably up to her chin and watched the raindrops collecting and running down the windows. She began to relax and feel warm. After a while she detected the aroma of frying bacon on the air, and shortly afterwards the unmistakable smell of burning toast. A quarter of an hour went by and Phoebe was just beginning to think that Duncan had forgotten to bring up her breakfast, when she heard his step on the stairs. He came into the bedroom holding a tray awkwardly, trying to avoid spilling the overfull orange juice. Phoebe pulled herself more upright to receive it but at the last moment, as Duncan placed the tray on her knees, the glass slid to the edge of the tray and tipped over spilling orange juice in a lake onto the tray and over its edge into the duvet. Phoebe's first reaction was one of pure rage: *I can't even be ill in peace without bloody Duncan screwing it up!*

'Oh, Duncan,' she wailed, 'for God's sake!' Duncan grabbed at the glass and only succeeded in spilling more orange onto the bed. 'Just leave it,' Phoebe snapped, struggling out from underneath. 'Get a cloth, can't you?' Duncan removed the dripping tray to the windowsill and put it down with a crash. Then he went out without a word. Phoebe meantime was soaking up as much orange juice as she could with a handful of paper tissues from the box by her bed. She heard Duncan going downstairs again. Where the hell was he going? Didn't he know there was a cloth next door in the bathroom? Of course not — when did he ever clean the bath?

By the time Duncan had got back with the dishcloth, Phoebe had already got the bathroom cloth, had stripped the duvet cover off and was examining the damage.

'It's gone right through,' she said angrily. 'I'll never get the stain out now!'

'Here's the c-c-cloth,' Duncan said, proffering it.

'The whole thing needs washing,' Phoebe said, brushing it away and bursting into tears. Her head ached. Her throat hurt. She felt wobbly on her feet. It was all too much.

'Why the hell couldn't you watch what you were doing?' she asked him.

'I d-didn't do it on p-p-purpose,' Duncan said, getting angry as well.

Why is it, Phoebe wondered, that he never admits he's in the wrong and *never* apologizes? 'Just go away,' she said, in exasperation. 'I'll sort it out myself. And take the tray with you,' she added as an afterthought. Duncan picked it up without a word.

When he had got to the bottom of the stairs and closed the door with a bang, Phoebe made herself sort things out. She took the duvet and its cover into the bathroom and ran six inches of cold water into the bath. Then she pushed the stained parts of both under the water and left them in a heap to soak. They only owned one duvet, so Phoebe was reduced to getting out the old blankets from a cupboard and finding herself a clean top sheet. By the time she had remade the bed, her headache was twice as bad and she was exhausted. She crawled into it and lay there with her eyes shut. If only Fay were here instead of useless Duncan! she thought. Then I'd be properly looked after. Perhaps I should leave him. Perhaps I should go and share a flat with Fay and get a job in London.

Fay had made a spur-of-the-moment decision. It was something she might well regret in the future, but she was sure she ought to do it anyway. She picked up the telephone in her parents' kitchen in Cornwall and dialled a number.

'Hello?' Duncan said.

'Duncan, it's Fay. Look, Jack and I are driving back to London today. We're just about to set off. I wondered if we might call in on you on the way?'

'Oh,' Duncan said, 'yes.'

'How's Phoebe?'

'She's got flu. She's in bed.'

'Oh poor thing. Tell her not to worry about lunch or anything. I'll come and cheer her up.' Duncan said he would.

Fay gave Jack half a travel sickness pill, strapped him into his seat, kissed her parents goodbye and set off. It was going to be a long journey, but she was buoyed up by the thought of seeing Phoebe again. Jack picked up her good mood and they sang songs and listened to story tapes as they progressed steadily eastwards through the rain.

It was still drizzling when they arrived at the cottage, Duncan let them in. Fay had wondered if Duncan would be gruff with her in solidarity with Conrad, but he seemed much as usual.

'I want to do some h-h-hammering in Duncan's shed,' Jack announced.

'That's a good idea,' Fay said quickly. 'I don't want him to catch Phoebe's flu,' she explained to Duncan. 'Do you mind?'

As Duncan allowed himself to be taken by the hand and walked towards the shed, Fay slipped up the stairs to Phoebe's bedroom and knocked softly on the door. There was no answer.

Fay put her head round the door and looked in. Phoebe was just waking up and looked rather puffy about the eyes, but there was no mistaking her delighted surprise.

'Fay! How marvellous. I was just wishing you were here, and all of a sudden you are!'

'Didn't Duncan tell you we were coming?'

'No. I was horrible to him this morning, so I expect he's fed up with me. Oh no!' Phoebe sat up suddenly. 'It's lunchtime and I haven't anything nice to give you . . .'

'We've already eaten,' Fay said firmly, 'and we can't stay long. We've got to get back to London.' She smiled at her. 'How are you?' Her hair was a mess and she looked younger and vulnerable. Fay wanted to hug her.

'Pretty grotty, but it's only flu. I hope you don't catch it. Don't get too close!'

'Is there anything you'd like?'

Fay made her up a jug of squash and some scrambled egg on toast. They talked about Jack's progress in Cornwall, about Peter's death and about Conrad's reaction to it.

'You haven't changed your mind about divorce?' Phoebe asked, eating the egg with gratitude.

'No,' Fay said. 'I'm sorry for all the brothers, but it doesn't make any difference. It's just tough on Con that it's all happening at once.'

'Duncan's very upset about the will,' Phoebe said. 'So is Herry. He phoned Duncan about it. They hardly ever speak to each other as a rule.'

'Phoebe,' Fay said, taking the plunge, 'there's something I want to tell you; something I ought to have told you before. I haven't been quite straight with you and it's been worrying me a lot.'

'Goodness,' Phoebe said in surprise, 'you make it sound very dramatic!'

'I just don't want us to stop being friends. I really value your friendship, you know?'

'I value yours too,' Phoebe said stoutly. 'Of course we'll still be friends, whatever it is you're going to say. Nothing could change that.' She reached out and touched Fay's sleeve, smiling.

Fay took a deep breath. 'The reason I've stayed married to Conrad for so long is that I've had support from other people,' she said. 'They've given me the love that I needed. They've bolstered me up and kept me going. They've even improved my relationship with Conrad. Jack is proof of that!'

'But that's good, isn't it?' Phoebe said. 'You told —'

'I'm talking about affairs, Phoebe,' Fay interrupted, 'love affairs. Without them I should have given up long ago, or gone of my rocker like Poppy. My last one finished in February four years ago, two months after Jack was born. It all got too difficult. There was never time. Since then I've been on my own except for Conrad and it's just got worse and worse.' She signed. 'That last affair was very special to me. It was the best love I've ever known.'

'Who was it with?' Phoebe asked. 'Not that it's any of my b—'

'The owner of my present flat.'

'But I thought you said she was a woman?' Phoebe said, surprised.

'She is,' Fay said quietly. 'They all were.'

After Fay and Jack had left, Phoebe had plenty of time for thinking. Her first reaction had been one of astonishment; her next one of anger at having been conned. When she had stayed in Fay's flat, how amused Fay must have been at her naïvety! Phoebe cringed at the thought. All her preconceived ideas about lesbians had been blown apart. She didn't know what to think. Her glib assurances to Fay about the certain continuity of their friendship seemed ridiculous. Could they now even talk to one another without embarrassment? Phoebe didn't know. Not knowing what to say, she had let Fay go without reassuring her, and had even taken some satisfaction in seeing Fay's composure crumple as she had left. Phoebe had wanted to punish her for her deception, but also for undermining her own unquestioning and complacent stance. If someone beautiful like Fay could have love affairs with women, then the hitherto clear boundaries between normal and perverted, straight and gay, were suddenly blurred and confusing. If she hadn't recognized what Fay was, then how could she identify anyone? Phoebe felt foolish and out of touch with the real world.

Then she remembered the look on Fay's face as she had gone out of the bedroom, and felt ashamed of herself. Who was she to be so judgmental? Fay had respected her enough to want to tell her the truth and had risked a lot in doing so. She had *liked* Fay. Was anything really so different now? It wasn't as though Fay had tried to seduce her. That, thought Phoebe, would be something else altogether. Next time I go to London, she decided, I'll go and see her and make it up. There's no reason in the world why we shouldn't go on as before.

In this conciliatory mood, she thought of Duncan too. He had been doing his best. She shouldn't have bitten his head off about spilling the orange juice. At least she could do something positive about that straightaway. She got out of bed, put on her dressing gown and slippers and went downstairs to the kitchen. Diggory was lying in his basket by the stove, fast asleep, which meant that Duncan was in the house somewhere. Phoebe looked about her. The flagstones on the floor were covered in fluffy clots of dust and dog hair punctuated by small oblongs of dried mud which had fallen from the tread of Duncan's wellies. The sink was piled with dirty dishes and mugs. The working surfaces were smeared with grease and littered with bread-crumbs. All Duncan's breakfast things were still on the table, even down to the blobs of marmalade which he had dropped when transferring it from jar to toast on the blade of a knife. Phoebe felt instantly mortified. What must Fay have thought?

'I'm ill for one day,' she complained aloud, 'and the place becomes a complete slum! I can't bear it. How can I lie and relax in bed, knowing it will get worse and worse? I suppose I shall have to deal with it myself. At least it will be done properly then. How can Duncan not notice such squalor?' She felt put upon and full of resentment, and it was in that frame of mind that she went through into the sitting room to find him.

Duncan was at his desk doing his accounts. His note-books were open in front of him and his calculator was

171

switched on, but he was leaning with his head in his hands, weeping.

'Duncan?' Phoebe said, taken aback and instantly concerned. He looked up at her and his eyes were extra blue, luminous with tears. 'What is it?' He seemed as though he was trying to speak but couldn't. Phoebe saw him sitting there, hunched in misery, wordless and hopeless, and was flooded with compassion for him. She went over and put her arms round his head, holding it against her and stroking it gently. She had never seen him cry before and the sight was unbearably pathetic.

'Darling Duncan,' she said, 'it's all right. I'm here.' He buried his face in her breast and put both arms round her waist, shaking with sobs. She stood like that for some time, holding him, kissing the top of his head and murmuring encouragement, and all the time she was thinking, He needs me. He *does* need me! It made her forget that she was angry with him. It made her forget that she was feeling ill. It made everything all right.

After a while Duncan disengaged himself and she sat down on the desk facing him as he blew his nose in a grubby handkerchief.

'It's F-Father,' he said. 'I n-n-never knew him.'

'I understand,' Phoebe said gently. 'I never knew mine either.'

'I c-can't talk a-a-about it,' Duncan said rather desperately.

'It's all right,' Phoebe said again. 'You don't have to. I know what you mean. Don't feel you have to say anything at all.' Duncan looked at her in surprise and relief, and Phoebe knew then that, quite by chance, she had found the way to get through to him. 'I'll make us some tea,' she said, and whilst they drank it, Duncan began to talk to her about his father.

'He never p-p-praised me,' he said. He spoke hesitantly at first and then with more and more confidence. Phoebe held his hand and let him go on without interruption until he had talked himself out. Then he heaved a huge sigh and smiled ruefully at her.

'Enough of me,' he said. 'What a-about you? Aren't you i-i-ill?'

'I do feel rather exhausted,' Phoebe admitted.

172

'Go b-back to b-bed,' Duncan said kindly, 'and I'll fetch us a Chinese for s-supper later on.'

Phoebe found herself escorted upstairs again, kissed on the forehead and tucked into bed. To hell with the mess downstairs, she thought. What does it matter? Duncan needs me.

Phoebe lay comfortably in bed reading Nancy's diaries. She was feeling a lot better.

12 April 1961. I suppose the biggest news of the day is that the Russians have won the race to put the first man into space – a terrific achievement and one with tremendous consequences for the future. P. was rather scathing about it, of course. He's anti science in the way that superior Arts people always are. I found out something extraordinary about the Moon family today when P. baldly announced that they had adopted a 14-year-old boy! He showed me a studio portrait he'd had taken of the whole family including Brendan, the newcomer. I have waited for years to see what all his children look like, and was fascinated by their strong resemblance to their father. I picked out Brendan at once by his brown eyes and his lack of strong Moon features. 'No,' P. said, pointing. 'That's Hereward. This is Brendan.' 'But that one can't be yours and Hope's,' I said, looking at the brown-eyed Hereward (poor young man having to go through life with a ridiculous name like that!), 'because you've both got blue eyes and blue eye colour is a recessive gene.' P. looked vexed and uncharacteristically flustered and then reluctantly told me the whole story. It seems that before he knew me, P. had an affair with an actress who bore him a son (in 1947) called Brendan. P. kept in contact with the boy and (all unknown to Hope) paid for his education. Now the actress has suddenly died and P. feels he has to take the boy on. Hope was not surprisingly dead against this idea, but P. says he insisted upon it. It was when I disbelievingly asked him 'How?' that I got my greatest shock. It seems that I'm right and that Hereward is not P.'s son at all, but the result of Hope's brief fling with a bishop! (She's gone up in my estimation.) P. says he didn't suspect

173

the child's parentage at all until two years later when Hope gave birth to the girl she'd always wanted, but the baby was stillborn. Hope in her grief apparently thought it was Divine retribution, and confessed all. The gruesome thing, to my mind, is that P. accepted the boy as his own but seems to have used his existence all this time as a form of moral blackmail – a way of keeping Hope in order. She had no idea, of course, that he also had had a child by someone else, and he's kept her in ignorance all these years until now, when he can make use of it. She didn't want to take Brendan on, but P had Hereward as a kind of hold over her – tit for tat. 'I took your bastard in, so you must do the same for mine.' He told it to me in such a matter-of-fact way, as though the logic of it was unassailable, but he had a glint of pure triumph in his eyes, which utterly unnerved me. I find myself feeling so sorry for H. and understanding her so much more. My feelings for P. are confused. For sometime now I've known that we've lost that lovely trusting passion which can overrule all common sense and carry one off, laughing. I suppose I find I can't love him unconditionally any more. There are facets of his character which really appal me (like today's revelations), but in spite of that I find I still want him. Our arrangement is ideal for me – casual but regular. I shall just be careful not to invest any more of my dreams in him. Perhaps this is what they mean by life beginning at 40 – a down-to-earth pragmatic sort of a life?

Phoebe lay back on her pillows, amazed. Her father-in-law had been a total shit! She felt sorriest for Brendan. What must it have been like as an awkward adolescent to have been foisted upon a family who didn't want you, with Hope as an unwilling stepmother? Phoebe couldn't imagine. Then she felt sorry for Hope too. What a position to be in! It explained things . . . why Hope favoured Herry and his family so much, and, yes, of course, it explained Peter's will. Phoebe thought, I must tell Duncan. It will help him so much if he knows the truth. To know the truth is to understand, and to understand is perhaps to forgive. But, she thought, if I do that I shall have to confess to having the diaries . . . and inevitably the bestiary too.

She had had at the back of her mind for some time that the bestiary would be her insurance for the future; a valuable asset to fall back upon, should her marriage fail. It had given her the peace of mind to stay where she was, knowing that in a crisis anytime she could just leave, sell it and live on the proceeds. She supposed that this was the reason she had kept quiet about it for so long. She wanted it by her, just in case. She felt guilty about having it, of course, but the more she read the diaries the more she felt entitled to the bestiary, as though she alone was Nancy's champion and rightful heir.

Phoebe wanted very much to tell Duncan everything straightaway, but something held her back. She thought she would wait and see whether things went on getting better between them. They had started to, and were promising but would they last? She and Duncan had had more talks, and Duncan had actually promised to try harder to communicate on a deeper level with her and even to be tidier. Phoebe in her turn had undertaken to be less critical and more understanding. If he really did make the effort, she knew she would go more than halfway to meet him. She decided to hold back until Duncan had proved conclusively that he really was committed to their marriage. Then she would confess to having both the diaries and the bestiary (which they could sell and divide the loot between all the brothers) and there would be no further thought in her head about splitting up. She would be Mrs Moon for ever.

On Tuesday when she was over her flu, they made love for the first time since the foam bath and massage fiasco. Phoebe was relieved to find that it worked adequately enough, even if it was less than wonderful, but she was not prepared for the thoughts which came unbidden to her mind at crucial moments. Images of Fay appeared. Phoebe wondered what lovemaking with another woman would be like . . .

Afterwards, as Duncan slept beside her, Phoebe lay awake and worried about herself. Was her curiosity about Fay normal, or was she a latent gay as well? Was that partly why Duncan had showed so little interest in her during their marriage? Wasn't she attractive to a man any more? What nonsense! she told herself. I've always been entirely heterosexual. There's absolutely nothing unnatural about me . . . but the thought persisted and unsettled her.

Chapter Sixteen

On Wednesday, the morning of Peter's funeral, Duncan was up early. He hadn't slept well the night before and had lain awake worrying about how the cremation service would go and whether he would manage not to break down in public and disgrace himself. He needed something to do now, to take his mind off things. It was too early to take Diggory to kennels for the night. They didn't open until nine o'clock. He made himself a pot of tea and sat at the kitchen table fretting. Phoebe was still asleep upstairs. He had managed to slip out of bed without waking her and noticed in passing how sweet and childlike she looked. He had felt heartened by their recent discussions and surprised at how much better he had felt when he had unloaded some of his pent-up misery onto her willing ears. She had been right about that after all. He found himself jolted into the realization that she had a point and that he *could* do practical things to make their life together run more smoothly.

He could do something useful now. The dirty-clothes basket in the bathroom was bulging, with shirts and socks and towels spilling out from under its woven lid. He remembered he had had trouble stuffing the last ones in. Duncan finished his tea and got up from the table. Then he tiptoed quietly upstairs again and sorted out a load of clothes to wash, congratulating himself on remembering that dark colours had to be done separately. He gathered them all up in one of the towels, crept downstairs again and through into the utility room. It took a moment or two before he could work out how to open the damn door on the washing machine, and there wasn't enough space in the room to allow him to get down to its level, but he finally worked it out and stuffed the clothes inside, together with a hollow ball thing which he filled with liquid soap. He switched it on and nothing happened. Duncan waited, puzzled. Still nothing happened. He frowned. It should be filling with water. Perhaps Phoebe turned the two inlet taps off every time.

177

He reached over and turned them on, and the machine hissed into life.

Feeling justifiably pleased with himself, he went back into the kitchen and made a pot of tea, carrying it upstairs to Phoebe and managing to negotiate the door at the bottom of the stairs to exclude Diggory. Mindful of last time's disaster, he put the tray down on the windowsill and carried the mugs from it one at a time. Phoebe sat up in bed blinking and rubbing her eyes.

'Oh Duncan,' she said, 'how lovely,' and leant over to give him a kiss. They sat comfortably side by side drinking their tea. 'How long will it take us to get to the crematorium?' Phoebe asked.

'Two and a h-half,' Duncan said, 'm-maybe three hours?'

'Better make it three and a half to be on the safe side,' Phoebe said, 'in case the traffic's bad.'

'If y-you like,' Duncan said. He didn't mind either way.

'Why isn't he being cremated here in Somerset?' Phoebe asked.

Duncan shrugged. 'L-London's his home,' he said, 'and a-all his friends are there and m-most of the family. It seemed the l-logical thing to do, and M-Mother wanted it. He a-always hated the country.'

'It would have been cheaper to cremate him here and then take just his ashes to London later on, for the service in the Temple church,' Phoebe said, 'but I suppose expense doesn't really come into it at a time like this.'

Duncan nodded.

'Who will be there?' Phoebe asked.

'Just about e-everyone,' Duncan said. 'Mother says the f-flat will be b-bursting at the seams with f-family. She went up after the i-i-inquest on Monday to get it s-sorted out.'

The inquest had brought in the expected verdict of Death by Misadventure. Duncan had not wanted to attend, so Phoebe had gone with Hope. Duncan had been grateful to her for that. He was grateful to her now just for being there.

After three leisurely cups of tea they got up. It was going to be a difficult day for Duncan, Phoebe knew, and she had resolved to make it as easy for him as possible. He seemed to be taking his father's death badly, much worse than his mother was. Phoebe has been surprised at how strong Hope had appeared to be at the inquest. She had been softer too, and had even taken Phoebe's arm as they walked in from the car, and had thanked her with unaccustomed warmth at the end. Phoebe wondered if she would be as stoical today. Halfway through breakfast she heard an unexpected roaring sound and looked up, startled.

'It's okay,' Duncan said. 'It's the w-washing machine.'

Phoebe raised an eyebrow. Duncan was looking rather smug, she thought with amusement. 'Good for you,' she said. 'Wonders will never cease!' and she reached over and kissed him on his ear. After the final spin, she got up to empty the machine, but Duncan put out a restraining hand.

'I'll d-do it,' he said, going out.

'I've started, so I'll finish!' Phoebe called in friendly mockery. She heard him opening the door and starting to pull the newly washed clothes out.

'What the b-bloody hell . . .?' he exclaimed.

'What?' Phoebe said. Duncan didn't answer, so she went to see what was wrong. Duncan was pulling the last of the clothes out into the plastic laundry basket. She looked over his shoulder. They were covered with whitish bits of what looked like paper, rather like the result of accidentally including a paper handkerchief in the wash, but a thousand times worse! A whole box of tissues would have been needed to produce this degree of chaos.

'What on earth . . .?' Phoebe began.

Duncan reached into the machine and felt about inside it. When he withdrew his hand he was holding the soggy, distorted, partially pulped remains of what looked like a small book, with blue covers and a black ribbon bookmark. The truth dawned on Phoebe with a sudden guilty clarity. She felt her cheeks blush a flaming red.

'What's this,' Duncan asked, 'and how did it g-g-get in here?'

Phoebe had realized that it must be Nancy's diary for 1960. She had finished reading it just before she had flu. She must have forgotten to take it out of its day hiding place, when she had felt ill and gone early to bed! Wildly, and for only seconds,

Phoebe considered lying to Duncan and inventing some story about a book, any book, to explain its presence there, but she realized straightaway that it would be unbelievable. Things were getting so much better between her and Duncan. She couldn't risk being found out and jeopardizing that progress. She had been going to tell him about Nancy's diaries all along. Now it would just be sooner than she had intended.

'Oh Lord,' she said. 'I put it in there. I never meant it to get washed! What a hideous mess.'

'But what i-i-is it?' Duncan said. 'And why p-put it there?'

'It's one of Nancy Sedgemoor's diaries,' Phoebe confessed. 'I found them in her flat when we went there that time, and I thought they'd be interesting so I brought them home.'

Duncan frowned. 'You didn't s-say,' he said. 'Why the s-s-secrecy?' He dropped the ruined diary into the bin and turned to confront her. 'What is all this?' he demanded.

'I'm sorry, Duncan. I *was* going to tell you about them,' Phoebe said earnestly. 'Please believe me. I was just waiting until the right moment. I've been reading through them, you see, and I used to hide them in there during the day to keep them safe . . .'

'To stop me from f-f-finding them, you mean,' Duncan said icily.

'No,' Phoebe said. 'Well . . . yes, I suppose so.' It had seemed harmless enough at the time. Now she saw only how shabby it must appear to Duncan. 'There's something else I was going to tell you as well,' she said. 'It's *good* news.'

'Go on.' Duncan was still regarding her coldly.

'It's about Nancy's bestiary,' Phoebe said, plunging in as a desperate attempt to put things right. 'I found it with the diaries and I rescued it too. It's –'

'You've got the b-b-b-bestiary?' Duncan sounded incredulous.

'Yes,' Phoebe said. Surely he would be pleased to hear it was safe? 'So you'll be able to sell it and give lots of money to all your brothers – except Brendan – and it won't matter any more about the –'

'Show me where it i-i-is.' His voice was curt.

Phoebe led him upstairs to their bedroom and pulled her trunk and from under the bed. Then she opened it, rummaged inside it and brought out the bestiary. Duncan almost snatched it from her. He turned it over and over in his hands and opened it, examining it minutely.

'It's all right,' Phoebe said. 'I've looked after it really well.'

Duncan shot her a furious look. 'You shouldn't have d-done it,' was all he said, and still holding the bestiary he left the room.

Phoebe was taken aback. She looked down at the open trunk and at the diaries inside it. She regretted keenly the loss of one of them. Now the story was no longer complete. But there were still a dozen or so of them which she hadn't read. What if Duncan insisted on giving them to Hope, or refused to let her read them? He was obviously pretty upset by their sudden appearance. Phoebe decided not to risk being deprived of the end of the story. She was packing an overnight bag anyway, and on impulse she put the unread diaries in the bottom of it and covered them with clothes. She would keep them with her at all times, she decided. That way, she would be sure of them. She felt quite glad that she had had to tell Duncan her secret now. She was sure he'd be quite bucked about the bestiary once he'd got over the surprise.

She turned her attention to what she should wear that day. Nothing seemed to fit her properly any more, and the clothes which were possible were not black. Phoebe sighed deeply. She knew that everybody else would look the part. They would be simply dressed but elegantly right for the occasion and she, as usual, would feel inadequate. At least Duncan wouldn't notice her shortcomings, she thought wryly. He never noticed anything. In the end all she could find that was black was an old necklace which had belonged to her great-aunt. She would have to rely on that to lend her a suitable air of gravity. She fastened it round her neck and made a rueful face at her reflection in the mirror. Her hair was sticking out all wrong again.

The journey up to London was tense. Duncan couldn't bring himself to speak to Phoebe. He felt wholly betrayed. She was not to be trusted, and to him that one fact negated all other points in her favour. He found it hard to concentrate upon his driving, particularly as he wasn't used to Phoebe's car. He would rather have driven up in his old van, but he had been forced to admit to its unreliability lately. He found, all of a sudden, that he was bearing down too fast upon a line of cars in the middle lane and that at the same time he was being overtaken by a stream of faster cars. He was forced to brake hurriedly and too hard. Out of the corner of his eye he saw Phoebe instinctively braking too. She was bracing herself with both hands against the dashboard.

'Watch out!' she said urgently. 'Look, Duncan, you're not yourself. Why don't you stop at the next service station and let me drive?'

'No,' Duncan said. Serve her right if she's scared, he thought. Serve her bloody well right! Once in London he had difficulty several times in going in the right direction, and found himself in the wrong lane being sworn at or blasted by taxi and car horns. He glanced sideways. Phoebe was sitting rigidly, staring straight ahead with her face pale and set, saying nothing. When they finally pulled into the car park at the crematorium, she got out of the car without a word and went to join Hope, who was at the centre of a group of waiting mourners. Duncan was called over to join Conrad in another group and discovered that he would be helping to carry in his father's coffin.

To Phoebe it was a grisly ceremony with few redeeming features. The chapel was high and dark. The service was perfunctory with virtually no mention or celebration of Peter's life. Conrad read the only lesson in a brave unfaltering voice, and when it was time for the coffin to disappear by sliding through the marble archway to the great furnace beyond, it progressed in a series of undignified jerks as though someone had forgotten to oil the wheels. It was hard to believe that Peter was really inside that anonymous box, Phoebe thought, wiping her eyes surreptitiously.

'Where is death's sting? Where, Grave, thy victory?
I triumph still, if Thou abide with me.'

She hadn't thought she would cry, but the words caught in her throat as she sang and her eyes overflowed with emotion. She tried to see how Duncan was managing but he was sitting with

182

the other bearers and was out of sight behind a pillar. Hope was closer to her, surrounded by elderly family and friends. Phoebe watched her covertly. She looked positively regal. Black suited her and she was carrying the whole ordeal off with consummate dignity. In fact, Phoebe thought, she looks better than usual. Perhaps she's not sorry. Knowing what Phoebe knew, it was not such an outrageous thought.

There was no sign of Fay. Phoebe had hoped against hope that she would be there, but realized that it was unlikely. Jack was too young to attend such an occasion and she would not have come on her own account out of respect for Conrad's feelings. Her two daughters were there, sitting beside their father. Conrad looked thinner, Phoebe thought. Rick had arrived late. He looked strained too. Phoebe didn't look forward to facing him in person. She hadn't seen him since Poppy had taken his boys. Brendan was absent. She supposed that he must be at sea. Presumably he knew about the will. Perhaps that was why he wasn't there. At the end, as they all filed out, Phoebe found herself next to Hereward and his children. He was wearing his usual baggy jersey and jeans. Phoebe looked round for Becky but couldn't see her.

'Hi, Phoebe,' he said. 'You're staying with us tonight, yes?'

'Yes, if that's all right with you,' Phoebe said. 'The flat is full of ancient aunts and cousins apparently.'

'Fine,' Herry said. He squeezed her arm. 'See you later then.'

Phoebe was glad to emerge into the graveyard at the back of the chapel. It was a cold grey day with spots of rain, but there was a large quince bush growing on the south wall, bearing masses of brilliant scarlet flowers which seemed defiantly cheerful in spite of its sombre surroundings. There were funeral flowers too, arranged in a block with Peter's name at their centre and cards with messages of condolence. Phoebe walked over and pretended to inspect them, but was actually waiting for Duncan to appear. Where was he?

She had been furious with him for driving so badly on the way up. It had been almost as if he were doing it on purpose; trying to scare her. But she had felt constrained by the situation to conceal what she was really thinking. It had taken her some time before she could trust herself to speak calmly to him, and by the time she had regained her composure he had disappeared. Phoebe hadn't known in advance where the bearers would sit, and she had found herself propelled with the rest of the congregation right to the far side of the chapel. There she had felt isolated and dismayed at her inability to share the service close at hand with Duncan. She asked herself why they had had to have such a stupid row today of all days, and all because Duncan had been trying to please her! Sod's law, she thought bitterly.

After a certain amount of standing about, the mourners organized themselves into cars and drove to the hotel where Conrad had arranged a buffet. Phoebe saw Duncan driving past with the blue car full of people, but he did not seem to notice her. She felt close to tears again. She accepted a lift and found herself sitting next to Purple Hat who this time was wearing a smart Black Watch tam-o'-shanter trimmed with heavy black braid. The old lady patted Phoebe's hand encouragingly, understandably misconstruing the cause of her brimming eyes.

'He had a good life,' she said. 'He probably enjoyed every minute of it.'

'Oh,' Phoebe said, gathering her wits, 'yes. I'm sure he did.'

'Are those jet?' she asked, pointing.

'Yes.' Phoebe touched the cold black stones at her neck.

'Very suitable,' the old lady said approvingly. 'Exactly the right thing to wear to a funeral.' Phoebe could have hugged her.

Duncan survived the funeral service without making a spectacle of himself but when they arrived at the hotel afterwards, he found himself faced by crowds of people, most of whom seemed to feel obliged to talk sympathetically to him about his father, and it all became too much. He stuck it for five minutes and then slipped out. He didn't feel up to facing people, so he wouldn't. It was as simple as that.

He hadn't seen Phoebe since they arrived at the crematorium, and for that he was grateful. He wouldn't have known how to act or what to say to her. He could barely cope with his churned up feelings about her; they were so powerfully negative and so final. She had deceived him and his whole family. She had lied and stolen and she was not to be trusted. No one could have any sort of a relationship with a person after they'd done that. It was out of the question, and there was an end to it. Their marriage had been a mistake right from the beginning. He had been conned into it. Well, he would be conned no further! He would make it clear that she was no longer welcome in his cottage, but first . . . Yes! Duncan thought, getting into the blue car and slamming the door. First I'll rifle the place and find out what else she's been hiding from me.

He drove aggressively, changing lanes and blaring his horn with the worst of them, and got out of London surprisingly quickly. There was not much traffic on the M4 as he drove west, nor on the M5 as he swung southwards round the north of Bristol. He got back to the cottage in record time. It was past six o'clock, too late to collect Diggory from the kennels, and the place felt empty without his bouncy welcome. It was cold and dark and there wasn't anything much to eat. Duncan lit the stove, heated up some baked beans in a saucepan and made two bits of toast to put them on. He felt hard done by and absolutely justified in what he planned to do.

After he had eaten, he went upstairs to the bedroom and dragged Phoebe's trunk out from under the bed. He picked out one of Nancy's diaries and opened it at random:

All Hugh's faults are sins of omission rather than those of commission, *Nancy had written*, but that doesn't in my eyes make them any less serious. They're just less obvious, so one gets less sympathy from family and friends! Men always seem to get away with that sort of failure, but a woman in the same circumstances would be pilloried for it.

Duncan threw it down in disgust. As he had supposed, it was typical navel-gazing feminist rubbish. He didn't want to read it and he didn't think it right that anyone else should. Nancy was dead. It was all irrelevant now.

He turned his attention to the other things in the trunk. There were bundles of letters and packets of photographs from Phoebe's past. There was a tatty straw hat, a teddy bear and a pair of sunglasses with one lens missing. There was even what looked like a pile of old vests! Duncan picked up the top one with clumsy fingers to cast it aside, when something solid fell out of it. It was a long cream-coloured plastic object, about the same size as a torch but with a smooth rounded blind end. Duncan had never seen one before but he realized with a shock after a few seconds what it must be. All his sexual inadequacies crowded in upon him at that moment. It was Phoebe's fault that he felt like this! Before he met her he had known that he was entirely normal. Then she had started upon him, criticizing him, expecting miracles, obviously disappointed in his capacities, making him feel like some sort of freak, undermining his confidence. And all the time it was she who was abnormal! What was she, some sort of nymphomaniac?

Duncan threw the vibrator back into the trunk in revulsion. He had intended to destroy the diaries, but now the whole contents of the trunk disgusted him. He dragged it roughly through the door and bumped it down the stairs to the kitchen. Then he got the burnables bin from the cupboard and emptied out its contents into it. He picked up a box of matches and an opened packet of firelighters and threw them in too. Then he opened the back door and pulled the trunk out after him into the night.

It was dry outside but cold and the wind blew his first match out, so Duncan had to crouch in the middle of the paddock to shield the next one with his body. Then he stood in the darkness and watched with satisfaction as the flames took hold. The trunk burnt like a bomb. It had been made of plywood and canvas with bent wooden ribs on the outside, holding it together. Duncan had had a very similar trunk at school, and it delighted him now to see one burn. He wondered how Phoebe had come to own it. She had not been away to school. She's not one of us, Duncan thought. I ought to have recognized that at the outset. Then he went indoors, found an unopened bottle which had belonged to his father, and drank a large quantity of whisky.

When the telephone rang later on, he was beginning to feel mellower but desperately tired. He dragged himself over to the phone and recognized Herry's voice with mild surprise.

'What on earth are you doing there?' Herry asked. 'You're

supposed to be here. Phoebe's got herself all upset, worrying about you.'

'I live here,' Duncan said. It seemed to him to be rather a clever remark and he giggled at his own wit.

'Are you all right?' Herry asked.

' 'Course I am.'

'Phoebe says you've gone off with all her things in the boot of the car. She hasn't even got a change of knickers!'

Duncan thought of the vests and their hidden, lewd contents. 'Oh that won't stop her,' he said sarcastically.

'Duncan? You're drunk!' Herry said. 'But as long as you're okay that's what matters. I'll tell Phoebe you're safe at home.'

'Tell her what you like,' Duncan said. 'I don't care.'

Chapter Seventeen

Phoebe felt encouraged by the old lady she still thought of as Purple Hat, and newly determined not to be put down by Duncan's indifference. She caught sight of him by the buffet in the hotel but decided that she was not going to crawl to him. If he didn't want to acknowledge her, then she would bloody well ignore him too. She felt angry and resentful that he should let something as trivial as the discovery of the diaries and bestiary prevent the two of them from supporting each other as a couple on this difficult day. Phoebe considered it childish and unworthy of him, but her pride wouldn't let her show it. If he didn't need her, then she would show him that she didn't need him either!

In this militant mood, Phoebe eased herself through the crowd and went to talk to Rick.

'Hello,' he said, 'sad occasion.' He put his arm round a young, pretty West Indian girl at his side and drew her forwards. 'Meet Treasure,' he said. 'This is probably not the right moment to say this, but Treasure and I have decided to live together.'

'Oh,' Phoebe said. The girl smiled shyly at her. She looked about eighteen! Phoebe wanted to warn her off; tell her about the fate of her predecessors, but all she managed was a weak, 'Welcome to the Moon family.'

'Thanks,' Treasure said, barely above a whisper. She looked up at Rick with lustrous brown eyes, and he pinched her cheek gently like a benevolent old uncle. Dirty old man! Phoebe thought, disgusted.

'Have you heard from the boys?' she asked him, smothering her disapproval. 'I still kick myself for not realizing what was going on that day.'

'How could you?' Rick said casually, and to her surprise: 'Don't give it another thought, Phoebe. I shall get them back, you'll see. I've got the best lawyer. It's just a matter of time.

Now, Treasure, my treasure, pluck up your courage and come and meet Mother.' They moved off. Phoebe tried to imagine how the poor girl would get on with Rod and Pete when – if – they returned, and failed. She was amazed that Rick could change so quickly from Distraught Father to Proud Sugar Daddy, but then, she supposed, that was the nature of actors. She wished she'd known it before. She need not have got herself into such a state!

When she spoke to Conrad, Phoebe found herself feeling quite sympathetic to him. He was very composed, but when she murmured how sorry she was about his father, his eyes filled briefly with tears and looked extra blue as Duncan's had.

'Have you seen Fay lately?' she asked him.

'We've spoken on the phone. She tells me you've been to her flat.'

'Ye-es' Phoebe felt guarded.

'It's all right,' Conrad said, 'she's told me where it is, and in any case she's not staying there much longer. It's too far from Jack's nursery school and too awkward for his nanny. Fay's moving back home this weekend.'

'But that's good!' Phoebe said with enthusiasm. 'I'm so glad for you.'

'Oh, I shan't be there,' Conrad said at once. 'I've been offered a twelve-month contract in Saudi. Very convenient, really. I'm off on Friday.'

'So you're still splitting up then?' Phoebe said, disappointed.

' 'Fraid so. It's been brewing for years, in fact.'

'I'm really sorry.'

'Oh well, these things happen.'

Phoebe was once again struck by the apparent shallowness of Moon emotions. Perhaps he did care, but was able to conceal it? Phoebe couldn't imagine anyone being indifferent to the loss of someone like Fay. Did he know about her affairs? Was that why? Phoebe decided that she must see Fay herself soon, and make her peace with her. Perhaps the next day Duncan would agree to a slight detour so that she could just pop in and talk to her for five minutes. No good, Phoebe remembered. Tomorrow is Thursday; she'll be at work. I'll just have to ring her from Herry's.

189

'Ah, Phoebe,' Hope said, appearing beside her with several elderly ladies in tow. 'I don't believe you've met my cousins.' She turned to them. 'This is Duncan's wife. Where is Duncan, by the way?'

'I haven't seen him,' Phoebe said, shaking hands all round.

'I do hope he hasn't disappeared,' Hope said with asperity. 'That would be so like him!' Phoebe had never heard her mother-in-law criticize Duncan before, and she felt surprised and rather pleased.

'I could go and find him for you?' she offered.

'No matter,' Hope said almost cheerfully. 'Have you tried the food? It's really rather good.'

It was not until the funeral party began to disperse that Phoebe realized Duncan was really not there. She supposed he had gone on ahead, and would be waiting for them at Herry's, but when she and Herry and the children arrived they found an empty house with no one on the doorstep.

'Where on earth can Duncan be?' Phoebe asked, worried.

'He's probably buggered off home,' Herry said, 'if I know him. We'll ring him later. No point now; he'll still be on the road.'

'I do hope you're right,' Phoebe said. 'Oh no!'

'What?'

'He's got my bag in the car. I haven't even got a toothbrush with me!' Or the diaries, she thought worriedly.

'You can borrow stuff from Becky,' Herry said, leading the way indoors and kicking aside various cardboard boxes full of junk. 'No worries.'

'Where is Becky?' Phoebe said. 'I've been meaning to ask.'

'She's taken African leave,' Herry said easily. 'Same as the French sort, but darker,' he laughed. Phoebe looked round at the three teenagers to see what their reaction to this was. They looked quite unconcerned. They threw their coats onto the hooks in the hallway and ambled upstairs in a huddle arguing amiably about whether cremation was preferable to burial.

'God no! Think of the *worms*,' one said, and their bedroom doors banged behind them.

'Come into the kitchen,' Herry said to her. 'I'll find us

something to drink.' Phoebe sat down at the large pine table and watched as Herry uncorked a bottle of red wine and poured two generous glasses full.

'Don't you mind?' Phoebe asked him.

'About what?'

'Becky and her poet.'

'Not at all. Why should I?'

'You don't get jealous?' Phoebe persisted.

'Dreary bourgeois habit. No, we don't own each other. No one does.'

'And do you do the same?'

'If I get a good offer.' He was smiling widely at her, quite unembarrassed and amused at her bewilderment. Phoebe remembered something she had always wanted to ask him.

'Why did you get expelled from school?' she said.

'I impregnated the assistant matron.'

'*What?*' Phoebe was scandalized.

'Oh, she had an abortion,' Herry said reassuringly. 'I shouldn't have fancied being a father at fifteen.'

'But how old was she?' Phoebe asked, visualizing a portly 50-year-old.

'Nineteen or so,' Herry said. 'She was a sort of trainee. Nice girl. Got married six months later, or so I believe.'

'But Duncan said it was "some prank or other",' Phoebe protested. 'I'd hardly call getting a woman pregnant a prank.'

'Dear old-fashioned Duncan,' Herry said. 'He so hates to call a spade a spade. What's the wine like?'

'It's fine,' Phoebe said, still disconcerted.

'Should be, I nicked it from Con. He fancies himself as a bit of an epicure, I believe.'

'It's sad about him and Fay,' Phoebe said, drinking deeply.

'Yeah, but Con, straight-up pillar of society that he is, could never cope with someone AC/DC like Fay. He's basically a simple creature. I expect he was shocked.'

'And you weren't?'

'Takes a lot to shock me.'

'Does Duncan know, about Fay?'

'Doubt it. He's a bit like Queen Victoria. He can't imagine it; therefore it doesn't happen.'

Phoebe laughed. Herry intrigued her. She wondered if he knew his father was a bishop.

'Poor Duncan,' she said. 'He's really upset about Peter.'

'We all are,' Herry said.

'Were you fond of him?' Phoebe asked.

'What a question!' Herry said. 'Of course I was. He was my father.'

So he doesn't know, Phoebe thought. Blood isn't thicker than water. I bet he would be shocked if I told him! Then she thought, No I've no right to interfere like that. I'll keep quiet.

'More wine?' Herry asked.

'Thanks.'

Phoebe went on sitting at the kitchen table while Herry cooked the supper. She found it hard to believe that Duncan had really gone home without her, and kept expecting him to turn up at the house. He surely wouldn't disappear without a word to anyone? She worried about it all through supper, which was spaghetti bolognese and very good. Herry's children treated her as one of themselves and were friendly but casual. At the end of the meal they got to their feet and wandered off without a word.

'Washing up,' Herry called after them.

'Come off it, Dad! We've got piles of homework.'

'I'll do it,' Phoebe offered, and they put their thumbs up and disappeared upstairs again. Loud rock music started beating above Phoebe's head as she brushed the plates and cutlery in the hot soapy water. Duncan still hadn't appeared. He must be home by now, if that was where he had gone. She wanted to know that he was safe, but she didn't want to have another argument with him, especially not over the phone. She sighed heavily.

'That sounded very heartfelt,' Herry said behind her. He was drying the clean plates and putting them into a cupboard above his head.

'I'm really worried about Duncan,' Phoebe said, 'but I . . .'

'Shall I give him a ring?' Herry offered.

'Oh *yes*, would you?'

Phoebe thought, He must have realized that I didn't want to

192

phone, so he offered to do it for me. Duncan could never be so sensitive! It just isn't in his make-up, yet it seems to come naturally to Herry. Herry was already on the telephone. She could hear the sound of his voice in the hall but not what he was saying, and then the ting as he put the phone down.

'He's pissed,' Herry said, coming back in. 'But he is there, and he is in one piece, as far as I can tell.'

'Thank you so much,' Phoebe said, deeply relieved. 'You are kind.'

'You two been having trouble?' Herry asked.

'Just a bit,' Phoebe acknowledged, biting her lip.

'You should have an open arrangement like mine,' Herry said. 'It's far less complicated. Why don't you leave those saucepans and come and sit down with me. We've wine to finish.' He led the way over to a cluttered sofa by the fire and threw papers and clothes off it onto the floor, before patting the seat beside him as an invitation to her to join him. 'Tell Uncle Herry all about it,' he said.

He was so easy to talk to. Phoebe could hardly believe that he was Duncan's brother. She found she could ask him anything she wanted and he didn't turn a hair. Sometime, hours later, she asked what it had been like when Brendan joined them as children.

'We were pretty foul to him,' Herry admitted. 'We looked up the meaning of his name and taunted him with it for years.'

'What does it mean?'

'Stinking hair,' Herry said, grinning.

'How rotten!' Phoebe said, pretending indignation.

'We were,' Herry said, 'but we've got our comeuppance now.'

'In the will, you mean?'

'Yep.'

'Will you contest it?'

'Yes, I think so. We've got six months to do it in. I was hoping to discuss it with Duncan tonight.'

'Do it by phone,' Phoebe said. 'It'll be quicker.'

'No stammering, you mean? That's not very kind!'

Phoebe burst into tears. 'I'm not kind,' she sobbed. 'I'm horrible to him, but I can't seem to stop. He's so *infuriating*!'

Herry put both arms round her and held her close to him. He

did it in such a calm and confident way that Phoebe was instantly comforted. He felt strong and secure and in command of things, and she found herself relaxing into his embrace. He might look scruffy, she thought irrelevantly, but he smells of Pears soap! Herry stroked her hair until she had finished hiccupping and then he felt about in his jeans pocket and produced a clean white handkerchief for her to dry her eyes on.

'Bed time,' he said firmly. 'Come on.' He led her upstairs and showed her into the large untidy room which she had last shared with Duncan when they came up to see Nancy Sedgemoor's flat. 'Have a good sleep,' Herry advised her. 'No hurry in the morning. I'm working at home tomorrow. Night night.' Then he bent over and kissed her lightly at the top of her nose, and withdrew.

Phoebe took a long breath and looked about her. The room was a complete shambles as usual. She walked across to the double bed and pulled the duvet back, fearing the worst. The bottom sheet was tight and clean. The pillowcases had creases in them from where they had been folded after ironing. It was even warm! Phoebe heaved a great sigh of relief, threw all her clothes onto the floor, switched off the electric blanket, and crawled thankfully inside. The rock music was still pounding out next door, but it didn't disturb her. She was out for the count.

In the middle of the night she woke with a bursting bladder, and groped her way in a borrowed dressing gown to the lavatory. Her tongue tasted foul so she rinsed her mouth out with water and rubbed her teeth with a forefinger and an inch of stolen toothpaste. Then she went back to bed and lay there thinking about Herry. She had never considered him as a man before, only as a brother-in-law. He was undoubtedly very attractive. Phoebe wondered why she had never noticed it until now. She lay there enjoying the feel of the smooth warm sheets on her skin, and began to invent a scenario in which Herry came into the bedroom in the dark and, mistaking her for Becky, started to make long, athletic, silent, *dominant* love to her . . . After a very short time she was wide awake and tingling in every muscle with anticipation, so she was obliged to make herself come several times to defuse the tension and bring her fantasy to its natural conclusion. Then, exhausted, she slept again.

At eleven o'clock the next morning, Herry climbed the stairs with two mugs of coffee and went into his spare bedroom. Phoebe was still asleep and all but invisible under the duvet. He put the mugs down on a wooden bedside table which was covered in a pattern of pale heat circles like a dislocated Olympic Games logo. He sat on the foot of the bed, bouncing it up and down.

'Coffee time,' he announced loudly. 'Let's be having you!'

'What time is it?' Phoebe asked blearily, emerging into a sitting position and then remembering that she had no clothes on. She jerked the duvet up to cover herself, and Herry got to his feet again briefly to let it slide under him, but not before he had had a good view of a pair of large white breasts with smooth pink nipples. He regarded her with amusement.

'Gone eleven,' he said. 'The kids have been at school for hours. Some people have an amazing capacity for sleep! I've brought you a coffee, since I was making one for myself.' He reached forward, and, picking up his own mug took a drink. He wondered how long it was since she'd had a good fuck. She looked as though she could do with one, poor girl. She had marvellous skin, he thought, very fine textured, almost hairless, velvet smooth . . .

Phoebe reached out and took her mug and drank from it, looking at him thoughtfully over the rim.

'Herry,' she said, putting it down suddenly.

'Phoebe?'

'Do you think I'm at all attractive?' Having said this she clearly wished she hadn't, because she blushed scarlet and looked down at her hands. They were clutching the duvet.

Hey up! Herry thought to himself. I'm in with a chance here.

'From where I'm sitting,' he said, 'you look positively irresistible.'

'Don't tease,' she said, with still-lowered eyes. 'I want to know, seriously.'

'Right,' Herry said, 'in that case I have to tell you that I find you seriously attractive. That do?'

'Honestly?'

'Cross my heart.'

She looked up at him with a tremulous smile. 'I don't know how to do this sort of thing,' she said. 'I never have before.'

'Were you, by any happy chance considering making me an offer I couldn't refuse?' Herry's underpants felt several sizes too small.

'Well I . . . Yes, I suppose I was . . .'

'I consider that to be very charming of you,' Herry said, putting his mug down and then bending low over her. 'I don't think I've ever had a better invitation.' Her lips, when he kissed them, parted a little. They too were full, in fact everything about her was generous. She helped him with some eagerness to take his clothes off, and she pulled him inside her with such enthusiasm that he nearly lost his famous control.

'Wait!' he commanded her. 'Take it slowly . . . very slowly . . . like this.'

She was a real peach, Herry thought, a ripe juicy peach just made for the job. She didn't seem to have any bones, unlike Becky! He thought about Becky briefly and without any particular emotion. He hoped she was having as good a time as he was. Afterwards as he and Phoebe lay together, he thought about Duncan and wondered how he could neglect such a prime source of pleasure. He shook his head. He would never understand his brothers, any of them. Perhaps he had been switched at birth.

'What are you smiling at?' Phoebe asked him.

'I think I'm a changeling,' he told her.

She giggled. 'Well, they say a changeling's as good as a rest,' she said.

Fay was just about to go to a meeting when the call from Phoebe was put through to her.

'I'm sorry about bothering you at work,' Phoebe said, all in a rush. 'I just wanted to tell you that I don't care about what you told me, I just want us to be friends like we were before.'

196

'That's very good news,' Fay said carefully, conscious that she could be overheard.

'And I'd really love to see you again soon,' Phoebe said entreatingly.

'Of course. Are you all right?'

'Not really. I've just done something incredibly stupid, just to prove a point which didn't need proving. I don't know what came over me! And Duncan and I have had a row and I'm just going home now to make it up. I'm not worried about that; I'm sure it will be all right. It's the other thing . . .'

'Where are you?'

'At Paddington. My train goes in five minutes. Herry even had to lend me the money for the phone. I felt such a fool . . .'

'What's Herry got to do with this?'

'We were staying there after the funeral, but Duncan —' Rapid pips announced imminent cut-off. 'No more money,' Phoebe said hurriedly. 'Sorry. See you soo —'

Fay put the receiver down thoughtfully. Of course, they would all have gathered for Peter's funeral. She wondered how it had gone. She picked up her briefcase and walked along the corridor towards the committee room with a light step, and only when she went inside and saw the answering smiles on the faces of her waiting staff, did she realize that she was grinning from ear to ear.

Chapter Eighteen

Phoebe wanted very much to go on talking to Fay, but she needed to keep some change to phone Duncan from the station at the end of her journey. She saw that she would have just enough. She could use her credit card to buy her ticket, and, with luck, Duncan would meet her at the other end. She found it almost intolerable to be without any income of her own. The sooner she got herself a new job, the better it would be.

I seem to be making a habit of anxious train journeys, she thought, settling herself into a window seat and watching as Paddington Station slid backwards out of her view. She stared out of the window with unfocused eyes, letting the London suburbs coalesce into a long grey blur as the train gathered speed. She felt soiled and remorseful. She had come back to reality suddenly and with a shock of self-disgust when Herry had climbed out of bed that afternoon and said something which shook her to the core.

Up to then, it had been a kind of game, an ego trip, an acting out of the fantasy of the previous night. She had wanted to be desirable again; worthy of love. She wanted the reassurance that she could still be important to a man. She longed to be totally uninhibited again, appreciated by and completely at one with someone. She wanted to throw herself into lovemaking with all her former verve and enthusiasm; to forget everything in the excitement of the moment. So she had done so, and it had worked! She had offered herself to him with no reservations, and all her self-confidence had been magically restored. She lay in his arms feeling the old familiar mixture of triumph and exhaustion. Their skin was welded together by drying sweat. Her left arm was squashed by his weight and tingling with pins and needles, but she didn't care. She noticed that Herry was grinning away to himself and asked him why, and then made some feeble pun, and they both laughed. It had seemed entirely right, innocent even.

Then Herry rolled over her to look at his watch and said, 'This is no good. I've got work to do,' and extricated himself gently from her embrace and began to pull his clothes on. As he pushed his arms into the sleeves and then dragged his shirt over his head without undoing any of its buttons, he said casually, 'One of these days I suppose I really ought to get around to so-called safe sex.'

The train was going along parallel to the Downs. Phoebe could just make out the long cat-like shape of the Uffington White Horse, cut into the chalk on the brow of the distant ridge of hills. She made a point of looking out for it every trip, for good luck, but today it gave her no pleasure. All she could think, over and over again, was that for the first time in her life she had been unfaithful and that it hadn't been lovemaking at all. She had 'had sex' and that was all it was. It didn't mean that she was desirable or loved or any of the things she needed to feel. It didn't prove anything. Even unpleasant, ugly, undeserving people had sex. You only had to look about you in a railway carriage, clamorous with tiresome undisciplined children, to see the evidence for that. But worse, far worse, had been Phoebe's sudden comprehension of the network of relationships which she had carelessly joined. She hadn't just gone to bed with Herry, but with all the other women he might have bedded, and with all the men that Becky had ever had. Any one of these could be a carrier of disease: hepatitis or herpes . . . but especially AIDS. It was not a problem Phoebe had ever had to contemplate before. No one she had ever known in Northumberland or in Somerset had those sorts of illnesses, but in London . . . She had been lulled into a false sense of security because Herry was family. Now she saw him more as a casual stranger with a high-risk life-style. He could be bisexual too for all she knew, which would make it a thousand times worse. What if I've caught AIDS? she kept thinking, panic-stricken. How could I have been so *stupid*?

Duncan was beginning to feel bad about having burnt Phoebe's trunk, but salved his conscience with the thought that some punishment was entirely justifiable. Now that he had calmed down a bit, he could see that there were advantages in discovering the bestiary after his father's death rather than before it. If it truly was worth as much as Peter had suggested, then the problem of the will faded into insignificance. He and his brothers could afford to be generous to Brendan and there would be a lot less fuss. Secondly he had burnt all those unsuitable diaries – he so disapproved of people writing down their every transient whinge. It lent them a significance out of all proportion to their real pettiness – so at least that chapter was closed. The only thing that still caused him unease was the thought that Phoebe might never have confessed to having taken those things secretly from Nancy's flat. How could he be sure that she was telling him the truth when she said she had intended to tell him all along? How could he trust her?

He wondered idly what had happened after he had absented himself from the funeral. He supposed that Phoebe would eventually find her way home again, but he was not concerned to think about how she would do it. That was up to her. He wasn't any longer planning to throw her out. That was something he had contemplated in the heat of the moment, and he now saw it to be unreasonable. He would just have to watch her in future and make it impossible for her to cheat him again.

He thought it all out as he dug a client's vegetable patch. It should have been done the autumn before and it was really too wet. Each spit of clay soil was heavy and stuck to the spade. It was also infested with the brittle white roots of bindweed, each broken-off section of which was capable of growing into a new plant. It was slow going but he wanted to get shot of the job, so he continued to dig as the light faded and went on until it was too dark to see what he was doing.

When he finally got home to the cottage, the lights were on inside and one of the panes of glass in the kitchen window was broken. He went inside cautiously, holding Diggory back by his collar, in case it was burglars. Phoebe was sitting with her elbows on the kitchen table, cradling a mug of coffee in both hands.

'Where have you been?' she demanded at once. 'I kept ringing from Weston Station but you didn't answer, so in the end I had to get a taxi, which cost me twelve quid that I haven't got, and then you weren't here to pay him, so I had to write a cheque and he was really sniffy about taking it.'

Duncan sighed. Here we go, he thought. 'Well, you're h-home now,' he said.

'No thanks to you. Why did you go off without me like that? I couldn't believe you had!'

'It's n-not i-i-important,' Duncan said. 'What happened to the w-window?'

'I had to break it to get in. I didn't take my keys with me, because I knew you had one . . . And anyway, it *is* important to me, Duncan. I wanted to be with you at the funeral — face it together and all that. I'm sorry you had to find out about the diaries just then, but it shouldn't have separated us just at the moment when we most needed to be together.' She looked pleadingly at him. 'Come on, Duncan, we've been doing so much better lately. Don't let's screw it up now.'

She looked as though she meant it, Duncan thought. After all, she could have told me about the diaries and not mentioned the bestiary. I'd never have known. She could even have sold it and hidden the money, but she didn't . . .

'Well?' Phoebe asked.

'The thing i-is,' Duncan said hesitantly, 'how do I know that you r-really were g-going to tell me e-everything?'

Phoebe made a kind of despairing face and put her mug down firmly on the table. 'You don't,' she said, 'unless you trust what I say. I was going to tell you, but the mess in the washing machine made it happen sooner than I planned, and that's the truth. What more can I say?'

'So you have a-a-absolutely no s-s-secrets from me now?' He looked directly at her, challenging her to be straightforward with him. He was sure she blushed. Her eyes didn't waver from his, but her cheeks got redder and her whole body looked tense.

'No,' she said.

'N-None at all?'

'None.'

He supposed that would have to do, even though it didn't satisfy him. He didn't know what else to say. So he began his

201

usual displacement activity; when in doubt, put the kettle on. 'More tea?' he asked.

'It's coffee, but I'd like another cup, thanks.' She had relaxed again. Her shoulders had dropped and her voice sounded less tight. She is still hiding something from me, Duncan thought uneasily.

When Phoebe had got home, one of the first things she had done after getting into the cottage and unlocking the front door, was to open the boot of the blue Polo and look for her overnight bag. It was still there. Duncan must have forgotten about it. She looked inside, pulling her clothes out in handfuls to check that the diaries were still hidden underneath. They were. She breathed a quick breath of relief. Then she went back indoors and swept up the broken glass with a dustpan and brush, wrapped it carefully in newspaper to render it safe, and put it in the bin. Duncan would be able to reglaze the window. It was no problem. She wondered where the hell he was. It was far too dark outside for him still to be working, surely? Then, as she sat down to a much-needed coffee, she heard his van in the lane.

She rehearsed her new resolutions in her head. There were things she needed to ask him, but she was not going to quarrel with him. She knew she had behaved badly, but it was not too late to retrieve the situation. She would try to forget all about Herry and concentrate on her marriage to Duncan, and if, please God, she had got away with it and had not caught AIDS, then life could go on as before. It would just be one of those crazy mistakes everyone makes at least once in a lifetime, which serves to bring you up short and makes you consider your priorities.

Good intentions are all very well, she thought later, but they so easily get brushed aside. When Duncan had actually come into the kitchen, Phoebe felt all her irritations with him return. She had had to bite her lip after a couple of unanswered questions, to prevent herself from launching straight into another argument. Then he had challenged her about secrets and she thought at once of sex with Herry, but had looked him steadfastly in the eye and hoped against hope that her confusion didn't show. She drank her second cup of coffee quickly and then went upstairs. She was dying to change out of her funeral clothes at last. In the bedroom, she put on clean underclothes, her baggy jeans and sweatshirt and felt straightaway more like her real self. Then she looked under the bed. No trunk. So I was right, she thought, he has done something with the diaries. Thank goodness I've got at least some of them safe. But what about the rest of the things?

'Duncan?' she called from the top of the stairs. No answer. She went down into the kitchen. He was bent over the stove, lighting the fire. 'Where's my trunk?' she asked him.

He wouldn't look at her. 'I g-got rid of i-it,' he said.

'Yes, but where?'

'In the p-paddock'.

'Outside? But it'll get ruined in the rain!'

'No,' Duncan said, 'it's b-b-b-burnt.'

'What?' Phoebe stared at him in horror. 'You burnt my trunk? But what did you do with all my things?' Duncan didn't answer. 'You didn't burn them all up too?' Duncan was still silent. 'You did! How *could* you?' She looked down at him wildly. 'But it belonged to my father. He had it at university and I kept all the things he ever gave me in it. All my old photographs . . . and letters . . . and GCE certificates . . . and my teddy bear . . . all my past . . . everything! How could you destroy that when it means so much to me? *How could you?*' She ran at him with fists flailing, meaning to hurt him in any way that she could. Duncan reached out and imprisoned her right hand easily in his own, but in trying to grab the other, he caught her an accidental glancing blow just on the ridge of her left eyebrow. She gasped with pain and then, wrenching herself free from him she ran back towards the stairs, followed by a prancing, barking Diggory who thought it was a game.

'I hate you,' she screamed. Then she slammed the door at the bottom of the stairs and stumbled up to the bedroom.

Fay was happy to be back in her own home again. Living in someone else's space always felt like camping, and she had been terrified that Jack would break some priceless artefact in spite of

203

her precautionary measures. She was glad to distance herself from the flat for other reasons as well. It brought back too many memories; it made her look to the past instead of to the future. Jack also seemed pleased to be home again and in a familiar routine. His nanny came daily and took him to nursery school or swimming or junior judo. He was also going regularly to the speech therapist that Phoebe had told her about, and it really did seem to be working. Things, Fay thought, were settling down nicely. Then Phoebe had telephoned in a great state of upset, saying that she couldn't stand living with Duncan for a moment longer and could she please stay with them for a while? Better and better!

Fay made up a bed for her in the spare room and moved clothes to make spaces in the wardrobe and chests of drawers. Then she went out into the garden with Jack to pick a little posy of spring flowers, winter jasmine, celandines and primroses, for Phoebe's dressing table. Fay wondered what had happened and whether Phoebe had walked out on Duncan for good, or was just taking a break from him. Either way, she sounded as though she needed cosseting. Fay planned to cook her special meals in the evenings and generally give her a much-needed boost.

When Phoebe arrived, in mid-afternoon, Fay was shocked by her appearance. She came into the hall with a suitcase in each hand and smiled weakly at her.

'Whatever happened to you?' Fay asked.

'Duncan hit me,' Phoebe said.

'Duncan did?' Fay was astonished. 'You poor little thing, but that's awful.' She hesitated and then held her arms out. Phoebe came forward gratefully and they hugged.

'I'm so glad to see you,' Phoebe said in muffled heartfelt tones.

'Stay as long as you like,' Fay said, holding her at arm's length and studying her with concern. 'We'll look after you, won't we, Jack?' Jack had come halfway downstairs, until his face was just above Phoebe's.

'You've got a big ow,' he observed.

'Yes,' Phoebe said. 'It's a black eye.'

'No, it isn't,' Jack said. 'It's a p-purple and yellow one.'

'Jack kiss it better?' Fay suggested.

Jack knelt down and put his hands through the banisters. Then he pulled Phoebe's face carefully towards him, holding her cheeks in his palms, before planting a soft, wet kiss on her swollen eyelid. 'All right now,' he said with satisfaction.

'Thank you, Jack,' Phoebe said, smiling up at him. 'That makes me feel very all right.'

'You're honoured,' Fay said. 'I think it means you're accepted.'

Phoebe stayed with Fay in London for most of March, and during that time she did not get in touch with Duncan once. At first she slept late every morning and stayed in her room alone after Fay had gone to work, reading Fay's books and some more of Nancy's diaries. She had now read all the continuous years which formed a complete record of Nancy's life from 25 to 41 years old, and had started on the disconnected part thereafter. There were a lot of years missing between 1962 and the time of her death in summer '91. This was the period when her affair with Peter had faltered and died, and she had been alone. Phoebe wondered if she had been too depressed to record her daily doings, or just too busy.

In the evenings after Jack had had his bath and a story, and gone to sleep, Phoebe talked to Fay. She told her everything that had happened, and was comforted by Fay's determination to see things entirely from her point of view, and not try to play devil's advocate for Duncan. In time she would be able to admit that he had points on his side as well, but at the moment she needed a sympathetic partisan like Fay. Fay reassured Phoebe that her fear of AIDS was in all likelihood unfounded, and that in any case there was nothing to be done at once, as it would be two months at the very least before a test would show a correct result.

Gradually the swelling on Phoebe's eye went down and the bruise faded. She met friends of Fay's and became included in her social circle. She was at first charmed by the ease with which she was accepted, and then worried about being a parasite.

'I ought to be paying for my keep,' she said rather desperately, 'and rent as well.'

'Don't worry about it,' Fay said easily. 'I've got to buy food for myself and Jack anyway. One more makes very little difference.'

'It's not right, though,' Phoebe insisted. 'It makes me feel uncomfortable.'

'So why not get a job?' Fay suggested.

'What here, in London?'

'Why not?'

'Well I hadn't really planned on staying that long. I mean, I always thought I'd get a job in the country. London isn't really me,' but even as she said it Phoebe realized that it was no longer entirely true. Fay's part of London was different from Rick's. It was more like a village but with all the advantages of the city. There were endless things to do and places to discover. There were interesting people to talk to and walks to be taken. There was even a garden with a rose arbour to sit in, and grass to lie on in summer. True, all the windows were lockable and there was a security system on the doors, but you could get used to that in time. Phoebe was even getting daring about driving around locally. On that first day when she had arrived with the blue Polo overloaded with her possessions, she had been terrified by the traffic and weak with relief when she had eventually discovered Fay's road and a parking space close by.

'I've got a friend who's a lecturer at UC,' Fay said. 'I could ask him if he knows of anything suitable. You were in a biology department before, weren't you?'

'Zoology,' Phoebe said.

'Of course there may be nothing,' Fay said, 'but it's worth a try.'

Fay was as intrigued by Nancy's diaries as Phoebe had been, and interested to find out more about Hope and Peter's past.

'It explains such a lot,' she kept saying, looking up from the pages. 'Conrad and Duncan and the rest ought to be told about it, then they'd understand their parents so much better. Have

206

you read the unbelievable bit about Peter offering to leave Hope
and marry Nancy? No wonder Hope didn't care about Nancy's
death!'

'Read it out,' Phoebe said. 'I'd like to hear it again.'

'Sunday, 15 April 1962. A beautiful spring day. Drove out
of London with P. and continued westwards until we found
a secluded country pub. Warm enough to sit out in the
gardens. Found a lovely spot by a little stream with a
chiff-chaff shouting from a nearby hawthorn bush (no
swallows yet), and had a ploughman's lunch. P. was unusually subdued, and I was all prepared to agree with him
that our affair is going nowhere and perhaps it should stop
altogether. Then he suddenly took both my hands in his
across the table and asked me to marry him! I was never
more astonished and I'm afraid I burst out laughing. When
I asked him 'Why?' and 'How?' he told me that life with H.
was getting ever more intolerable. They've got two boys at
home now that Herry has been expelled from his boarding
school, and Brendan refused to be sent there. Apparently
they are at each other's throats most of the time (there's
only a year between them) and they're picking on Roderick
whenever he's there. So P. thinks that 'Divorce is the only
answer.' I've had some backhanded compliments in my
time, but this one takes the biscuit! It doesn't seem to have
occurred to P. that the family unrest is of his own making.
He also appears not to have considered how much worse it
must be for H., who is there all the time, and resolutely
trying to keep her music going, despite all other commit-
ments! P. himself is hardly ever at home – he's always away
on some ploy or another. He seems to do exactly as he
pleases without any regard to his duty to his family. How
else would he be able to get away at weekends to see me?
He's undoubtedly the most selfish person I've ever met, but
he gets away with it because he makes people laugh.
Beware of humour – it's a smoke screen for ruthless
egotism. So, of course, I declined his offer and instead of
accepting defeat gracefully he flounced into a tremendous
huff and we drove back to The Smoke in almost total

silence. Later on – alone again – I felt despairing about life in general. I remembered the years when I was *desperate* to marry him, when I would have given anything to hear him say the words he used today. I believe the gods do it on purpose. They seem to take a malicious pleasure in granting requests – their way – to catch you out. I've got what I longed for, but it's too late. It has no value any more.'

Chapter Nineteen

Duncan woke too early as usual and lay restlessly in the hour before dawn, trying not to think. It was impossible. The images came to mind anyway; a jumbled procession of all the humiliating, demoralizing incidents which had ever happened to him, one after the other. He remembered as a child making a pipe rack for his father out of two pieces of plywood and a pair of wooden bobbins, and how he had cut the holes with such care and then wrapped it as a proper brown-paper parcel, with string and sealing wax. He had waited with such anticipation for Peter to come home and had stayed up late to see him, but when his father had finally arrived, he had thrown himself down into an easy chair with a tumbler of whisky and had carelessly tossed Duncan's parcel onto the sideboard, where it had remained unopened for three days.

Duncan shifted impatiently trying to get comfortable. That had happened nearly forty years ago! What possible importance had it now? But the parade went on. He remembered Herry at 8, telling him the facts of life and roaring with laughter at the 12-year-old Duncan's disgust and disbelief. He remembered being made to read the lesson in chapel at school and being utterly unable to get a single word out. He remembered Conrad, two years younger but catching him up academically and always there, on his heels, superior in every way. He remembered taking a special girl out (a musician, like Hope) and not daring to kiss her, and at the end of that unsuccessful evening, her telling him that he was about as stimulating as an autistic rabbit. He remembered his father saying that Oxford or Cambridge were the only universities worth going to. He remembered sitting in the exam room at his second-rate horticultural college and staring blankly at an examination paper for the full three hours. He remembered being officially in charge of a gang of County Council men planting shrubs by the roadside, and how, when he had arrived a quarter of an hour late, he had found that they had all gone off and started without him; he being entirely superfluous. Duncan shook his head. His thoughts were like flies, plaguing him.

So he thought instead about his mother, but this memory went back even earlier. He had so much wanted to emulate her musical abilities, so he had screwed up his courage and done something that was strictly forbidden to all the children. He had opened Hope's viola case, taken out her precious instrument and tried to play it. He discovered that he couldn't hold it up and get his fingers round it the way she did, so he stood it instead with its back against him as he knelt on the floor. Then he could press his fingers onto the strings whilst he supported the instrument against his chest, and saw away with the bow in his dominant left hand like a miniature cello. He was triumphant in having solved the problem in a manner unique to himself. His mother had heard him almost at once, of course, and had rushed in and snatched the viola from him. It wasn't that he minded her being cross, he welcomed the special attention. It was the *way* she was cross that he had never forgotten. She had looked at him pityingly and said, 'For heaven's sake, Duncan, even you must know that's not the correct way to hold it! I'm afraid you'll never make a musician.'

Well, he hadn't made one, had he? He hadn't become anything. He and education had never had a meeting of minds. He hadn't been able to see the point of it much of the time, so he had muddled along, left with no qualifications to speak of, and eventually found work. He had got through a lot of menial jobs in his time. He couldn't even remember them all. He had always tried to model himself on his father and adopt his assertive approach to life, but he had come badly unstuck. They had said he was toffee-nosed, standoffish, and so sharp he'd cut himself, when all he had been trying to convey was a passable, though false, sense of self-assurance, an ability to be self-contained, and a modest degree of wit. He gave up on the wit very early. He hadn't got the speed of thought or the delivery. No one ever understood him, and just assumed him to be taking the piss. His tightly crafted veneer of self-assurance in conjunction with his stammer and old-fashioned posh accent, was mistaken for arrogance and mocked mercilessly. There was nothing else to fall back upon but his capacity for solitude. He became self-employed.

He had chosen gardening in order to please his mother, as it was a passion of hers. Duncan could never bring himself to admit that it hadn't worked. He still hoped that it would, one day. He had stayed close by her in Somerset when his brothers moved away. He thought, perhaps subconsciously, that once they had all gone, and his father was spending most of his time in London, he and his mother would be on their own together again, and that he would be able to make up for years of lost time and preoccupation. He had spent weeks building her the pond, but she had taken it all for granted and been much more interested in some scheme of Herry's; some ridiculous property speculation. Now, of course, she would blame him for his father's death. If he had never built the bloody pond in the first place, then Peter would still be alive.

After his death Duncan had hoped perhaps to retrieve the situation, once he and Hope had each got over the worst of their grief. Then there really would be just the two of them again. Duncan could take his father's place, in a manner of speaking . . . could prune her apple trees, direct her gardener, pluck the odd pheasant for her – not that Peter had ever done any such thing – get close to her. He shifted restlessly again. Everyone and everything seemed to be against him. In the event it hadn't turned out like that at all. Hope, far from settling down sorrowfully to a comfortable widowhood with her one faithful son, was gallivanting off to London all the time, going to concerts, playing in recitals, even contemplating a musical voyage round the world! She was busier than ever! He was left like a spare prick at a wedding . . . which reminded him of Phoebe.

It was just over a month since he had seen her. Where did she fit into all this? In truth, she didn't. Duncan hadn't chosen her. He'd had marriage to her imposed upon him, and she didn't fit into his scheme of things at all. Initially he had felt nothing but relief when she had packed her bags and gone. She had slept in the spare room on the night of their final row and had not got up to prepare his breakfast the next morning. He'd done without, just to show her, and gone to work as usual. By the time he came home in the evening there was no sign of her; no blue Polo, no clothes in the wardrobe, no Phoebe, no hassle. Ah well, he thought. If she isn't here, then at least I don't have to worry about whether she's telling me the truth or not!

Duncan had expected that he would settle back very quickly into his old routines. He had years and years experience of living alone. It was a situation he knew he was very comfortable with, and now he would have the additional companionship of Diggory.

But imperceptibly, and without conscious thought on the subject, Duncan began to realize that all was not well. At first he assumed that he was just out of practice with cooking. He found it an unmitigated bore and chore. He couldn't be bothered with it; with the forethought necessary to ensure that you had a meal to eat when you were hungry and not two hours afterwards. He hated shopping, so he did it as little as possible. He congratulated himself on spending virtually no money. His low point came three weeks after Phoebe had left, when after a particularly fatiguing day's work, he discovered that he had only dog biscuits and grapefruit juice for supper. Roughage and vitamins, he told himself gloomily, it's all there. So he ate it.

You miss Phoebe, a voice said inside his head. If she were here you'd be on meat and three veg, not a daily diet of beans on toast and ruddy Winalot! It's worth it, Duncan silenced the voice firmly, for the peace. Yes, he missed her. He missed her the way a man might miss his housekeeper. It's very pleasant to have meals on time, sandwiches prepared for lunch, clothes washed and ironed, beds made, rooms cleaned. But, he told himself firmly, it is not essential.

He managed to maintain this attitude for a further week before even more subversive thoughts arrived to disturb him. Phoebe may have been a misfit at the beginning, but she had contrived to change her environment to suit herself, and once changed it remained to taunt him. There were reminders of her everywhere he looked, even though she had taken her personal things with her. She had left their wedding presents. She had left all her lampshades and curtains and the rug in the sitting room. She had even left some of her pictures on the walls and

212

books on the shelves. Perhaps she was intending to come back. Perhaps she was just teaching him a lesson.

Once Duncan allowed himself to hope, he was lost. He was forced to admit that it wasn't just the external environment she had changed, it was him as well. He had grown to depend upon having her around, encouraging him when he was down, pushing him gently to get things done at the right time, exclaiming with delight over things he had made or built; being on his side.

He had thought that he despised such need. It was unnecessary weakness. He hadn't realized how insidiously it had crept up on him while Phoebe was with him, and had now become a part of his life. It was as though he was unfitted to be solitary any more. He had been domesticated by stealth! Duncan did not resent this. He accepted it as inevitable. He'd finally joined the human race, and blown it, all in one go. How typical, he thought bitterly. The ultimate failure!

He got out of bed and went downstairs to make himself a pot of tea, turfing Diggory outside for his morning leak as he did so. Then, without thinking, he put the tea things on a tray and brought it back upstairs, as he had often done when Phoebe was there. As he carried it into the empty bedroom he was poignantly conscious of her absence. He set the tray down defiantly and climbed into bed again, picking up his full mug for a sip. As he sat there alone he could hear the song of a blackbird in the garden outside. It was a cool, windy, March Saturday morning. He had a number of jobs to do, but couldn't think coherently about doing any of them. His brain refused to function.

No, he thought at last. It's no good. I can't shrug off this failure as I have all the others. This one won't go away. He began in earnest to mourn the loss of his wife.

Fay sat up in her comfortable king-sized bed on Friday evening, three days into April, and leaned back luxuriously against her pillows. Life at last seemed to be working out to her satisfaction. If she could just get Phoebe a job in London, then there was every chance that she would stay. Fay smiled at the thought of her and wondered what it was about Phoebe that she found so endearing. It was her straightforwardness, she decided, her candour. Phoebe

213

was the only person she'd ever met who could genuinely be called true-hearted. Fay could easily understand why Phoebe had hidden Nancy's diaries from Duncan. It wasn't because she was devious or dishonest. It was because she knew Duncan wouldn't have understood them and would have sneered. It was a fine gesture of female solidarity on Phoebe's part. Fay didn't share Phoebe's totally partisan feelings about Nancy, but she was interested in her diaries and keen to read the juicy bits and find out about the parts of her life which had impinged upon the Moon family. She decided to skip all the day to day bits about Nancy's working life as a university lecturer and read just the meat of the story. As she began to flip through the pile, she was amused to find Nancy's account of her own wedding.

Saturday, 18 May 1968. Decided to go to the second Moon son's wedding after all. I'm not sure why P. asked me – we hardly see each other at all these days, and when we do we're very polite and distant. Was curious to see them all after so long, and comforted by the thought that in all the crowd no one would notice me at all. P. looked marvellous as always and made a very witty (though not always kind) speech. H. was manifestly hostile, about which I can't complain. I don't envy her new daughter-in-law! The groom (Conrad) although young, looked like a portly stock-broker and isn't nearly good enough for his bride. She was quite lovely – reminded me of my Eleanor in her youth. Spoke to P. briefly but it was forced and awkward. Perhaps I should have contained my curiosity and not gone. Managed to keep out of all the photographs and slipped away early. Somehow I don't think I shall see P. again. It's a melancholy thought.

Thursday, 11 October 1973. To Harley Street for my usual session. The Shrink: 'And to what do you attribute your present condition, Dr Sedgemoor?' Me: 'Lack of love,' at which he turned and gave the other trick-cyclist a signifi-cant look, as if to say, 'See what I mean?' I don't know if this therapy is doing me any good. I've been very down lately ever since the first anniversary of Eleanor's death. Am

I having a nervous breakdown? They say not. Anyway – I've decided to rewrite my will. I've no one to leave my things to, now that E. is gone, so I've decided to leave all to P. (even though I haven't seen him for five years) in memory of happy days. I shan't care what becomes of my belongings once I'm dead and they may be of use, even if it's only to remind P. that I once existed.

Saturday, 31 January 1981. So today I'm 60, officially an 'Old Person'. I don't feel any different inside except perhaps that I have attained a state of Single Blessedness at last. It's a long time now since married women were suspicious of me, and men were overeager to help me out. Nowadays I am simply a person in my own right, and a threat or an invitation to no one. The gods be praised. To think that in ten years' time F. and H. will be celebrating their Golden Wedding! I wonder sometimes how Hugh and I would have been, if I hadn't gone. Could we have made it to fifty years together? Sometimes I regret leaving him. The guilt has never entirely faded. Then again, I did what I had to at the time. Marriage was not for me. The burden of responsibility for another person's happiness was always too great for me to bear.

Saturday, 25 December 1982. Christmas on my tod. Today I am truly lonely. I have realized too late that I do need the commitment that marriage (or its equivalent) brings. I hope I don't live to a 'good' old age. It's a bleak prospect. I worry also about the future of this world of ours. It is now twenty years since Rachel Carson wrote *Silent Spring* and ten since *The Limits to Growth* and have we changed anything? Precious little. I'm sure the biosphere will survive my time, but for how much longer? It's a mess. I can't decide whether it will be overpopulation or pollution (or both) which will bring the human race to its knees in the end.

NB Must remember to add a codicil to my will. I don't want to contribute to the destruction of the rain forest when I'm dead – I want to be buried in a paper sack.

*

There was a knock at the bedroom door.

'Come in,' Fay called, putting that diary down on top of the pile. 'Oh, Phoebe, you don't have to knock. Come in.'

'I thought you might be asleep,' Phoebe said.

'Was Nancy Sedgemoor buried in a paper bag?' Fay asked her.

'I don't know. I doubt it,' Phoebe said, looking startled. 'Why?'

'She says here, in 1982, that she wants to be.'

'Oh yes, so she did.' Phoebe stood awkwardly at the end of the bed. 'Fay?' she said tentatively.

'What is it? Come and sit down,' Fay patted the bed beside her.

Phoebe looked embarrassed. 'I'm sixteen days late,' she said apologetically. 'My period should have come on March the eighteenth and it's never late as a rule. I wouldn't bother you about it, but it's been worrying me and I can't get to sl —'

'Phoebe!' Fay exclaimed in delight. 'Wouldn't it be marvellous if you were pregnant?'

'Well . . . I'm not sure now.'

'But you always wanted a baby.'

'Yes, but I'm not sure how Duncan will feel . . .'

Fay almost said, 'What's Duncan got to do with it?' but stopped herself in time. 'Tomorrow morning, first thing,' she said firmly, 'we'll go and buy a Predictor Kit and then we'll know for sure. Then we can make *plans*.' She put her arms round Phoebe. 'Oh, I do hope you are,' she said.

Phoebe was surprised and pleased at Fay's reaction to her problem. She had expected her to be concerned, considering the state of her marriage, perhaps even to suggest abortion. The more she thought about the possibility of being pregnant, the more excited she became. Fay had sat back against her pillows again and was regarding her with affection. Phoebe found she had a pent-up flood of things she wanted to discuss.

'What signs did you have at this stage?' she began. She wrapped her arms round herself as she spoke. The heating had gone off some time before and Phoebe had forgotten to put on her dressing gown. She shivered.

'Here,' Fay said, pulling her duvet aside, 'pop in here or you'll catch your death. There's masses of room.' Phoebe hesitated. 'It's quite safe,' Fay said almost crossly. 'I'm not going to molest you.'

'It's not that . . .' Phoebe said at once, but couldn't think what else might be holding her back, and so was stuck for an explanation. To overcome this awkwardness and to avoid hurting Fay's feelings, she climbed in beside her and they sat side by side. Fay put out a warm foot and touched one of Phoebe's.

'You're freezing!' she exclaimed.

'I'm fine,' Phoebe said, flinching.

'Right,' Fay said briskly, withdrawing her foot, 'symptoms of pregnancy, let's see – sickness obviously, sore breasts, having to pee all the time – although that comes later – Oh yes, I remember I had an odd sort of metallic taste in my mouth too. Trouble is, I can't remember when any of them started. I was never actually sick. I just felt bloody.'

'I've been feeling a bit sick,' Phoebe confessed, 'but it's probably all in the mind. Maybe it's because I've been worrying about it. Duncan really doesn't want children, you see . . . I don't know what he'll say . . . if I am. I sort of assumed that things were all over between us, but if I am . . . then I suppose they can't be, and I'm not sure if I really want that. It's all such a muddle.'

'Mmmmm,' Fay said encouragingly.

'You see,' Phoebe said earnestly, 'if I'm to fit in properly with Duncan, then I have to suppress about ninety per cent of my own personality. I can do it. I *have* done it, but it's awfully hard . . . and I don't think I want to any more.'

'Why should you?' Fay agreed.

'The trouble is,' Phoebe said, 'Duncan doesn't know how to love someone. He has no idea of what love is. He seems to

217

have a great chunk of humanity just left out somehow, like a robot.'

'Have you been hoping all this time that he'll miss you and want you to go home again?' Fay asked.

'Not really,' Phoebe said with resignation. 'With Duncan it's out of sight; out of mind.'

'I always think,' Fay said, 'that indifference is worse than abuse, although you seem to have suffered both.'

Phoebe blushed. 'Actually, the black eye was my fault,' she admitted. 'I was trying to hit him.'

Fay burst out laughing. 'Well, you had me fooled,' she said.

At that moment the bedroom door opened and Jack came in, rubbing his eyes.

'Stop laughing,' he said. 'It's not f-funny.'

'What isn't funny, darling? And why aren't you asleep?'

Jack shook his head and climbed up to join them, crawling over Phoebe until he could slide himself into bed between them.

'One, two, three in bed,' he counted with satisfaction.

'That reminds me of a song,' Phoebe said, and began singing it:

'There were ten in the bed, and the little one said,
"Roll over! Roll over!"
So they all rolled over and one fell out.
There were nine in the bed and the little one said.
"Roll over! Roll over!" '

Phoebe sang down all the numbers to one in the bed and ended up with:

'There was one in the bed and the little one said,
"Goodnight!" '

'Sing it again!' Jack demanded, delighted. He cuddled up next to her and Phoebe could feel the warmth of his chubby little body through her nightdress, punctuated every so often by blows from his constantly fidgeting elbows and heels. She looked down on his charming baby face with its perfect skin and

218

long eyelashes, and wondered what it would be like to have one of her own.

She sang the song all through again and Jack joined in with the numbers, getting most of them right.

'You're obviously going to be a mathematical genius when you grow up,' Phoebe told him, impressed.

'No, I'm not,' he said. 'I'm going to marry Mummy. Sing ten in a bed again?'

'Not tonight,' Phoebe said reluctantly. 'I've got to go to my own bed and go to sleep. It's late.' She disengaged herself gently from him and slipped out of the double bed. 'See you in the morning,' she said to them both.

'Sleep well,' Fay said. 'Keep your fingers crossed.'

The next morning was Saturday and they all three went out together to do the shopping. Jack insisted that Phoebe be the one to push him in the supermarket trolley.

'Good practice,' Fay teased.

They bought a pregnancy testing kit at the chemists, and Phoebe put it into her bag as carefully as if it were a bomb.

'I shall be scared to use it,' she said to Fay, 'in case I'm not.'

'It may well be too early,' Fay said. 'If it's negative at this stage, I don't think it means that you're definitely not pregnant.'

'But if it's positive, I definitely am?'

'That's right.'

'In that case, I'm going to do it the minute we get home!' Phoebe said, but when she read the instructions, she found that the urine had to be a morning sample. She would just have to contain her impatience until first thing on Sunday.

They unpacked the groceries and put them away in the cupboards with help from Jack, so it took twice as long as usual.

'Let's have a coffee before we get lunch?' Fay suggested.

'Good idea,' Phoebe said, putting the kettle on.

'Juice,' Jack demanded, and as he said it the front doorbell rang. He ran to answer it, followed by Fay. Phoebe sat down for a rest on one of the kitchen stools to wait for the kettle to boil. She heard whoever it was at the front door being invited in. Then they all came into the kitchen preceded by Jack.

'Grandma Dragon,' he said.

It was Hope!

Chapter Twenty

Fay's first reaction to seeing Hope on the doorstep was, Oh God, the Moon brothers have sent in the heavy mob to bring us to our senses!

'Good morning,' Hope said crisply. 'I just thought I'd pop over and see how you all are.'

'Hope!' Fay said. 'How, er, lovely. Come in.' They went into the kitchen and Fay caught the fleeting expression of shock on Phoebe's face, as an echo of her own. She made a face of mock horror at her, behind her mother-in-law's back, and saw Phoebe trying to suppress an hysterical giggle.

'Hello, Phoebe,' Hope said. 'How are you?'

'Fine,' Phoebe said, disconcerted, 'thanks.'

'I'm in London for a concert,' Hope said, finding the only comfortable chair and sitting down stiffly. 'It's a wonderful series, quite outstandingly played, conducted by that young Scandinavian with the Italian mother . . . what *is* his name now? . . . Oh yes, Guido Mâelstrøm, a singularly unprepossessing one for such a beautiful and talented young man, but that's often the way, isn't it?'

'Like places called "Paradise" are always awful dumps,' Phoebe suggested.

Hope ignored this. 'Is that coffee?' she asked.

'Yes,' Fay said, with a guilty start. 'Would you like some? You will stay to lunch, won't you?'

Hope graciously consented to take coffee and lunch with them. She didn't once mention their marital problems. Fay wondered why she was there. She wasn't one to pay a mere social call.

'Grandma,' Jack said, 'we were three in a b-bed.'

Oh my God! Fay thought, what will she think? Does she know? What shall I say?

'Really?' Hope said, looking inscrutable.

'It's a song we were singing,' Phoebe said quickly. 'You know

221

the one − *And the little one said, 'Roll over.' So they all rolled over and −*'

'I did in fact have a purpose in coming here,' Hope interrupted. 'As you know, I'm moving out of the Temple flat and dispersing all its contents. I wondered if there was anything you two would particularly like. After all, in spite of all events, you are still my daughters-in-law.'

'*There were ten in the bed and the little* −' Jack began in a loud tuneless chant.

'Jack,' his grandmother said firmly, 'be a good little boy and go and play somewhere else for ten minutes, will you? We grown-ups have some serious talking to do.' And to Fay's amazement, Jack went! 'Now,' Hope said, 'Phoebe, is there anything?'

'Well,' Phoebe said cautiously, 'do books count?'

'Which ones were you thinking of?'

'The five volumes of Witherby's *Handbook of British Birds,*' Phoebe said. 'I've always thought they were special . . .'

'Consider them yours,' Hope said. Phoebe let out a little cry, jumped to her feet and rushed over to hug her. Fay watched with amusement. She would sooner have hugged a gorse bush, but then Phoebe was like that, impulsive and warm-hearted. Fay glanced at Hope over Phoebe's shoulder and was surprised to see, on the aristocratic face in that unguarded moment, an expression almost of tenderness. For the first time ever, Fay acknowledged that the older woman did indeed have real feelings, and could be touched by affection. Perhaps if she had married a demonstrative sort of man, she too could have let her emotions show, and her children in turn would have been able to acquire that most necessary of human attributes; the ability to relate to others. In that moment Fay sympathized with Hope in a way that she hadn't managed to, during all of the twenty-four years that she had known her. She realized that it was Peter, not Hope, who was primarily responsible for the chain. Perhaps Hope was here now to offer them an olive branch because she secretly envied them. Perhaps she wished that she had had the opportunity to leave Peter years before when the children were young, but couldn't. Fay didn't know much about her in-laws' background, but she did know that in those days divorce was particularly traumatic, and divorcées considered beyond the pale. Only 'fast' women like Nancy Sedgemoor had the courage, or the foolhardiness – or the money? – to put themselves through it . . .

'And what about you, Fay?' Hope was asking. 'What would you like?'

'I'd love the firedogs from the drawing room,' Fay began, ' . . . no, the walnut corner cupboard in the dining room . . .'

'Which?' Hope asked.

'The cupboard,' Fay said, deciding.

'Good,' Hope said. 'I shall arrange it. You may well get both or more. It all depends upon what everybody else wants, but I decided to give you both first refusal.'

'Is it ten minutes yet, Grandma?' Jack asked, sliding in through the door on his bottom.

'Yes,' Hope said, smiling down at him. 'I do believe it is.'

Phoebe had been horrified to see Hope coming into the kitchen. She had assumed immediately that Hope was an envoy from Duncan, and had been afraid that she would be called upon to explain herself and justify her actions. The relief which had flooded through her when Hope had explained her presence there by announcing her intention of actually giving them something from the flat, and then her joy at the thought of those lovely books with their detailed descriptions, old-fashioned illustrations and the advertisement on the flap of their dust jacket for the BBC in wartime London – the voice of freedom . . . Phoebe had forgotten herself completely and rushed to do the most natural thing in the world. Afterwards she was amazed at her temerity; that she should have been so forward! But she appeared to have got away with it.

Over lunch, Hope talked all about herself as usual, going over old ground again, but Phoebe felt able to forgive her for it. She was 73, after all. She had seen a lot of life. She told them how her father had been wounded on the Somme in 1916 and had died three years later, just before Hope was born. She and her sisters seemed to have been neglected by their distraught

223

mother, who in later life immersed herself in painting and had very little time for her children. Hope had assumed it was because they weren't boys. She in her turn had wanted boys and had got them, but then having achieved this easily, had longed for a daughter. In 1948 between Hereward and Roderick she had had one, stillborn. Hope told her story without drama, with an even voice and little expression yet Phoebe, with all the easy emotions of the probably pregnant, had actually shed tears for her and had reached across the table to squeeze one of Hope's hands in sympathy. Hope had snatched it away before she could do so. Don't get carried away, Phoebe told herself, wiping her eyes rather shamefacedly. One hug does not a relationship make!

Phoebe supposed that Duncan had told Hope about the emergence of the bestiary from hiding and also about Nancy's diaries, but Hope did not mention them, so Phoebe felt unable to bring the subject up. She was partly relieved about this and partly sad not to be able to present her own side of the story. Peter's will was not mentioned either, so Phoebe was unable to find out what was going on about it; whether Duncan or Herry were going to contest it or not. Phoebe wondered how much money was involved, and what Brendan would do with it. Would he buy his own boat? Any normal person could be quizzed in a conversational manner about this sort of thing, Phoebe thought, but not Hope. She looked across at her mother-in-law's formidable façade and quailed at the thought.

They got on to discussing the guests at the funeral. Hope had something dismissive to say about each one of her cousins. They had either failed in aspects of their own lives or had married no-hopers who had underachieved on their behalf. She's always so *negative*, Phoebe thought. She always has to complain about something. Phoebe had thought for a moment earlier on that Hope was going to open up and become almost human; that released from Peter's influence she might even soften and admit to weakness. But no, she was as adamant and unyielding as ever.

'Pity that Brendan couldn't make it to the funeral,' Fay remarked.

224

'I doubt very much whether I shall be seeing *him* again,' Hope said. Subject closed.

After more coffee at the end of lunch, Hope announced her intention of leaving. She allowed Phoebe to hold her coat for her to slip into, and offered her cheek for each of her daughters-in-law to kiss. Then she preceded them out of the front door. The bright day had clouded over, threatening a sudden April shower. Hope paused beside a large showy white camellia in a pot on the front steps and then turning, issued not so much a request, rather a royal command.

'I should deem it a kindness,' Hope said, 'if neither of you would divulge to my family *in any particular* the contents of any of the diaries that the Sedgemoor woman may have perpetrated.'

Phoebe thought to herself, Oh I see. *That's* why she came!

Fay and Phoebe discussed her request after she had gone and agreed that it might be better to say nothing.

'We haven't much opportunity to tell Conrad and Duncan anyway,' Fay said, 'and what's the point? I'm all for burying the past.'

'I don't suppose it would do them any good,' Phoebe agreed. 'They wouldn't be able to let it change anything for them, after all; their characters are set in concrete.'

'Yes, it's far too late.'

'But don't you think it's possible for open-minded people to learn from others' experience?' Phoebe asked her. 'I've always felt that Nancy and I have had similar problems in our lives. I've sort of identified with her, and she really regretted leaving her husband when she was too old and it was too late. Perhaps there's a message there for me.'

'Nonsense!' Fay said, with a shade too much asperity. 'You're not a bit like Nancy. You can take those sort of parallels too far, you know. What was right or wrong for her has absolutely no bearing on what would be best for you.'

'I suppose not,' Phoebe said. 'Oh I wish I knew what was what a bit more.'

'You might have more idea tomorrow morning,' Fay said.

Fay could see that Phoebe was feeling tense, and would

continue to be on edge until she knew whether or not she was pregnant. Fay wanted very much to discuss the future and sound Phoebe out cautiously about her own ideas. If I do it at the wrong moment, Fay thought, then it may have exactly the opposite effect to the one I want. Perhaps I should wait until after she knows. But then, Fay thought, if she is pregnant she'll be so overcome by the idea that she won't be able to think clearly. And if she isn't – she'll be so upset that, ditto. I must try and talk to her tonight, after Jack has gone to bed.

The afternoon seemed to last a long time. They went for a walk in the park and fed the ducks. Whatever happens, Fay thought, I know I've done the right thing by Jack. The child appeared to her to be so much happier. He trotted between herself and Phoebe, swinging from their arms and laughing delightedly. He ran and hid behind trees for them to find him. He played piggy in the middle with a ball and didn't get cross. He was sleeping better these days and not waking in the mornings until seven, sometimes 7.30, and was invariably dry. He had even said that he was looking forward to going to proper school. Perhaps the damage was already being repaired. Perhaps breaking the chain had worked. When they put him to bed that evening, he insisted that Phoebe should be present at his bathside so he could demonstrate the action of a special diving man toy. Then they had a good splashy game and he went to sleep afterwards with no complaints and none of his customary stalling tactics.

'Jack's getting really fond of you,' Fay said to Phoebe over supper.

'I'm really fond of him too,' Phoebe said. 'He's so lively and quick on the uptake. I hope any child I have is half as bright.'

'Have you decided what you're going to do?' Fay asked, taking the plunge.

'I keep putting off having to think about it,' Phoebe confessed. 'After tomorrow, of course, I'll have to.'

'I had some ideas,' Fay said cautiously, 'but you may think they're rubbish.'

'Tell me,' Phoebe urged. 'I'm sure I won't think that.'

Fay braced herself. 'They cover both eventualities,' she said, 'whether you are or whether you aren't. If you're *not* pregnant, then I hope you'll stay and get a job as we planned. If you *are*, then I can see two possibilities. You can still stay and get a job once the baby is old enough, and then you can share Jack's nanny and contribute to the running of the place from your salary. Or, if you wanted to be a full-time mum, then you could do that here too, and in time you could take on the nanny's duties – Jack will be at school a lot of the time by then anyway – and save me having to employ her, and so earn your keep that way. It would be lovely for Jack to have a little brother or sister. It would mean security for you and the baby . . . and, of course, it would be marvellous for me.'

'Oh Fay,' Phoebe said, reaching out and squeezing her shoulder. 'That's so generous of you. I don't know what to say.'

'How about "Yes"?'

Phoebe laughed. 'But what about Duncan?' she said. 'He's the problem. I'm almost sure I don't want to go back to him, but if I'm pregnant then perhaps I should, for the baby's sake.'

'Why?' asked Fay, bluntly.

'Well, because . . . babies need fathers.'

'Jack is much better off without his father.'

'Yes, but –'

'Does Duncan show any signs of wanting to be a father?'

'Well, no –'

'And have you considered that the baby might not be Duncan's child anyway? It might be Herry's!' Perhaps this was unfair ammunition, Fay thought, deploying it anyway.

'Yes,' Phoebe said. 'That thought had occurred to me, but Duncan would never know that. I mean, I've got brownish eyes too, so it wouldn't be obvious . . .'

'But what if it became clear in later life, and Duncan hadn't liked having a child around anyway? Wouldn't he feel cheated then?'

'I don't know,' Phoebe said. 'I really don't know.' She looked agonized.

'Don't get upset,' Fay said soothingly. 'We'll sort something out, you'll see.' Please, she thought, *please* say you'll stay. She tried to will Phoebe to agree to do so.

227

'I don't know what I'd have done without you, Fay,' Phoebe said, smiling wanly. 'You've been so good to me. The only thing I *do* know is that, whatever happens, I'm never going to commit myself absolutely to anyone again. I'm never going to be emotionally dependent and I'm always going to keep something of myself in reserve; keep my options open. You and Nancy have taught me that.'

Phoebe felt safe at Fay's, so there was a great temptation for her to stay put. Fighting against this were her feelings of duty towards Duncan and the idea that, although he didn't seem keen on fatherhood, it would be wrong to rob him of the experience of his own child – if in truth it was his. On the other hand, Fay did seem very keen for her to stay. Phoebe knew she wasn't just being polite. She wondered why Fay was being so kind. Perhaps she fancied her. That idea didn't seem so outrageous any more. Now that Phoebe knew Fay so well, she couldn't think of her as 'one of them' in some unmentionable category of perverts. There was nothing strange or queer about her. There was no dividing line between her and any other woman Phoebe had ever come across. Phoebe realized that there was no way she could have 'known' about Fay, even had she been ultra-sophisticated and streetwise when she had first met her. Something that Fay once said to her – All humans are to a greater or lesser extent bisexual – began to make more sense. Human beings could not always be grouped into distinct boxes with identifying labels 'straight' or 'gay'. Most people came down firmly on one side or the other. Some didn't, but they were not to be condemned for this 'failure' surely? Love was love, whoever it was you chose.

Once Phoebe had thought this through in her mind, she was able to relax and forget about it. If you didn't categorize someone, you were better able to accept them for what they really were, admire their good qualities and come to terms with their bad. Phoebe felt very close to Fay. Their minds worked the same way. Talking was so easy. Tonight, though, Phoebe thought, I won't stay up late nattering.

I'll have an early night and then I'll be in a good state to cope with whatever the pregnancy test shows tomorrow morning.

'I'm off to bed,' she told Fay. 'All this uncertainty has worn me out!'

'Sleep well,' Fay said. She too looked tense. Phoebe went upstairs to her room and got undressed, putting on her long cotton nightie and then, sitting down at her dressing table, began to rub some cream into her face. She looked at her reflection in the mirror and tried to imagine herself as a mother. Did she look the part? Frankly no. Her hair was sticking out as usual. Phoebe despaired of ever getting it to go as she wanted. She made a hideous face at herself.

There was a tap at the door and Fay came in, holding a small glass jar.

'I've brought you something to pee in,' she explained, 'otherwise you might forget. If you leave this somewhere obvious, then it'll remind you in the morning.'

'Thank you,' Phoebe said. 'I don't think I'm likely to forget, but thanks anyway.'

'Why were you making faces at yourself?'

'It's my hair,' Phoebe said, brushing at it ineffectually. 'It won't take orders.'

'You could get it cut differently,' Fay suggested. 'I'll take you to my hairdresser, she's brilliant.'

'Worth a try,' Phoebe agreed, pushing handfuls of it off her face. 'Like this perhaps?'

Fay came forward and picked up the hairbrush. 'Let's experiment,' she said. She stood behind Phoebe and began brushing her hair.

'Aaaaaah,' Phoebe said, closing her eyes. 'That's bliss. Don't stop.'

'I think it would look good like this,' Fay said, holding the hair in position, 'shorter here at the sides and with more bounce on top.'

'Mmmmmm.'

'Open your eyes, you idiot!' Fay said, laughing. 'See what I mean?'

Phoebe looked at herself critically. 'My face is the wrong shape,' she said.

229

'There is nothing wrong with your face,' Fay said.

'Nancy had a good-shaped face,' Phoebe said reflectively, 'and her hair was the same colour as mine, I think. It said auburn in her passport. Perhaps I could have my hair like hers.'

Fay held the hair back against Phoebe's head. 'Too severe and monkish,' she said. 'Doesn't go with your personality.'

'D'you think Nancy was severe and monkish?'

'Tough, yes, but not solitary by nature. Has it occurred to you to wonder whether she and Eleanor were lovers?' Fay went on brushing her hair.

'No. Why?'

'It's just a thought. They were obviously very close. She calls her "my Eleanor" in the diaries.'

'I suppose it's quite possible. How sad if so, because she died so early.' The significance of her remark registered suddenly with Phoebe. 'Poor Nancy,' she said, 'just when she had got herself sorted out and perhaps found someone special to care for. Wasn't it too cruel of fate?' She looked up and caught Fay's eye in the mirror, and seemed to see her as she had never done before, as though the very indirectness of her gaze had a clarifying effect on its object, through the process of reflection. She saw the warmth in Fay's eyes, and the attentive expression on her face, and felt the gentleness of her hands as they played with her hair. It struck an answering chord deep inside Phoebe, and she voiced her thoughts spontaneously.

'I couldn't bear it if you died,' she said.

'Oh Phoebe . . .' Fay's eyes were suddenly full of tears.

Phoebe got to her feet and turned in one swift movement, to embrace her. They stood holding each other for a long time before Phoebe let out a long juddering sigh. 'You feel so little,' she said. 'Kiss me,' Fay said.

Later, Phoebe said in anxious tones, 'I can't take my nightie off. I don't want you to see how fat and horrible I am.'

'You forget,' Fay said tenderly, 'I undressed you that night. I know just what you look like, and I think you're lovely.'

230

When Fay woke early next morning, she and Phoebe were still entwined. She opened her eyes and stared in absolute content-ment at the rays of sunshine cutting through the gap between the rose-coloured curtains and gathering in a pool of light on the foot of the bed. Phoebe stirred in her arms and opened her eyes as well. Their irises were a glowing hazel colour with specks of darker brown pigment scattered through them like the pattern on a bird's egg. Fay thought that they were quite simply the most beautiful eyes she had ever seen. When they had first opened, they looked momentarily startled but then Phoebe had smiled. It's all right, Fay thought with relief. She doesn't regret anything. Phoebe turned in the bed until they were looking straight at each other, and then ran her fingers very gently across the skin of Fay's cheek, over the edge of her jaw and along her neck. Fay held her breath.

'Promise me you're immortal,' Phoebe said.

Phoebe had never known such elation. She felt super-human, bursting with energy, cherished, *happy*. She couldn't believe her luck. The world had been transformed overnight and now offered infinite opportunities for optimism. She kissed Fay again and got out of bed to put her nightie on, before Jack came in. Then she went into the bathroom, squatted over the lavatory and urinated with difficulty into the glass jar, catching only the midstream. She held the result up. It looked very concentrated, a dark yellow. She fol-lowed carefully the instructions of the kit and left the little test tube in its plastic stand to work its magic undis-turbed.

'Keep your fingers crossed,' she said to Fay as she got back into bed.

'I've got everything crossed,' Fay assured her.

Jack bounced in and threw himself happily onto the bed before inserting himself confidently under the duvet between them.

'Sing ten in a bed,' he said to Phoebe. They sang it all the way through three times, then Jack patted Phoebe on the chest and said, 'You've got bigger boozies than Mummy.'

'Yes,' Phoebe agreed.

'Are you going to stay here for ever and ever?' Jack asked.

'Well, I'll have to stay until the summer at least,' Phoebe said, winking at Fay. 'Your mum has offered to take me on a boat on the Thames then.'

'I want you to stay longer than that,' Jack said. 'Promise?'

'I promise,' Phoebe said solemnly.

'Is it time yet?' Fay asked.

Phoebe looked at her watch. 'Yes. I'm scared to look!'

'Shall I?'

'No. I'll go.' Phoebe got out of bed, padded across the carpet and entered the bathroom. If there was a brown ring in the test tube, then the test was negative. If there was not, then she was pregnant . . . Phoebe sent up a silent prayer and looked.

Next minute she was bounding back into the bedroom. 'There's NO brown ring!' she cried. 'It's *positive!*'

'Oh, I'm *so* glad,' Fay said, laughing delightedly. Phoebe was doing a little dance of triumph. Jack joined her, and together they swung round the floor in ever dizzying circles.

The telephone by the bed rang and Fay answered it. 'It's for you, Phoebe,' she said. 'It's Duncan.'

'Oh.' Phoebe felt quite blank . . . and giddy. She let go of Jack's hands and came across to take the receiver. 'Hello,' she said, without enthusiasm.

'Phoebe!' Duncan said, in tones of relief. 'I've been wanting to ring you for weeks, but somehow I haven't managed to.'

'Oh?'

'Look, Phoebe, it's time we talked. I've got something very important to say to you; something I should have said a long time ago.'

'Say it now,' Phoebe said.

'Well, it's difficult on the telephone . . . Couldn't you come home?'

'No,' Phoebe said, 'I don't think I could.'

'Damn it, Phoebe,' Duncan said, 'you're my wife and . . . and I love you.'

232

Phoebe gave a little gasp, halfway between a laugh and a sob. 'I'm sorry, Duncan,' she said. 'You're twelve hours too late.'

There follows the first chapter of Maggie Makepeace's new novel,
available in Century hardback

TRAVELLING HOPEFULLY

Chapter One

'Just listen to this,' Barnaby Redcliffe said in tones of disgust, brandishing a note from the dustbin men. He quoted ' "In order to more effectively pick up the domestic refuse would you please place your bin outside your house for collection each Thursday." Do they think that's English? *I* don't want to pick up my refuse, effectively or otherwise, *they* do. How can they write such rubbish? It's so sloppy!'

'It's obvious what it means,' Imogen observed from behind her breakfast coffee. 'It may be ungrammatical but it serves its purpose perfectly well.'

'People don't care any more,' Barnaby said. 'They're so keen on expressing themselves freely, that's the phrase isn't it? Their . . . dammit, I've lost the word . . . making things . . . imagination . . . *blast*!' He looked exasperated.

'Workmanship?' Imogen suggested. 'Flair?'

'No! Look, it's bad enough forgetting the bloody words without you suggesting all the wrong ones. It's on the tip of my tongue . . . *creativity*, yes that's it. People nowadays think their creativity shouldn't be stunted by wearisome rules. Novels these days are full of sentences with no *verbs!* What they don't seem to realise is that grammar is there not to obstruct the language but to clarify it; to make it unambiguous. That's the beauty of it.'

'More coffee?' asked Imogen, wearily. She looked across the kitchen table at her husband and wished she were able to leave him.

'Had enough. You don't care either do you?'

'Not as much as you do, clearly.'

'You should. Our generation is the last bastion of civilisation against the illiterate hordes.'

'Oh well,' Imogen said easily, '*après nous le déluge* and all that.' If only he were in good health, she thought, I could go tomorrow, but only a total shit leaves a partner with an incurable disease.

'Time to go to work,' Barnaby said with a sigh, getting to his feet. He refused at all times to use a walking stick and had a tendency to lurch sideways or trip over the slightest little irregularity underfoot.

Ten years before, the day of his 40th birthday, and after years of uncertainty, he had been diagnosed as having multiple sclerosis. Imogen's first response, to her shame, had been *I've been cheated!* It was as though she had bought damaged goods in good faith and had only discovered the fault after the guarantee had run out. A good woman would first have been flooded with compassion for Barnaby, and only then filled with regret for herself. I'm not a good woman, she had thought. How shall I endure it?

'I must get off too,' she said. 'Will you be home at the usual time?'

'Probably.' Barnaby picked up his briefcase and his driving glasses and walked towards the door. 'See you this evening.'

'Right.'

As she piled the breakfast things into the machine to be washed later, Imogen glanced through the window and saw him get rather awkwardly into his car and drive off towards his office. I suppose, she thought, I should be grateful that he's got a relatively benign kind of MS, the slow sort and not the dramatic disease which sometimes paralyses people and puts them into wheelchairs or even kills them in a very few years. I should be grateful too to Butcombe, Nempnett & Thrubwell, Solicitors and Commisioners for Oaths, who took him on as a partner years ago and who now make allowances for him. I should too but somehow I don't. She glanced round the kitchen to check that everything was turned off, heaved her own bag on to her shoulder, took her mac off the hook and checked her face in the hall mirror. She closed the front door firmly behind her and set off for her stint at the Citizens Advice Bureau.

Her friend Carol passed her in the corridor as she arrived. 'Not long now,' Carol said. 'You lucky devil. Have you had all your jabs and things?'

'Tetanus, hepatitis and boosters for polio and typhoid,' Imogen said counting them off her fingers.

Carol sighed. 'I really envy you but I reckon you've earned it.'

'I like working here,' Imogen said, 'but even so I shall be glad of the change.' By Saturday, she thought gleefully, we shall be in Seychelles in heaven, and nothing else will seem important. Barnaby will have no syntax to moan about, and our dustbin will be securely out of sight in the garage, so the bin men can go and be effective wherever else they choose.

Barnaby drove to work gloomily, anticipating the pile in his in-tray that would certainly not get dealt with by the time he went on holiday. He would have to sort through it for the priorities but it niggled him to leave even the smallest thing uncompleted. These days he kept forgetting things, and was quite capable of losing a whole conversation which had taken place only the day before. Imogen kept nagging him to write things down, but Barnaby felt that this would be giving in to old age. After all, that was all it was. It was just a question of keeping the old brain going. Once you started leaving yourself little notes all over the place, you might as well retire to the geriatric ward. Today he would have to make an extra effort to make sure he'd forgotten nothing vital. He could hardly ring the office from the Indian Ocean . . . He sighed. He was not convinced of the merits of this holiday but Imogen had been so insistent. It was all right for her, but the thought of spending fifteen days with a load of cripples (even if it was beside warm turquoise seas and palm trees) did not fill him with any enthusiasm. Oh, he saw the logic of it all right. It was a clever idea to run two parallel holidays for 'sufferers' and 'carers' so that they could 'share in the experience, but each according to his/her physical capabilities', the carers being let off duty to do energetic walks, while the poor, bloody disabled commiserated with each other and, no doubt, compared symptoms from a sitting position somewhere in the shade. Barnaby had looked up from the Leisure Doubletrips brochure which Imogen had brought home in triumph, and said, 'I'm damned if I'm going to join a party of no-hopers in wheelchair races on the coral strand in a sort of tropical "Gladiators" crossed with "Hearts of Gold"!'

'Don't be ridiculous,' Imogen said. 'It wouldn't be anything like that. It's for people with your sort of MS who aren't badly incapacitated but who can't quite walk as far as the rest of us. There won't be *any* wheelchairs. It will just give us both a chance to do as much as we can.

'Instead of me holding you back all the time, you mean?'

'Yes!' She looked exasperated at being made to say it.

'Perhaps you should go without me then,' he suggested, 'to give you a clear field?'

'Oh, please don't be a martyr. I'd rather you were bad tempered! Look Barnaby, why won't you try it once? You don't know anyone else with MS because you've already refused to join a group. You never know, you might find the others very supportive and interesting. You moan about having it. Why shouldn't they?'

'I'm afraid I don't like the idea of being herded about with a crowd of strange people – being . . . arranged? . . . sorted? No. Hell! Don't tell me . . . ' He thumped the table in frustration and then remembered what he was trying to say. '. . . *Categorised*. . . just because we've all got the same disease, but probably damn-all else in common.'

Imogen giggled. 'Like that ghastly woman at your office party who introduced those two painfully shy wives to each other by saying, "Here, Sue, you must meet Sally. You'll have so much to talk about since both your husbands have just had vasectomies." '

Barnaby made a face 'Precisely,' he said.

'But I'm sure it won't be like that. There's bound to be someone interesting on the trip and at least half of them will be –' she had almost, he knew, said 'normal' – 'won't have MS. Anyway,' she gave him her little-girl look, which had disarmed him in their youth but now just looked silly, 'Seychelles are paradise on earth, or so they say. They're somewhere I've always wanted to go. We both need a break and it would be so good to experience it together.' Wishful thinking, or did she believe that?

'Oh well, I suppose . . . '

'Marvellous!' She rushed over to kiss him. 'You won't regret it. I'll make sure of that. Oh, I can't wait to go!' Then she made a mock frown and said, 'I never knew you watched "Gladiators" or the other one, hearts of something?'

'I see them by mistake when I'm waiting for the News', he said firmly,

'You are sweet,' she said, laughing indulgently.

Barnaby had noticed that she was always sweet to him – well, 'sweet' was the only word for it – when she was getting her own way. Once he had thought it was charming. Now he saw it as manipulative. 'I wonder what the leader will be like,' she said, 'Roger Dare. Apparently his wife has MS and he's been doing this sort of thing for several years. I admire someone like that, I really do. And Claire Mainwaring his assistant is a GP. That's handy!'

'It would be if she could dispense convenient little pills which could cure MS.'

'One day,' Imogen said encouragingly. 'One day there will be. They're doing masses of research.'

'Then they'd better get a move on.'

Barnaby was jolted back into the present. He had been driving on autopilot, but apparently successfully. He glanced at his watch, five minutes to nine, he should just do it. The modest queue of cars funnelling into the small Somerset town could barely be termed 'rush-hour' traffic. He was glad he didn't live in and work in London. He was glad he was going on holiday too, if he were honest. He could do with the rest, and Imogen, diluted by a dozen or so others, might be a lot more liveable with. He made a wry face at the thought.

'Now then', Daisy Mann sad to her friend and companion, Dorothy Petrie. 'All set? Got your tickets? Travellers cheques? Bathing suit? Torch? Notebook? Sunblock and hat?'

'Yes, I think so,'

'Right. Now, I've got my bird book, my binoculars and the map.' She ticked them off her check–list. 'I still think you'll wish you'd got yourself a snorkel and mask like these old ones of mine. There will be lots of opportunities to explore the coral reefs, you know. After all, that's what we've been training for all these months, isn't it?'

'I like swimming,' Dorothy said. 'I used to be quite good at it. I got my bronze life-saving certificate at school, you know, but I don't like putting my head under the water and I'm too old to change that now.'

'What rubbish! You're the healthy one and you're years younger than me, and I'm certainly going to have another go at it.'

'Which stick are you taking?' Dorothy asked, She wondered why Daisy had been so keen to go, yet again, on one of Roger Dare's holidays. It was true that she and Dorothy had enjoyed the trips, but others hadn't. There had often been quite a lot of 'unpleasantness'. When Dorothy talked to herself it was usually in euphemisms. She concluded that Daisy must secretly be studying Roger. Once a psycotherapist, always one, she thought.

'I shall take both sticks,' Daisy said. 'The folding one one may come in useful if I lose the other, and I suppose it's entirely possible that I may need two at once if it's frightfully hot and tiring.'

'Perhaps we should have opted to go to the Isle of Wight after all?' Dorothy said. 'Oh, I do hope it won't be too much for you.'

'I shall see to it that it isn't,' Daisy said crisply. 'Ah, here's the taxi now. You are sure you've got your tickets?'

'In my handbag.' Dorothy opened it, drew a blank and started scabbling desperately through it. 'They're not here!' Panic stricken, she emptied the contents of her bag on to their dining-room table. 'Oh my goodness!' she exclaimed, running her fingers through her fluffy white hair until it stood up all over her head like froth. The taxi hooted outside.

Daisy made an imperious gesture at it through the window. 'Perhaps you put it in your little green bag?' she suggested patiently.

'Oh *yes*, perhaps I did.' Dorothy unzipped the smallest pocket of her hand luggage and peered inside. '*They're here*! Thank goodness for that!'

'Come along then,' Daisy said. 'Just get yourself into the taxi and do try to remember to take your head.'

'I'm so sorry,' Dorothy gabbled, picking up her handbag and sweeping everything off the table and back inside it. 'I remember now. I thought that pocket would be such a safe place, and so easy to get at . . .'

'What would you do without me?' Daisy said. She picked up her walking stick in one hand and her hand luggage in the other, and limped to the front door. She rested the stick carefully against the hatstand while she opened the door and beckoned to the driver to come and help.

'I'd be lost,' Dorothy said. 'If you hadn't come along after Albert died, I just don't know how I should have managed.' Her eyes filled with grateful tears.

'Silly old thing,' Daisy said gruffly. 'Ah, driver, would you be good enough to carry these two? Thank you so much.'

Dorothy climbed into the taxi and mopped her face with a lace-edged handkerchief. Her eyes were prone to leaking spontaneously and she had long ago ceased to feel any embarrassment about being seen to weep in public. It was just that she felt emotions more keenly than most people; her skin was thinner. She wondered what the group would be like this year. She asked herself how Roger's saint of a wife could possibly put up with him. She hoped that Philip Blunt, Daisy's protegée from the local bird-watching club, would be fit enough to enjoy the trip. Multiple sclerosis sometimes raged through the young at a terrifying pace. What future has he got? she thought. What a wicked waste!

The taxi called at Philip's house and he climed in, beaming all over his face. 'Morning, Daisy, Dorothy,' he said. 'Isn't this great? I've got a brand new five hundred mm mirror lens specially for this trip. Can't wait to use it!'

Dorothy noticed that his flight bag was bulging with photographic equipment, so much so that the zip wouldn't do up. She watched as his anxious mother waved them off, and wondered whether the poor woman would be comforted in years to come by the albums of photographs her son would leave behind. She dabbed at her eyes again. Philip waved encouragingly at his mother as the taxi set off and sat down on the jump seat opposite the two elderly women.

'She worries,' he explained, 'but I've told her I'll be in good company.'

He's so handsome, Dorothy thought, and has such expressive eyes. It's so unfair.

Dr Claire Mainwaring travelled south on the train from Edinburgh to London in optimistic mood. Outside it was raining and the November countryside looked brown and dreary. Claire looked forward to hot white beaches, lazy swimming and wonderful Creole food. She was glad to leave Edinburgh just now. Magnus was becoming a nuisance, but Murdo (with whom she went rock climbing at weekends) was simmering encouragingly and could be relied upon to come to the boil in just over a fortnight, coinciding nicely with her return, all langorous with sunshine and fetchingly tanned. She smiled to herself. She knew Roger Dare would not be a problem on this, her second Seychelles trip working as his assistant. He was fun, it was true, and he was pretty good in the sack too, but once Claire had got to know his wife she saw that Ruth has known what was going on right from the beginning and was quietly putting up with it. Claire, who had seen Roger as a fellow free-spirit and hadn't given a thought to anyone else, was shocked at Ruth's acquiescence, and troubled by feelings of guilt for the first time in her life. So, after a week, she had told him to sling his hook and he had accepted her decision, albeit rather childishly.

Ruth must be some sort of masochist, she now thought, to put herself in that situation year after year. Claire had no illusions about Roger. She was sure that if she herself were not on offer, he would chat up someone else. Why didn't he piss off on his own once a year, she wondered? It would be much kinder to spare Ruth from being a witness to his verbal foreplay, and would give him far more freedom. Perhaps he couldn't afford to unless he made money out of it? She didn't know anything about his home life except that he lived in Cheshire and had once been a probation officer. She supposed that he could hardly lead Leisure Doubletrips without Ruth as that would invalidate his own brilliant idea of running parallel holidays for the able and the infirm. Perhaps he didn't care if he hurt Ruth? Claire smiled grimly. It didn't say much for Roger's character but it still made Ruth a wimp, and of the two, Claire preferred the heartless chancer any day. She looked out of the window and wondered idly what the punters would be like this time. Then she got the group address list out of her bag studied their names, each of which was followed with the persons age and 'MS' or 'AB' (the latter for 'able bodied').

Mr Barnaby Redcliffe [50, MS] Somerset.
Mrs Imogen Redcliffe [48, AB] ditto.
Dr Daisy Mann [70, MS] Spalding, Lincolnshire.
Mrs Dorothy Petrie [64, AB] ditto.
Mr Simon Overy [45, MS] Islington, London.
Miss Shirley Gage [62, AB] Sheffield, Yorkshire.
Mr Brian Gage [60, MS] ditto.
Miss Annabel de Beauchamp [25, MS] Cambridge.
Mr Philip Blunt [21, MS] Spalding, Lincolnshire.
Mr Leslie Cromwell [55, MS] Birmingham.
Mrs Janice Cromwell [53, AB] ditto.

They were mostly pretty ancient, but that was to be expected. Few people in their twenties and thirties could afford such a trip. Perhaps Simon Overy would be amusing? She wondered what they all did for a living. She had tried to guess the previous year and had got it badly wrong. Daisy and Dorothy (the retired psychotherapist and nursery-school teacher) of course she knew already, they were regulars and harmless enough. Brian and Shirley Gage had also been on other trips but not with her. They and the others would reveal themselves at Gatwick and be identifiable by their red Leisure Doubletrips luggage labels. Claire hoped that there would not be any moaners, mopers or malingerers among them.

The train was half an hour late into King's Cross, but Claire had plenty of time to spare and finally arrived at Gatwick unflustered and full of anticipation. She walked across the concourse and saw them all at once; the little knot of people at the Air Seychelles desk. Roger and Ruth had their backs to her. Daisy and Dorothy were bent double and seemed to be unpacking one of their bags on the floor. Claire approached slowly to get a good look at all of them before having to declare herself. The two youngsters stood out. The young man (who must be Philip) was demonstrating an expensive camera to the young woman. Mmmm, Claire thought, he's a bit of all right. Pity he's not older. The woman (Annabel) was not as sophisticated as her elegant name would suggest. She was intelligent looking and quite attractive, with shoulder length ginger hair, good cheek-bones and a pale skin, but she looked vulnerable and shy. The short, bearded man in glasses, standing a little apart from the rest, must be Simon. He didn't look promising. The rest of them looked pretty undistinguished: plump or thin, greyheaded or bald, all middle-aged and to Claire (who was young and didn't know any better) all very much past it. She amused herself trying to predict which of the women Roger would make a play for. It wouldn't be Annabel, that was for sure, not because Roger was overawed by breeding or brains, or even seduced by youth and beauty, but (a) because she was unmarried and (presumably) available on too permanent a basis, and (b) because she was likely to become a health liability fairly soon. Roger always went for married ladies, or women like herself who were clearly allergic to commitment and would therefore cause no longterm problems. Claire smiled inwardly. It looked as though Roger was in for rather a thin time this year. Serve him right! Was everyone here? She counted heads; two missing.

'Claire!' Daisy had seen her and was waving enthusiastically. Claire went forward and joined the group. 'How nice to see you again,' Daisy said. 'How are you?'

'Very well. Lovely to see you too. Hi, Rog! Hello, Ruth, here we go again.

Roger winked at her and put an arm round her shoulder. 'Now this,' he said, presenting her to the group, 'is the delicious doctor I was telling you about. Claire Mainwaring, pronounced Mannering (don't get it wrong, or she gets very uppity). She's the best GP I know; totally unsympathetic, doesn't believe in pills, but is wonderful in a crisis. What more could you ask?'

Claire smiled apologetically at Ruth and began shaking hands as she was introduced to the others. 'Who missing?' she asked Roger.

'The Redcliffes,' he said, 'Barnaby and Imogen. I hope they get a move-on.' He looked round. 'Oh, this looks like them now.'

Claire turned and saw a couple with red-tagged luggage approaching them. The man was tall, going a little thin on top and with a friendly, distinguished sort of face. He looks nice, she thought. He lurched when he walked, like someone intoxicated, but he was not using a stick. At his side walked a slim well-dressed woman who looked ten years younger than the forty-eight Claire knew her to be. She had large blue eyes, short curly hair (which was too evenly dark to be natural) and she was smiling broadly. Roger stepped forward to welcome them and took her hand first, in both of his.

'Mr and Mrs Redcliffe?' he said. 'Hello to you both. I'm Roger Dare.'

Claire, watching him, thought, Oh Roger, you jammy bastard!

Sue Gee's new novel available in Century hardback

LETTERS FROM PRAGUE

Harriet Pickering is on a quest in search of her first love. For a few brief weeks in the summer of 1968, she and Karel, a Czech student, were inseparable. But their happiness was snatched away when the Russian tanks crossed the border. Now, over twenty years later, Harriet and her ten-year-old daughter travel by train across a very different Europe.

Brussels and Berlin bring turmoil public and private, but it is in Prague that Harriet faces an inner journey yet to begin.

'Sue Gee's themes are families, friendships and human folly . . . the emotional journey is compelling . . . a lesson about life'
THE TIMES

'Sue Gee explores the fascinating relationships that bind people together set against the uncertain and often worrying changes in Eastern Europe . . . a book that deals with different issues and one that tugs at the heartstrings' LINCOLNSHIRE ECHO

'. . . a sensitive and intelligent stylist . . . *Letters From Prague* is an evocative tale that performs a delicate balancing act between the literary novel and more romantic genres'
Barry Forshaw, NORTH LONDON NEWS

THE MORNING GIFT
Eva Ibbotson

Volatile, passionate and clever, Ruth Berger grows up in untroubled affluence in pre-war Vienna – until Hitler's annexation of Austria puts an end to her dreams of a golden future with her fiancé Heini, a brilliant young pianist.

But while her parents escape to England, Ruth's harmless political antics mark her as a troublemaker and her departure is stopped, leaving her adrift in a Vienna she no longer recognizes. Quin Somerville, a young British Professor of Palaeontology, comes to the rescue by persuading her to undergo a marriage of convenience which will enable him to take her safely back to Britain. Reluctant, embarrassed, terrified, Ruth accepts, vowing never to trouble her chivalrous rescuer again . . .

In this enchanting, moving and often very funny novel, Eva Ibbotson paints a remarkable picture of 1930s émigré life.

'The very best sort of romantic novel . . . there are asides in here worthy of Jane Austen'
Carol Clewlow author of *A Woman's Guide to Adultery*

A COUNTESS BELOW STAIRS
Eva Ibbotson

Forced to flee Russia after the Revolution, Countess Anna Grazinsky lodges in London with her English governess. It is 1919 and the First World War is over, but Countess Anna's battles are only just beginning . . .

Penniless, she must say goodbye to the world of skating parties, balls and caviar picnics and seek her fate as a housemaid for the aristocratic Westerholme family. Rather than shirk her responsibilities, Anna tackles her new job with unquenchable determination – until the arrival of the new Earl of Westerholme and his fiancée.

It will take all Anna's strength to resist the growing attraction she feels for the new Earl, for it is a changing world and Anna must accept that her life now exists 'below stairs' . . .

In *A Countess Below Stairs* Eva Ibbotson has created an enchanting world filled with characters who live on in the mind long after the story has ended.

PLUCKING THE APPLE
Elizabeth Palmer

A Chelsea dinner party at the home of art gallery owners James and Victoria Harting sets in motion a chain of events that will leave none of the guests unscathed.

Among those assembled is artist Jack Carey and Ellen, his long-suffering wife, who has the job of keeping Jack's mind on the canvas. The evening ends, however, with Jack slipping James's vampish sister Tessa his business card, promising future exchanges of a more intimate nature – much to the despair of Tessa's love-sick husband Alexander.

Casting a cool eye over the proceedings is Ginevra, Victoria's intellectual but plain university friend. Her fathomless eyes absorb the subtle nuances at work under the conversational hum, but not even she can foresee the shocking events about to unfold – and just as well . . .

Plucking the Apple is a brilliant comedy of English modern manners – or the lack of them – in the tradition of Mary Wesley and Joanna Trollope.

B FORMAT TITLES AVAILABLE IN ARROW

☐ Last Guests of the Season	Sue Gee	009925641X	£4.99
☐ Letters From Prague	Sue Gee	0099274515	£5.99
☐ Spring Will Be Ours	Sue Gee	0099487314	£5.99
☐ Damage	Josephine Hart	0099871505	£5.99
☐ Sin	Josephine Hart	009925381X	£5.99
☐ Magic Flutes	Eva Ibbotson	0099225913	£4.99
☐ The Morning Gift	Eva Ibbotson	0099193817	£5.99
☐ A Countess Below Stairs	Eva Ibbotson	0099204312	£5.99
☐ Telling Only Lies	Jessica Mann	0099147610	£5.99
☐ Plucking the Apple	Elizabeth Palmer	0099195917	£5.99
☐ The Stainless Angel	Elizabeth Palmer	009919581X	£4.99
☐ Old Money	Elizabeth Palmer	0099373718	£5.99
☐ The Young Italians	Amanda Prantera	0099377012	£5.99
☐ One True Thing	Anna Quindlen	0099527219	£5.99
☐ A Price For Everything	Mary Sheepshanks	0099467917	£5.99
☐ My Life As A Whale	Dyan Sheldon	0099159317	£4.99

ALL ARROW BOOKS ARE AVAILABLE THROUGH MAIL ORDER OR
FROM YOUR LOCAL BOOKSHOP AND NEWSAGENT.

PLEASE SEND CHEQUE/EUROCHEQUE/POSTAL ORDER
(STERLING ONLY) ACCESS, VISA OR MASTERCARD

☐☐☐☐☐☐☐☐☐☐☐☐☐☐☐☐

EXPIRY DATE.......................... SIGNATURE...

PLEASE ALLOW 75 PENCE PER BOOK FOR POST AND PACKING U.K.
OVERSEAS CUSTOMERS PLEASE ALLOW £1.00 PER COPY FOR POST
AND PACKING.

ALL ORDERS TO:
ARROW BOOKS, BOOK SERVICE BY POST, P.O. BOX 29, DOUGLAS,
ISLE OF MAN, IM99 1BQ. TEL: 01624 675137 FAX: 01624 670 923

NAME ....

ADDRESS ....

....

Please allow 28 days for delivery. Please tick box if you do not wish to receive
any additional information ☐

Prices and availability subject to change without notice.